KATE MOORE

Author of *To Seduce an Angel*

Danger will reunite
them—or divide
them forever...

Blackstone's
Bride

B

**BERKLEY
SENSATION**

$7.99 U.S.
$8.99 CAN

ISBN 978-0-425-25088-4

EAN

Blackstone's Bride

KATE MOORE

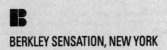

BERKLEY SENSATION, NEW YORK

THE BERKLEY PUBLISHING GROUP
Published by the Penguin Group
Penguin Group (USA) Inc.
375 Hudson Street, New York, New York 10014, USA
Penguin Group (Canada), 90 Eglinton Avenue East, Suite 700, Toronto, Ontario M4P 2Y3, Canada
(a division of Pearson Penguin Canada Inc.) • Penguin Books Ltd., 80 Strand, London WC2R 0RL,
England • Penguin Group Ireland, 25 St. Stephen's Green, Dublin 2, Ireland (a division of Penguin
Books Ltd.) • Penguin Group (Australia), 250 Camberwell Road, Camberwell, Victoria 3124, Australia
(a division of Pearson Australia Group Pty. Ltd.) • Penguin Books India Pvt. Ltd., 11 Community
Centre, Panchsheel Park, New Delhi—110 017, India • Penguin Group (NZ), 67 Apollo Drive,
Rosedale, Auckland 0632, New Zealand (a division of Pearson New Zealand Ltd.) • Penguin Books
(South Africa) (Pty.) Ltd., 24 Sturdee Avenue, Rosebank, Johannesburg 2196, South Africa

Penguin Books Ltd., Registered Offices: 80 Strand, London WC2R 0RL, England

This is a work of fiction. Names, characters, places, and incidents either are the product of the author's
imagination or are used fictitiously, and any resemblance to actual persons, living or dead, business
establishments, events, or locales is entirely coincidental. The publisher does not have any control over
and does not assume any responsibility for author or third-party websites or their content.

BLACKSTONE'S BRIDE

A Berkley Sensation Book / published by arrangement with the author

PUBLISHING HISTORY
Berkley Sensation mass-market edition / August 2012

ISBN: 978-0-425-25088-4

BERKLEY SENSATION®
Berkley Sensation Books are published by The Berkley Publishing Group,
a division of Penguin Group (USA) Inc.,
375 Hudson Street, New York, New York 10014.
BERKLEY SENSATION® is a registered trademark of Penguin Group (USA) Inc.
The "B" design is a trademark of Penguin Group (USA) Inc.

PRINTED IN THE UNITED STATES OF AMERICA

10 9 8 7 6 5 4 3 2 1

ALWAYS LEARNING   **PEARSON**

For Loren, Kevin, and Allison, as ever

Were the same fair prospect to arise at present as had flattered them a year ago, every thing . . . would be hastening to the same vexatious conclusion.

—Jane Austen, *Pride and Prejudice*

Prologue

The English Channel. February 1825

Lyle Massing, Baron Blackstone, was losing at cards, a situation he could only attribute to the rise and fall of the ship under him. The HMS *Redemption*, a naval vessel of questionable seaworthiness, had been pressed into service to bring Blackstone and a few other survivors of the Greek misadventure home.

He tried to concentrate on the cards in his hand and not think about home. At the moment he didn't have one. Blackstone Court, the ancestral seat he'd inherited from his father, had been mortgaged to pay his ransom to the Greek warlord Vasiladi. The house was now leased to a wealthy maker of crockery. Blackstone's widowed mother and sisters had removed to a modest townhouse in Bath. His mother made no complaint, but in her letter about the move, his sister Elena had double underlined the words "thirty feet," the distance between their two drawing rooms in Bath. When he thought of his mother in such narrow circumstances after the vastness of Blackstone Court, he grew a little reckless with his cards, and already a pile of his vowels littered the table.

Beating its way across the channel to Dover, the *Redemption* lurched and shuddered, making the yellow light waver in the smoky compartment. Blackstone blinked at the unforgiving cards in his hand. His opponent, Samuel Goldsworthy, a large mound of a man with thick red hair and beard and a green silk waistcoat that glowed in the swaying light, grinned at him. The fellow seemed incapable of ill humor or of losing. It was he who had proposed a little harmless game of cards. Hours earlier, the endless card game and the rolling seas had defeated the other two passengers. Only Goldsworthy and Blackstone remained at the table.

The big man could not conceal his satisfaction with the situation. "Son, those cards you're holding are worthless. Let me offer you a way out."

Blackstone felt an unsettling prickle of wariness as if the man could see his hand. He made a joke. "Is this the moment when you suggest that I marry your quiz of a daughter?" If Goldsworthy had such a daughter, Blackstone might do it. He had few options to recover his estate.

Goldsworthy gave a head-splittingly hearty laugh. Blackstone had suggested a marriage in jest, but as if in protest at the idea of his marrying, his careless memory threw up a flash of laughing black eyes and soft creamy breasts. He shook it off. That opportunity had long since passed. No doubt Violet Hammersley had married while Blackstone was in the hands of the bandits.

"Nothing so clichéd, lad. All I ask is that you enter my employ for a year and a day."

Blackstone noted the fairy-tale phrase. A year and a day was also the amount of time he had been a captive, a year and a day, in which Byron had died, and the Greek freedom fighters who had sought to throw off the Turks had fallen into rival factions, apt to cut each other's throats.

He peered again at Goldsworthy. The man looked ordinary enough in spite of his oaklike size and the absurd invitation to employment. He was taller than Blackstone by four inches or more, and wider than any of the berths offered on the ship. Blackstone put his age at somewhere between forty and fifty. He looked like a great leafy tree with his russet coat, walnut trousers, and the green waistcoat. For all the stirring of Blackstone's instincts at the man's odd turn of phrase, the fellow was most likely not an enchanter out of a fairy tale, but an ordinary London merchant. He probably had a warehouse on the Thames stuffed with bolts of muslin or sacks of coffee beans.

But Blackstone's year with the bandits had taught him to be wary of appearances. He could not help a suspicion that Goldsworthy was not what he appeared to be. The timing of the arrival of Goldsworthy and the *Redemption* in Koron harbor at the singularly delicate moment in Blackstone's negotiations with the bandit, when the money was about to change hands, was more than fortuitous. It was miraculous. At that moment, Blackstone had realized there was no reason for Vasiladi to follow through with the release of his hostages. He had mortgaged his estate to buy freedom for his younger half-brother and a score of young girls and boys who had been pressed into slavish roles by the warlord's army. Blackstone's whole mission to Greece had hung in the balance.

He tried again to determine Goldsworthy's true nature. "I suppose you're a cesspool cleaner or a shambles operator."

"Nothing so fragrant, or so common I assure you, lad. Something rather more suited to your talents."

"We didn't meet in London, did we?"

"Not at all."

"Why offer to hire me? You can't have a high estimate of my talents based on our little game."

"You are a charming fellow—"

Blackstone shot Goldsworthy a skeptical glance. "I've hardly charmed you."

"Still among your own, among the ton, you move with grace and ease, wear a well-cut coat, show a pretty leg on the dance floor, and perhaps off of it, drive and ride to an inch."

"You've heard of me then. What you've heard can hardly recommend me for anyone's employ."

"Except mine. You'll be invited everywhere, and I want you to attend as many of the season's events as you can."

Maybe there was an ugly daughter after all, a very ugly daughter. Maybe she was so plain and so awkward that Goldsworthy needed to prevail on a man of Blackstone's scandalous reputation to escort her to balls and routs. "And for submitting to the endless social whirl?"

"I will pay off all your debts, including the mortgage on Blackstone Court."

In captivity, Blackstone had learned not to betray the least sign of discomposure, but he felt a rush of mortifying heat. The pile of scraps on which Blackstone and his luckless fellow travelers had pledged their funds to Goldsworthy lay on the table. Blackstone glanced from them to the dismal cards in his hand. Luck had been against him all night, and now the stranger who had managed to fleece them all was offering him what he most needed.

"I beg your pardon." Blackstone stared hard at the man who seemed to know more of his business than anyone, outside of his solicitor.

"Come with me to my club, and I'll explain."

"Your club?" The blunt fellow did not strike Blackstone as a clubman. Goldsworthy might be English to the core, but he was no gentleman.

"The Pantheon Club in Albemarle Street. I've a post chaise meeting the ship. It will take us directly there."

Not to Bath and his mother's reproaches, but to London and a chance to repair his fortune. Goldsworthy certainly knew how to dangle temptation, but Blackstone needed to know what was behind the man's apparent generosity.

"Who are you?"

Goldsworthy frowned. "You can't have forgotten already."

"Not your name. Who are you? What's this mysterious position you're offering?"

"Quite right to ask. Service to king and country, that's what it is." Goldsworthy's good-humored expression remained unimpaired. "It's spying actually."

"Spying? On whom would I be spying in the drawing rooms of London?"

For once, Goldsworthy's expression turned grim. He shook his great, lionlike head. "It's a black world we live in these days, lad. England's enemies pass themselves off as friends every day and move among us, high and low. And secrets have a way of falling into their hands. It's our job to prevent those secrets from going astray."

Blackstone blinked at the man, as if his eyes were not working properly in the dim, smoke-filled cabin. He was being asked to become a spy for England. His prospects shifted with the creaking roll of the *Redemption*. He could return to his mother and sisters and endure their helpless hand-wringing, or he could act to recover his lost fortune.

The ship paused on a peak. Then the treacherous ocean

shifted, and they fell into a stomach-seizing nothingness as if the world had vanished. Goldsworthy calmly clamped a hand around his ale pot. Blackstone caught the lamp. Everything else hit the low ceiling. In that moment of free fall, nothing to grab, nothing to lose that wasn't lost already, he saw again the flash of laughing black eyes and wanted against all reason to see them once more, which was madness.

The long fall ended as the *Redemption* slammed into another wave, shuddered mightily, and decided not to splinter into driftwood.

"I'll do it."

"That's the good lad. A year and a day, then you'll be free and clear."

Chapter One

Everybody declared that he was the wickedest young man in the world; and everybody began to find out that they had always distrusted the appearance of his goodness.

—Jane Austen, *Pride and Prejudice*

Blackstone opened one eye to squint at the vault of the ceiling above him, pale as a bride cake and distant as the moon. The cushioned surface under him didn't heave or shudder. He remembered. *Goldsworthy's club. Albemarle Street. London.*

He was not in a cave. He had not witnessed a beheading in weeks or seen a thirteen-year-old slave given to a brutal man as a prize. Sometimes on waking, it took him awhile to dismiss the images his sleeping mind released.

"Wilde, open that drapery, and you're a dead man." The menacing voice came from another sofa in the cavernous coffee room of Goldsworthy's club where Blackstone and his fellow spies had ended the previous night.

Rain, English rain, cool and fitful, battered a window somewhere and rattled a drainpipe. The freshness of it was another reminder that he was home.

"Good morning to you, Lord Hazelwood. Coffee?" A

now familiar voice, young and unreasonably cheerful, came with a hint of London's East End in the flattened vowels. *Coffee* sounded like *cawfy* in Blackstone's ears, but the smell induced him to lift his head.

A groan came from a third couch, but the purposeful clink of china went on, and the coffee smell intensified.

"Lord Blackstone?" The young male voice was now at his side. Blackstone pushed upright and swung his feet to the floor. Nate Wilde, Goldsworthy's protégé, was both a sort of majordomo at the club and their access to Goldsworthy himself. The youth, dressed in a fashionable ink blue coat and buff trousers, thrust a steaming cup of coffee at him and Blackstone took it. Impossible not to—the stuff smelled so good.

He watched Wilde coax the room's other two occupants to wakefulness. For a few minutes there was silence, while the coffee worked to make the world a bearable place in which a man could speak civilly to his fellows.

Blackstone drank, grateful for the relative quiet and calm of the coffee room. It was the one fully furnished room in the club at the moment, as the rest of the place was undergoing renovations that Goldsworthy had failed to mention in his recruiting pitch.

Scaffolding surrounded the building, and each day an army of carpenters, plasterers, masons, and bricklayers appeared early and set to banging away and raising a good deal of dust. Curtains of canvas concealed halls and staircases.

The coffee room, however, was a quiet, wholly male space with a lack of fuss or frill, darkly paneled with deep leather chairs, a rich swirling carpet of reds, blues, and golds, well-stocked bookcases, and a gleaming silver coffee urn on a table clad in crisp white linen.

Blackstone's fellow spies were Captain Clare, a hero of Waterloo, in scarlet regimentals, and Viscount Hazelwood, the Earl of Vange's disinherited heir. Wild-haired Hazelwood wore a rumpled black evening coat over white satin breeches that might have once been pristine, but now bore stains to make a man's valet weep or faint. Though Blackstone and his fellow spies had shared little of the circumstances that had brought them to Goldsworthy's employ, Blackstone had pieced together what he could about the other two.

Each had signed a contract with Goldsworthy that Clare claimed was legal, and that Hazelwood declared was tight as a vicar's ass. Each had been assigned a rung of London's social ladder as his territory. Clare haunted low taverns frequented by soldiers, sailors, and radicals. Hazelwood moved between gaming hells and brothels. And Blackstone had been assigned the fashionable West End.

His first assignment was Lady Ravenhurst, whose politically ambitious husband often carried foreign office dispatches to and from his library at home. Gossip claimed that lonely Lady Ravenhurst was seeking diversion in the arms of a Russian count, whose designs were perhaps on secret documents rather than the lady. Goldsworthy had assigned Blackstone to make himself agreeable enough to cut the count out of the running as the lady's lover.

As the coffee began to have an effect, the captain addressed Wilde.

"Where did you learn to make coffee this good, Wilde?"

Hazelwood answered for the boy. "He's a Turk and was a slave in Istanbul under the sultan."

Wilde's grin revealed a gleaming set of white teeth. "London born and bred, gentlemen. An old soldier named Harding taught me. You lot will likely meet him on some case or other."

"Couldn't he have taught you to make porter?"

Wilde shrugged, his grin fading. "No porter for you, Lord Hazelwood."

Clare lifted his cup in a toast, "Sobriety, solvency, and celibacy. That's the motto here." Clare was a wiry redhead with a far-seeing look. Blackstone had no trouble imagining him leading his men through the chaos of a smoking battle-field.

"It will make you fit as a prizefighter, Captain."

"It'll make us duller than moss growing." Hazelwood stared morosely at his coffee.

Wilde laughed, apparently unperturbed at his charges' grousing. "Not for long, I'll wager." He tapped the gleaming silver vessel on the cloth-covered table. "The urn's full. Newspapers are here. Ring when you're hungry."

After he left, silence descended on the room for a time. Then Hazelwood turned to Blackstone. "So how are you getting on with Lady Ravenhurst?"

"Well enough." The lady had sent him a pointed invitation to join her guests for an evening of song, making it clear that her husband would not be present. So he had spent the previous evening shoulder to shoulder with the fashionable of London in a row of gilded chairs enduring the heat of candles and close bodies and a lady's fan occasionally drawn across his thigh by the movement of her arm. The Russian count had been conspicuously absent. Blackstone would have a good report to make to Goldsworthy. "And you?"

Hazelwood was following the missteps of a set of fash-ionable young bloods, one of whom had an older brother in the cabinet.

"It's been a purgatorial fortnight, and I've got nothing." Hazelwood staggered to his feet, refilled his cup from the urn, and tucked one of the newspapers under his arm. "How is a man to think with an army of carpenters banging away and not a drop of liquor to be got out of that inscrutable whelp of a tailor's dummy, who claims to be at our service?"

Blackstone had to laugh. Wilde cheerfully directed them to anything they needed and nothing they wanted. They had a valet, Twickler, and if they needed funds or a carriage, Wilde arranged them. Around the corner from the club, but accessible to it through connecting back gardens, was a chemist's shop on Bond Street that supplied them with all the accessories of men of fashion. Kirby, the artist who dressed Goldsworthy's stable of spies, had frowned at Blackstone's color and thinness. But to his credit he had turned a man who had eaten subsistence rations for a year into a model of wealth and fashion. No one would guess he still bore the effects of his captivity.

This morning Clare's gaze seemed to sharpen as the coffee took effect. "Blackstone, whatever happened to that painting of your mistress, the Spanish dancer, the one that made you notorious?"

Hazelwood's brows lifted. "What's this? Blackstone, you sly dog. You never mentioned a scandal. I guess that answers the question about why you landed here. Did your family disown you?"

"The title was mine."

"Ah, the title and the tittle-tattle. The print shops must have enjoyed your folly. Goldsworthy's genius begins to reveal itself." Hazelwood put his cup on the floor and settled back down on his couch, opening the newspaper and pulling it over his face. Blackstone turned to Clare, who leaned forward, his coffee cup in both hands.

"Hazelwood has a theory about why Goldsworthy tapped us for this work, which your situation rather confirms. Hazelwood thinks that Goldsworthy picked us for our notoriety."

"I thought spies were discreet fellows."

"Hazelwood thinks, and I see his point, that once a man's reputation is fixed in the public mind, no one will suspect him of being anything other than what he is reputed to be."

"So you're a hero, Hazelwood is a wastrel . . ."

"And you're a rake."

Blackstone had to acknowledge the logic of it. People tended to see what they expected to see.

He'd now spent a fortnight back in London, and had discovered that the scandalous painting that had made him famous as a rakeshame at four and twenty had fixed the public view of his character forever. He had never guessed, in the stunned moment of seeing that painting for the first time, that it would come to define *him*. Nor had he understood how impossible it was to shake a scandal. At twenty-four he had been free in his assumption of power and privilege. He had believed that he alone determined his place in the world. No painter, a mere dabbler in oils, in a reeking studio, could hurt a peer of the realm. He'd been wrong.

When he refused to pay for the painting, the painter Royce made it public, and scandal broke over his head. Sobriquets for his mighty manhood appeared repeatedly in the sort of doggerel the gossip sheets indulged in. Women he'd never met left their cards. He was invited to the masquerades and the balls of the demi-monde and expected to arrive wherever general debauchery might ensue. At the time he could hardly protest that he was not a scoundrel. He had made a promise. While raffish strangers flocked to make his acquaintance, his betrothed and his family had broken all connection with him.

Wilde strode back into the room carrying a covered basket. Outside, the daily hammering began.

"Where's Goldsworthy?" Blackstone wanted to make his daily report.

"Never where you need him." Hazelwood's newspaper rustled over his concealed face. "Damned elusive fellow. Comes and goes like a ghost."

"Mr. Goldsworthy does a bit of fishing now and then." Wilde deposited his basket of fresh rolls. "As a matter of fact, he's waiting for you this morning, Lord Blackstone."

"Time to pay the piper, Blackstone," Hazelwood mumbled from under his paper.

Wilde glanced at Hazelwood's recumbent form. "Your turn will come, Lord Hazelwood."

Chapter Two

"... she is really a very sweet girl, and I wish with all my heart she were well settled. But with such a father and mother, and such low connections, I am afraid there is no chance of it."

—Jane Austen, *Pride and Prejudice*

Violet Hammersley understood better than most that the time of day to which Londoners referred as *morning* was not determined by clocks or the spinning of the planet, but by one's station in life. The lowliest maid rose at four to start fires and heat water. Her mistress might not rise until ten. At one in the afternoon Violet's *morning* call on her grace, the Duchess of Huntingdon, Penelope Frayne, came to an end.

"Violet, dear, you must be so pleased. Your ball will be a notable success." Penelope offered a faint, perfumed embrace as her butler waited to escort Violet to the door of the grand house on Park Lane.

"I'm just grateful to have your help, Penelope. Thank you."

"Do not concern yourself. You must have a hundred details on your mind. An upcoming royal visit, how will you manage?"

"Thankfully, the Prince of Moldova is my brother's guest. Milvert's Hotel will bear the brunt of any royal

demands. You do not think I overstated the charitable purpose of our ball?" Violet had been aware of all eyes turning
to Penelope when the other women present realized they
were being asked to support a cause.

"Not at all. My friends are pleased to be patronesses of
such a worthy endeavor. What could be more fitting than
that we support our downtrodden sisters who make the very
cloth of our gowns?" The duchess lifted her own moss-
colored gros de Naples skirts and let them fall in a liquid
whisper. She linked her arm in Violet's and dismissed her
butler with a nod. "I'll see Miss Hammersley out, Coyle."

Worthy endeavor. Violet's head buzzed with the details
of the ball, but Penelope's words reduced the glittering ballroom of her imagination to a sober meeting of the Society
for the Care of Indigent Widows. Perhaps she had gone too
far in making herself a pattern card of feminine propriety.

Not that Violet had dreamed of balls as a girl. What she
had dreamed of was an office of her own in her father's bank.
In the months after her mama's death Papa had not known
what to do with his solemn, big-eyed sugarplum of a daughter. Bereft himself, and with his son away at school, Papa had
not wanted to leave Violet at home each day, and so, admon-
ishing her to be quiet and good, he had taken her to his bank
and allowed her to sit in a large leather chair in his office.

Violet loved the bank. She had not then known anything
of Athens and its time-whitened temples, on which the bank
was modeled. But the bank's grand columns and stately air
appealed to her, and the bank was never lonely. It even had
its own special sound. Violet thought it was the sound of
energy itself, a compound of papers and footsteps rustling
and pens scratching and low purposeful voices and muffled
London traffic.

From that time, Violet had wanted an office of her own

like Papa's, and it seemed as if she must inevitably become
a banker because she was Papa's daughter and because when
his partners stopped to say hello, they would set sums to
tease her, and she would always know the answers.

Much later, when she was thirteen and changing into her
unrecognizable grown-up self, Papa had been surprised to
hear she wanted to be a banker. He had told her that girls
did not become bankers, and when she had wanted to know
what they did become, he had thrown up his hands and told
her that he expected she would be interested in girl things,
not banking.

Violet had been at first puzzled to hear of this division
in the world of things that belonged to males and those that
belonged to females. It reminded her of the befuddling way
that French people divided their nouns into masculine and
feminine nouns. She had asked her papa what principle one
used to sort out which thing belonged to which sex.

Papa had shrugged again. He thought a person simply
knew. So Violet made a list of things that interested her and
showed it to her brother Frank. He cheerfully told her that
nothing on her list was a girl thing—not banking, not money,
not law, not justice, not architecture, not steam engines. He
scribbled an alternate list next to hers—bonnets, dresses,
gloves, shoes, charities, books, and balls. "These are girl
things, Violet."

Violet had to laugh at herself. It had taken her a long time
to get to that last item on Frank's list. But now that she had,
she had no time to dwell on doubts about her life course.
She had a ball to prepare for. A celebratory skip would not
be amiss.

The duchess, however, set a leisurely pace as they strolled
towards the stairs. A footman followed at a discreet distance
carrying a box of cards of invitation, Violet's share.

Violet could not say that she and Penelope had developed a friendship. Her acquaintance with her grace, the Duchess of Huntingdon, was but a few weeks old. It was far too early to claim intimacy, though Penelope had insisted that they use each other's given names.

Three weeks earlier, the duchess, who had an interest in charitable projects, had called on Violet and invited her to call in return. Violet had discussed the invitation at length with her old governess and faithful friend, Augusta Lowndes, and the two had concluded that Violet could lose nothing in accepting such an invitation.

Penelope Frayne was a handsome, small-boned woman just past her thirtieth birthday, with green eyes and Titian hair. Before her marriage, such a gang of suitors had courted her that at one ball her father had reportedly cleared his house of the lot of them. Penelope possessed, in addition to title, fortune, and beauty, an effortless influence in society. Her willingness to take up a *modiste* or a milliner could mean thousands of pounds of added income for the favored establishment. In three weeks, with Penelope's help, Violet had managed astonishing feats of preparation for a charity ball.

The pressure of the duchess's arm on Violet's roused some instinct that warned her that the duchess expected a return of favors for her support. Violet's mind raced through all she knew of the Frayne family finances. There could be no want of money, surely. Anything that would compromise the integrity of her father's bank was out of the question. Such a request would mean her vision of a ball to support the former silk workers of Spitalfields would disappear in a blink like a magic lantern slide.

Violet wanted to take the stairs two at a time and leap into her carriage before any thought occurred that might

make Penelope revoke her support. Their March ball was a
risky endeavor, and without Penelope's backing the thing
would be hopeless. Penelope's delicate brows had contracted
into a thoughtful crease.

"I think the idea of each lady wearing a distinctive gown
made of fabric produced in Spitalfields sets just the tone."
They reached the landing and made the turn to the final
flight of stairs. "If you agree, we could have our fittings here.
I will turn over a drawing room to your seamstresses."

Violet nodded. It was perhaps a wise strategy to bring
the seamstresses to their titled patrons, rather than expecting
the ladies to venture into the less savory neighborhoods of
London. Violet truly was grateful for the duchess's support,
but conscious that the duchess saw through her a bit. She had
not merely wanted help; she had wanted her fellow patronesses to recognize their dependence on the labor of others
and the conditions under which their finery was created. If
the ladies came to Park Lane for fittings, they would never
see the rooms where women huddled around a single lamp
working late into the night, but still the seamstresses would
feed their families.

The duchess made no move to release Violet's arm.
Below them an alert footman in magnificent blue livery rose
from a bench at the door.

"And whom will you invite to our ball?"

"Oh, I hardly know." Violet had not imagined Penelope
to have any interest in Violet's other acquaintance. Outside
of their charitable project their paths never crossed. "I have
dozens of friends who will lend their support to our cause."

"I meant is there anyone you would wish to have as a
special guest?"

Belatedly, Violet recognized the underlying question. "A
man, you mean? No, I have my eye on a bank, not a man."

"But men must have their eyes on you."

"I think not. I'm no longer a girl." Violet was twenty-four, and she hoped she had put her girlhood behind her, or locked it in a box, or buried it in a crypt, or sunk it in an ocean cave, like some weighty ship's cargo tossed overboard to lighten the vessel so that it might move forward again.

"You are an heiress."

"In that case, men don't have their eyes on me, but on my bank account."

Penelope gave her a doubting look. There was an extended pause before she spoke again. "Violet, you do know that Blackstone has returned."

The name made Violet start. She caught up her skirts, as if her awkward movement was just a preparation for descending the stairs, but she feared the duchess had noted her reaction. *Blackstone*. She had banished him from her thoughts. No one in Hammersley House ever spoke his name, and yet the mention of it instantly gave her the sensation of tumbling ignominiously down the stairs in front of her. She reached to grab the rail and dropped her skirts, suddenly clumsy with the ordinary motions of life. "I hadn't heard. You don't think one of the patronesses would invite him to our ball?"

"Oh never." Penelope started walking again. "I just wanted you to be prepared for the inevitable talk. He's scandalous as ever, I hear. It's said that he returned to England with a harem."

A harem. Violet tried to keep her knees steady. She would think about Blackstone's return later. Penelope had made no embarrassing request of a favor. It was not the end of Violet's hopes for the ball. Still the sharp green gaze was bent on her. "Thank you for informing me. It's unlikely that Blackstone's path shall ever cross mine."

"I should imagine not, but even at your end of town there is no avoiding the talk about such a man. He's forever the center of some intrigue. The most circumspect of maidens is likely to hear something, if only her governess's warning to avoid him."

"You may be sure that he is no danger to me."

"You were once to be Blackstone's bride, were you not? You are no longer interested in him?" Penelope sounded doubtful.

Once. "It was a brief engagement. I know his true character." Violet looked down from the landing at the pattern of black and white marble in the entry hall. The duchess's blue-coated footman stood in readiness to open the door. He had an umbrella in hand. Violet knew that she did not control the conversation. Only the duchess could end it when she saw fit. Rank had its privilege.

"Lady Ravenhurst made a play for him the other night. Offered up her wares like Covent Garden fare. Well, she can't help it, I suppose. There is no subtlety in a bosom like hers. She simply lays them out like buns on a tea tray."

Violet knew that she was meant to laugh at the image, but found that she had unthinkingly clenched her right hand. "I'm sure Blackstone knows what to do when tea is served."

"But tell me, seriously, Violet, you don't want him?" The duchess still had a hold of Violet's elbow. Violet made an effort to meet the alert green gaze squarely. Penelope Frayne was no fool.

"I don't want him." She had once wanted him, as a girl, desperately and unwisely, but she was no longer that girl. Surely she could say that that desire was dead now. She forced her lips into a smile and gently pulled her arm free. The stairs looked impossibly long and steep, the footman impossibly distant.

"I confess I'm glad to hear it. I mean to have him if I can. Just to see what all the fuss is about, you know, but I didn't want to interfere if you still regarded him as yours."

"Not at all."

A rainy evening blotted out a gray London beyond the club windows. Blackstone looked over the scaffolding that surrounded the club's portico. The usual hammering had stopped. A month had passed since his return. He wondered whether the rain would keep Lady Ravenhurst from a masquerade in a public garden, with private grottos and long, dark lanes of trees. A perfumed note had advised Blackstone of the nature of the costume the lady intended to wear and Wilde had procured him a domino. He found he had no objection when Goldsworthy sent for him instead.

"Blackstone, the club agrees with you." Goldsworthy laced the fingers of his large hands, rested them on a spread of papers on his desk, and cast a measuring glance over Blackstone. "Still some lingering effects of Vasiladi's hospitality, I imagine, but give us time, and we'll get the meat back on your bones." He waved Blackstone into a leather chair.

The office resembled a temporary military headquarters with paint-and-plaster-spattered canvas draped floor to ceiling, dividing one part of the room from the section where Goldsworthy had set up his desk. A rolled-up rug leaned against a paneled wall with maps of London and glass-fronted cabinets stuffed with weapons. "You must pardon the dust and chaos of these renovations."

"I cannot fault the club's services." Except for the hammering and the tramp of carpenters' feet, living at the Pantheon Club was like being a well-stabled horse. One was fed and groomed and exercised by careful attendants, and one had only to do his part, and nothing too onerous, at that. Blackstone didn't quite know why he was resisting Lady Ravenhurst, but he didn't think that Goldsworthy expected him to go so far as to seduce a married woman of quality. It was all a matter of appearances, suggestions, whispers. Whether he seduced married ladies or didn't, people were supposed to believe him an unrepentant rake, which London society had been willing to believe of him from the moment he'd inherited his father's title at twenty-four.

"Good. I have no complaints about your reentry into London society. You've managed to be seen everywhere, I think. However, now that you have the lay of the land so to speak, the real work begins. We've a case for you, lad."

"A case?"

"Yes, it's pressing I'm afraid. Neither Hazelwood nor Clare will do, but you should be able to wrap it up in a week or so."

"You have a remarkable faith in my libertine ways then."

Goldsworthy nodded. "Your way with women. Why in no time, you've turned Lady Ravenhurst away from that sly Russian count. Now do you think you can manage two ladies at once?"

"What are you suggesting?" Conversing with Goldsworthy was like talking to an old yew tree in Epping Forest. Tonight the man wore a forest green jacket over a russet silk waistcoat and tree trunk brown trousers.

"No need to get your back up, lad. A fellow's gone missing with . . . a report of great interest to the government. The trouble is he was supposed to meet our courier in Koron and the fellow turned up dead. We arranged another to meet him in Naples. Equally dead. So we've a problem."

Koron, the name caught Blackstone's attention. So there

had been a reason for Goldsworthy to be in that Greek harbor when he'd offered to aid in the rescue of Blackstone and the other captives.

"Any idea who killed your agents?"

"Someone who didn't want that report to reach us." Goldsworthy's large hands flattened over the papers on his desk. He shifted them about the way a hazard dealer might rearrange his cards. Blackstone had a momentary recollection of that card table on the *Redemption*, where he'd lost so much he'd been willing to take whatever bargain Goldsworthy offered. He had not missed Goldsworthy's hesitation over the missing "report."

"How were these agents killed?"

"Strangled. Killer used some sort of cord. Necks heavily bruised. One fellow nearly decapitated. Ugly business."

"Just where do the elegant London drawing rooms, society functions, and willing women come into the case of agents murdered abroad?"

"I'll get to it, lad." He ended his paper shuffling, pulling out from under a pile of loose sheets a small blue velvet box of the kind jewelers used. "Our missing man was to arrive with the Prince of Moldova for a state visit. The prince landed this afternoon, but not our man. We've kept the prince and his party tied up in customs as long as we could, but nothing turned up. We think our murderer is one of the prince's people, and we want you to stick as close to them as possible."

"Who's the missing man?"

"A banker. Frank Hammersley."

Blackstone could not have heard properly. He waited for Goldsworthy to look at his desk again or shuffle his papers some more. But the man sat there with his bluff country squire looks as if he had not just poked a stick in the wasp's nest of Blackstone's past.

"With whom am I to flirt then?" He kept his voice level. He could guess the answer.

Goldsworthy flicked the lid on the little box in his large hands. "There's a countess in the prince's party. We want to investigate her."

"And the other woman?"

"Ah, now there's the pickle. We need you to be a good bit closer than a flirt, Blackstone. We need you to be a fiancé to Hammersley's sister."

Blackstone stared at the man across from him. Did Goldsworthy know the whole of Blackstone's past? The engagement between him and Violet Hammersley had been public at the time, but there had been scandals since his and no one cared for old news. "The lady may have some objections."

Goldsworthy tossed Blackstone the small blue velvet box. "To find her brother, she'll have to swallow them."

Blackstone flicked open the box. A great square diamond winked up at him. Fate once again assigned him the role of faithless fiancé. He could see himself bending to kiss Violet Hammersley's cold hand while looking over it to catch another woman's glance.

"It's paste," said his tormentor. "Remember, a year and a day clears you and Blackstone Court."

Chapter Three

"There's a gentleman . . . who can it be? It looks just like that man that used to be with him before. Mr. what's-his-name. That tall, proud man."

—Jane Austen, *Pride and Prejudice*

"Your tie's askew, Papa. You don't want to lessen the triumph of Frank's homecoming."

George Hammersley turned to his daughter at the top of the grand stairs of Hammersley House. "Don't tease, Violet. You know Preston's handiwork is perfection."

Violet reached up to tug the neck cloth in question. "Precisely the problem. It's too perfect. We've got to be ourselves even if a prince is our guest. Show no awe."

George squared his shoulders and gave his daughter a wink. "I know you'll be yourself, at any rate, my girl. You can't help it, can you?"

Violet laughed. "I'm afraid not."

From below came the rap of hurried footsteps on the parquet. Granthem, the Hammersley butler, looked up from the foot of the grand stairway. "A Lord Chartwell to speak with you, sir, about the prince. There's been a delay."

Papa frowned and turned to Violet.

She shrugged. "It's to be expected with this rain."

"Will it ruin the royal supper?"

Violet shook her head. "Never fear, Papa. We'll manage. Let's meet the visitor." She took her father's arm.

In the smaller drawing room, the one with the straw silk walls and Aubusson sofas, Violet rang for refreshments. The man who entered with Granthem was round-faced with a bald, freckle-dusted dome, an air of consequence, and gold-rimmed eyeglasses as round as his head. He came forward as Granthem announced him.

"I have unfortunate news for you, Mr. Hammersley. Your son Frank did not arrive with the prince's party."

Violet clutched her father's arm. She felt an odd sensation as if a cold rushing wind filled her ears.

"I don't understand." Papa's voice sounded like it came from a well. "Frank did not reach London?"

"That's what I'm saying, Hammersley. We don't know where your son is."

"Why is it your concern, Lord Chartwell?" Violet did not imagine the foreign office usually sent lords to find delayed travelers.

Papa turned to hush her, but she kept her gaze on their visitor.

Lord Chartwell frowned. "Perhaps you would care to sit, Miss Hammersley. Naturally, the government is concerned when one of his majesty's subjects is missing."

"Missing?" Papa croaked the word.

"Yes, missing."

"Do you mean dead, Lord Chartwell?" Violet had to ask.

"Not dead, Miss Hammersley. A dead man generally shows up somewhere, and your brother has not appeared in Spain or in England and certainly not aboard the ship on which he booked his passage." Lord Chartwell seemed to take it as a personal affront that Frank was not where the government expected him to be.

They settled uneasily, Lord Chartwell opposite Violet and Papa. Violet felt the hard edge of the gilt wood against the backs of her legs. Granthem appeared with a tray of tea and refreshments.

Chartwell turned to Papa. "Your son, Hammersley, went to Moldova to make a report on the prince's use of funds borrowed from England to improve Moldova's defenses. We know he arrived there, and we know he left again. He met the prince's party in Gibraltar to begin the final leg of his journey. No doubt you had messages from him along the way."

"We did." Violet felt an odd unease. The way Lord Chartwell described it, the government had been following her brother.

"Somewhere in Gibraltar between his hotel and the prince's ship, your brother's path diverged from his plan." To Violet it sounded as if Chartwell were making an accusation.

Papa strained forward so that he filled the space between himself and Lord Chartwell. "What's been done to recover my son?"

"Recover him?" Chartwell's round eyebrows arched above the gleaming rims of his spectacles. "We are investigating his trail, questioning all who saw him, examining the ship, and interviewing its crew."

Violet pulled Papa back. "Was he attacked in the street then?"

"Ordinary street ruffians might be to blame, but your brother is an experienced traveler, Miss Hammersley, and the one particularly valuable item he possessed was his report on the state of military finances in Moldova. The document is also missing."

"Who knew that Frank was carrying the document?" The government's rapid and thorough response did not sound like concern for Frank. Something was not right in Lord Chartwell's approach to Frank's disappearance.

"We must assume that everyone in the prince's party knew that he carried those documents."

Violet picked up the blue and white china teapot and concentrated on filling Lord Chartwell's cup instead of pouring tea over his round, freckled, unfeeling head. He was placating them, telling a shocked family that the government would do everything in its power to recover Frank, but his true concern was the missing document, not the missing brother. She recognized what was wrong with his tone. Chartwell was annoyed. Frank's disappearance was inconvenient. He didn't say it directly, but it was plain nonetheless. The government suspected someone in the prince's party of murdering or abducting Frank.

He ended by saying that all the government required was a little cooperation on their part. No one in the prince's party must know of the investigation.

"To aid in the recovery of your son, we have created an inconvenience for the prince and his party with Milvert's Hotel and have advised them that they will lodge with you for the first week of the royal visit. That will give us time to investigate." He looked at Violet. "We have added two servants to your staff, Miss Hammersley, who will be of material advantage in the investigation."

Violet saw Papa swell with outrage again. His voice boomed out. "We are supposed to host the prince and his people at Hammersley House for the duration of a state visit when one of them might have murdered Frank?"

"The best way to find your son is to keep the prince's entire party under scrutiny."

"And allow the murderer a chance to get at us in our own beds?" Violet tried to picture Granthem defending them and failed.

"We will arrange for you, Miss Hammersley, to have protection close at hand wherever you go."

"Do you recommend that I carry a pistol?"

Lord Chartwell's round face registered a faint distaste. He resettled his glasses on his nose. "Not necessary, I assure you. We have a man who will be at your side at all times."

"I beg your pardon. Won't such an arrangement appear odd to the prince and his party?"

"Not if the man at your side has a right, indeed a duty, to escort you wherever you go in the coming week."

"Outrageous!" Papa sputtered.

Violet watched Chartwell straighten his coat. "What man has such a right?"

"A fiancé, Miss Hammersley."

She must have misheard. They were talking about Frank, missing, not her unmarried state.

"Lord Chartwell, a woman does not acquire a fiancé in the same way she acquires a hat." She should have thrown the teapot at him.

"We will provide the fiancé, a reliable man."

"Really! I think the young ladies of London should know that the government keeps a supply of eligible men available. How soon do you expect to find Frank?"

"The sooner the better."

"If Frank is alive, what are his circumstances likely to be?"

Lord Chartwell shrugged, and Violet contemplated the poker by the fireplace. "If he is alive, he's likely being kept away from notice, somewhere where his presence won't rouse curiosity, but not far from the prince's party."

"So, not far from Hammersley House. What may we do?"

"Do nothing, Miss Hammersley. Unless you wish your brother dead." Lord Chartwell abandoned all pretense of offering comfort. He simply rose, signaling an end to the conversation. "A little cooperation from you is all we require, Hammersley. We have retrieved your son's possessions from the ship. We'd like you to look at them with our man to see whether anything strikes you as out of the ordinary. Where should we send them?"

Violet turned to Papa, staring ahead unseeing, and took his hand. "To Frank's room, and we should send for Preston, Frank's valet. He'll know better than any of us whether anything is missing."

Blackstone supposed that if one had to meet one's first love after a bitter parting and years of separation, it was best to have the upper hand. He had all the advantage. He knew the moment was coming. He had time to prepare his countenance. He had a job to do.

He had the further advantage of seeing Violet Hammersley before she saw him. She was crossing the landing at the top of the grand vulgar stairway of the mansion her father had built with his banking fortune. The whole house was a monstrosity that dominated one of the newer squares north of Mayfair, and the entry's soaring white marble steps with their iron filigree balusters and red carpet, were a particular offense against good taste.

Violet's face was closed in a tight frown and her wine-colored silk skirts made a rustle like a rushing stream. Blackstone could see at a glance that she had grown into her beauty. Styles had changed, but the new fashion of locating a woman's waist somewhere about her ribs suited Violet well. The downward V of the bodice was meant to flatten a woman's chest, but in Violet's case only served to heighten her charms.

She turned to her papa and picked up her skirts with the practiced gesture of a woman sure of her movement, anticipating the stairs. He had perhaps two seconds to arrange his face into a bracing sneer. He had known the news of Frank's disappearance would hit her hard. He watched the next blow fall, not without satisfaction.

Her startled gaze met his, and in her unguarded expression he read a brief tumultuous history of their past before her papa caught her stumble and steadied her.

He had wished in that moment of freefall on the *Redemption* to see the flash of those dark eyes again. Now he steadied himself with the reflection that getting what one wished for rarely measured up to the expectation.

George Hammersley glared down at him, a staked bear, his black hair peppered with gray now, but his height and bulk undiminished. He disengaged himself from his daughter's hold, setting her unresisting hand on the banister and turning to the government's man. "This man cannot be the man you mean. You can't foist this fellow on us, Chartwell. Don't you know who he is? He's the very blackguard that broke my Violet's heart."

Chapter Four

"Had they fixed on any other man it would have been nothing; but his perfect indifference, and your pointed dislike, make it so delightfully absurd!"

—Jane Austen, *Pride and Prejudice*

Violet watched Blackstone start up the stairs, tall, lean, unhurried. He did not take them two at time as he once had, but her father's calling him a blackguard had no apparent effect on the cool, mocking face. She knew that expression well. It was the face he'd shown her at their parting, and it had erased all earlier images of him. She did not remember what he looked liked when he made a joke or when he was about to kiss her. This cool, detached face was the one he wore in her memory whenever a recollection of him surfaced like a bobbing piece of wreckage after a storm.

"Was this your idea?" She recognized that she could not control a slight tremor in her voice.

"I'm here to serve my country." His voice said that nothing less could induce him to return to Hammersley House.

"Noble of you."

"Join the damned army then, Blackstone." Papa's color was high, his face rigid. Violet took his arm and gave it a squeeze.

Blackstone stopped about halfway up the stairs. He had that look as if his surroundings offended him. She knew his opinion of Papa's taste. Blackstone Court, his own estate, was renowned for its elegance.

"If you want the government's help finding Frank, you'll smile sweetly at me."

Her father stood unmoving. "Why this man, Chartwell?"

"Papa?" Violet's voice was almost a plea.

Chartwell spoke sharply. "There's no time to dither, Hammersley."

George Hammersley looked torn. "I wouldn't ask it of you, my girl, but Frank . . . missing . . . How are we to find Frank without their help?"

Violet reached up and touched Papa's cheek. "We'll find him."

Lord Chartwell cleared his throat. "That's the cooperation we need, Hammersley. I'll leave you in Blackstone's hands then. I must stress that it's imperative that no one in the prince's party receive the least hint of our investigation."

"For Frank's safety," Violet said.

"Of course, Miss Hammersley." Lord Chartwell bowed. In the next moment he was halfway down the stairs.

Blackstone signaled her footmen. *Her* footmen, and they turned to do his bidding. "We'll want to look at your brother's trunk and bags before the prince arrives."

Granthem appeared, carrying Frank's valise and satchel, and directed Tom and Ned with the trunk. It seemed to Violet that Frank's possessions had betrayed him, apparently unconcerned to arrive home without their master.

Blackstone reached the top of the stairs. He gave her a brief indifferent glance. "Have you sent for Preston?"

"Yes."

"Good. We have little time. The prince and his party could arrive at any moment."

In Frank's room a grim-looking Preston saw to the placement of Frank's dark green trunk and leather cases. The room felt crowded, but no one else's presence could make up for Frank's absence. Violet felt Preston's reluctance to touch Frank's things, as if to touch them made them artifacts of a life, instead of a man's necessary belongings needing to be put away for his use. Frank was supposed to be here, joking with Preston, teasing Violet, and dressing for dinner.

Preston looked at Blackstone, who nodded, once again assuming command of the situation.

Preston popped the latches and swung open the trunk revealing its two sides, on the right a set of six shallow drawers, and on the left a large open compartment where Frank's coats and trousers hung. For several minutes they all simply gazed at the open trunk.

It smelled of Frank's sandalwood shaving soap and the faint starch of his linens. At a nod from Blackstone, Preston began to work his way through an examination of the drawers, opening each in turn.

Papa slipped from Violet's hold and stood at the window, his back to them, his hands tightly clasped behind him. Blackstone said nothing, watching Preston with undivided attention.

At last Preston shook his head. "This packing job is not Master Frank's work. Someone's been through his things, someone who doesn't know Master Frank well."

"You're sure, Preston."

"I am, my lord. Look here at the way these coats have been hung. You see the turn of the hanger hook?"

Blackstone nodded.

"Master Frank is left-handed, so when he does for himself, he naturally puts the hooks to face right, you see. And in the drawers, someone's run a hand under his shirts and linens. Took the drawers out and mixed up the order. Master Frank likes his smalls drawer above his cravats drawer."

"Do you think the search was made here or in Spain?"

"Here, I'd say. Things are not settled like in the drawers. The linings have all been slit, too." Preston gently pinched the printed fabric to show how the pale green silk had been pulled away from the trim that had once held it in place. Someone with an expert's steady hand had made the slits.

Blackstone continued to stare at the trunk. "What's missing, Preston? What do you think Frank was wearing?"

"One minute, your lordship. I keep an inventory each time Master Frank travels. Let me fetch it." Preston disappeared into Frank's dressing room and returned with a small black moleskin notebook. He flipped open the little book, and went back to examining Frank's coats.

"I can't say for sure, your lordship, but there are two coats missing, a blue coat and a bottle green, a pair of gray trousers, and two waistcoats—burgundy and cream."

"Thanks, Preston."

Was wearing. Violet caught the change of tense. They were speaking of Frank as if he were dead. Her knees felt wobbly, and she stiffened them.

"Was Frank in the habit of concealing documents in his trunk?"

Preston shook his head. Violet looked away. She must be careful not to meet the valet's gaze on this point. She would look again at the trunk without Blackstone, to see if Frank had made use of his secret code.

The door opened, and Granthem interrupted. "The prince is below."

Everyone turned to her then, but only Blackstone spoke.

"Think of me as a branch of the government, Violet. Give me a week to find your brother."

A week. She could recover from a week. To find Frank, a week would be nothing. Now that she looked closely at Blackstone, she could see that he seemed irrevocably altered. His thick hair was black as ever, and his eyes were that deep, cool blue she remembered. But he was not so much lean as gaunt, and his complexion had a yellowish cast, as if he'd been ill. He was impeccably turned out in black evening clothes, as if he had stepped directly from some other drawing room into her life again. His body had that easy disposition of limbs that made him incapable of an awkward move. Only the sneer altered his face, making it hard to see her brother's boyhood friend in the man before her. A week with this new Blackstone. Maybe that week would finally erase the years of holding on to the old one.

Violet caught her father's pleading glance. She nodded. "Find Frank."

Abruptly Papa staggered as if under a blow and reached to cling to a post of Frank's massive bed.

"Papa?" Violet started towards him.

He pressed a hand to his chest. "I can't meet the prince, Violet. I . . ."

"I can do it, Papa. I will come to you later to report."

She glanced at Preston, who stepped forward to take Papa's arm and guide him to a chair.

"Don't worry, miss. I've got him." Preston bent over her father, loosening his collar.

She turned to Blackstone.

"Well, Violet, can you do it?"

She nodded.

He took her hand, his warm and firm and alive, while hers felt cold and numb. He slipped a heavy band on her ring finger, and she looked at their joined hands, hers weighted with a large square diamond and his with the infamous signet ring, gold and black with distinctive acanthus leaves on the band and the proud masculine *B* on the black face.

"If you are worried about the diamond, it's paste," he told her.

"Appropriate then, a false diamond for a false engagement." A brief irrelevant thought flitted through her mind that Penelope Frayne would never forgive her.

Andre Sturdzi, the Prince of Moldova, wore a magnificent dark blue uniform fit for a fairy-tale prince, heavy with gold epaulets and endless loops of braid. He was tall and broad shouldered with guinea gold hair and bright, pale blue eyes like a doll's painted ones. He had a full drooping moustache that Violet thought a walrus might envy. A fur-trimmed cape dangled from one shoulder. With his stiff posture he reminded her of a wonderful nutcracker Frank had once brought home from Russia.

With him were the Count and Countess Rezina, a December and May married pair, and the prince's ancient secretary, General Gustav Dubusari. The elderly general was a quaint figure from an earlier time with a powdered wig and a gold-tipped cane. The whole group seemed like a set of figurines on a mantel, inclined to take their fashion cues from the prince himself. There was nearly as much gold military braid on the hem of the countess's pale blue gown as on the prince's jacket. After the introductions were made the prince turned to Violet.

"Dear, dear Miss Hammersley." He bowed over her hand, his moustache tickling the backs of her fingers. A faint flowery scent reached her. "A thousand apologies. I have lost

your brother. No, not lost, I think. He has the delay. He left
me this note for you."

The prince extended his hand with a piece of common
stationery, folded over repeatedly.

Violet opened the folds and read—

My dear sister,

*Do not be alarmed at my delay. Circumstances require
me to attend to one more matter before I return. Show
the prince every courtesy and every pleasure. I rely
on you.*

Your brother,
Frank

It was a fine note. The handwriting was Frank's and the
signature to be sure. It was only the stilted words that her
brother would never use that caused Violet's pulse to quicken.
Someone else had chosen the words for Frank to write, perhaps someone in the room. Violet suppressed a shudder, and
summoned a smile she hoped did not appear too empty.

"Thank you, your highness. We do not blame you for
Frank's delay, and it is a great comfort to us to receive his
message." She could feel Blackstone's gaze, but she tucked
the little note up her sleeve. "My father, too, cannot be here
tonight and sends his apologies. He is unwell this evening,
and hopes to greet you properly in the morning. In the mean-
time, welcome to Hammersley House. We will try to make
your stay with us as comfortable as Milvert's."

The prince watched her closely. "Your brother's
absence makes our visit not so glad. It is good that we have
not the hotel. We will cheer you and keep your spirits up

while we wait for your brother. You will show us your English ways."

At each of the prince's pronouncements the members of his entourage nodded and murmured their agreement. He seemed to expect this approval and paused between sentences to allow the appreciative assent of his followers.

"You English do everything the modern way. We must make Moldova modern, strong." He thumped his chest with a closed fist. "Our Russian neighbor is powerful, so we learn from you how to keep ourselves strong."

A pause followed the prince's stirring speech as if he expected a rapt audience to applaud. For a moment his unfocused gaze did not see her or the servants lined up to assist his party or Blackstone at her side. She felt the pressure of Blackstone's hand at the small of her back, prompting her to speak.

"Your highness, my fiancé, Lord Blackstone."

For the first time the prince's smile faltered a little. His glance at last took in Blackstone and returned to Violet. "But you are beautiful as a thousand virgins. This your brother did not tell me, so, of course, you have the fiancé." He bowed to Blackstone.

"She is beautiful, isn't she? We're but new engaged, so I keep her close to me at all times." Blackstone linked Violet's arm through his. "It's not the fashion, but we do not like to be apart."

The prince laughed. "But perhaps at dinner, you must sit elsewhere, and I may safely flirt with the beautiful Miss Hammersley. That, too, is English fashion, is it not?"

Lingering over port in George Hammersley's red dining room, Blackstone tried to assess the men of the party. General

Dubusari was the one to whom they all looked in spite of
the prince's bluster and the count's practice of keeping the
wineglasses filled. Blackstone had not dined with bandits
for a year without coming to recognize dangerous men. The
prince did not seem to be one of them, but a true killer could
shift from cordial amusement to deadly rage in the time it
took candlelight to flash down the length of a knife blade.
By the time they joined the women, Blackstone decided that
Frank was in deep trouble.

What advantage Blackstone possessed in the first
moments of seeing Violet Hammersley again evaporated
during an interminable hour in her drawing room enduring
the prince's attentions to her. It was impossible not to watch
her, not to want to touch her. She never once glanced towards
Blackstone, but she twisted the ring he'd given her as if she
felt its presence like an irritation.

Apparently current fashion had decided to dispense
entirely with anything so practical as straps or shoulders to
hold a woman's bodice in place. Somehow a woman's gown
molded to her breasts and ribs like bark to a tree. He did not
know why he had not noticed the vast amount of skin
revealed by the new mode any time in the past month. Perhaps living with bandits had thrown him off his game or
perhaps it was the contrast between the deep wine color of
Violet's gown and the pale shimmer of her skin that made
him take note of changing fashion as he had not done earlier.
He told himself that she was paying rapt attention to the
empty-headed prince because she cared about her brother.

He found himself less able to summon the attention he
needed for the little countess, a round-cheeked, big-eyed
blonde with sweet, doll-like features, and a manner of dressing that, he suspected, was contrived to take years off her

actual age. Like Lady Ravenhurst the countess had a way of leaning forward to invite a man's gaze.

"Lord Blackstone, you must tell me"—the countess glanced at her husband, who appeared to be dozing with a wineglass dangling from his slack hand—"how to behave here in England. I do not want to make any faux pas. May I rely on you?"

Her eyes were full of helpless appeal. She reached out a small hand to touch his. Blackstone felt General Dubusari's scrutiny and smiled at the little countess. Maybe Hazelwood had it right after all. Young Wilde was Hermes disguised by impeccable English tailoring to lead Goldsworthy's reluctant spies down to that special rung of Hades where the things a man wanted hovered out of reach while some lesser object dangled near at hand.

Chapter Five

Violet entered Frank's room on shaking legs. She needed to be doing something, anything to recover him. *Frank. Missing.* The two words beat in her head every minute making sleep impossible.

The quiet when the neighborhood bells sounded was hollow and mournful. Violet had settled her guests and their servants for the night, the countess's thin stick of a lady's maid, the prince's diminutive valet, and his hulking bodyguard, who was to sleep in his dressing room. There was also a rotund little chef, who insisted on inspecting and tasting all of the dishes offered to the prince by Violet's offended cook. Once she'd seen her guests off to bed, Blackstone had gone. Her mind had instantly cleared without the simmering distraction of his presence. Near him she felt like a little pot on a flame, bubbling and seething. She had reported to Papa on the prince's arrival and made him take a sleeping draught. Promising to do the same, she dismissed her maid.

She closed Frank's door. It was odd to enter with no expectation of seeing him. When he was not on one of his trips, she often stopped by to visit with him before each of them left for separate evening entertainments. He had talked of taking bachelor's quarters, but hadn't got round to it.

To her right beyond the faint glow of her candle loomed the dark mass of his tester bed with its carved paneled headboard and gold tapestried hangings. The walls of the room were a deep burgundy. Frank's green trunk stood upended and open in the center of the room where Blackstone had asked Preston to leave it. She was sure Blackstone meant to examine it again himself, and she wanted to be ahead of him.

She set her candle on top of the upended trunk and studied the open wings of the interior. If Frank had anticipated danger, he would have left a sign in the arrangement of the drawers. Since he had begun traveling for the bank, he used the pattern of the silk print as a kind of index, and by shifting the drawers, he could arrange the slanting lines in several ways to leave a message for Preston or for Violet herself.

Staring into the trunk released thoughts Blackstone's presence had driven from her head. It was a double mystery, both Frank's disappearance and the government's investigation. She wanted to understand both, but the questions and possibilities made her chest feel too tight for her heart, and her legs were really behaving quite badly. She dragged the leather bench from the foot of Frank's bed to face the trunk and sat, folding her hands in her lap, conscious of the absurd chunk of glass on her left hand. She closed her eyes and took a deep breath. Frank was alive somewhere, and they would get him back. No other thought would do. As the government's man, Blackstone's concern would be the missing report. Well, he could find it himself. She would worry about Frank. She opened her eyes and set to thinking.

During the interminable supper and the coffee that followed, she had studied the prince's people. The prince himself seemed a brainless mix of flattery and anticipation for the wonders of London. She could get little out of him about Frank. Each time she so much as alluded to her brother, the prince stopped to pat her hand consolingly. When he leaned towards her, she smelled the cloying floral pomade of his moustache. She had quickly realized she could not endure those sympathetic pats, and she could not say more without giving away her knowledge of the true circumstances of Frank's absence.

It was the others in the party who made her uneasy. They were half a second too late to laugh at the prince's jokes and entirely too watchful for guests consuming the amount of wine the count insisted on pouring. She had hoped for better luck questioning the countess, when the two of them retired to the drawing room while the men lingered over port at the table, but she learned little. The Countess Rezina had a fair, childlike beauty with long corkscrews of flaxen curls and an old-fashioned high-waisted gown with a gold sash and loops of heavy matching cord along the hem. She and the prince both had a painted look of doll-bright cheeks and eyes, and she seemed more like a daughter to her husband the count, than a wife.

When Violet asked how they came to be traveling with the prince, the countess reminded Violet that Prince Andre, one of a confusing number of claimants to the Moldovan throne, had come into his position as a result of a Russo-Turkish agreement. The prince, caught between the two enemies, had turned immediately to England, as to a friend, for military aid.

The countess, a cousin of Andre's, was helping the bachelor prince to establish his court. She explained that she had been raised in a dreadful moldy old pile of a castle surrounded by a swamp. She confessed that she found her new position daunting and that she hoped to see how the great hostesses of London managed their affairs. She was sure everyone in Moldova would judge her cruelly. She had heard, but couldn't quite believe, that ladies in London sometimes dampened their petticoats. Her pale blue eyes big with wonder, she assured Violet that such a daring practice would result in pneumonia in her country. Violet doubted the woman was as naïve as she appeared.

The only information the countess offered about Frank was a remark that he had gone to pay a call on their last day in Spain, and they had not seen him again. "In truth," the countess confided, "I think he went to see a certain sort of woman. I heard him inquire of one of the porters the way to the Romany district."

This breathless confidence seemed implausible. Frank was no libertine, and he had no personal connections in Spain that Violet knew. To suggest that Frank had wandered into danger somewhere away from the prince's people absolved the royal party of responsibility. The prince and the countess hinted that Frank had disappeared or been delayed in Spain, but the government believed him to be in England. Violet might have believed the prince, if she had not read the note. The note that Frank had penned but not composed was the most alarming piece of the puzzle. In Violet's mind the note ruled out the possibility of kidnapping. If strangers had kidnapped Frank, his captors would make a ransom demand of their banker father.

Her legs grew steadier, and Violet pushed the bench back. Kneeling, she rearranged the drawers of Frank's trunk according to his usual habit, but the pattern swam before her eyes. She would need more light to see any message he intended. She glanced over her shoulder at the mantelpiece, looking for candles, and found none. For a moment she simply regarded the empty mantelpiece, where Frank's familiar possessions—his bronze clock, his red and black Greek vase, his onyx owls—all seemed to be in their proper places. Her brain stalled trying to recall where she had moved the candlesticks. They had not taken themselves off to other shelves. She was contemplating the mystery when a slight noise drew her gaze to Frank's bed.

A gasp escaped her, and her hand flew up as if she could catch the small sound. Blackstone stood looking at her, from the shadows, a dark figure, except for the white silk of his waistcoat and cuffs. He stood as still as one of Frank's bed-posts, but from deep inside her, memory leapt up to meet him, foolishly glad at his presence. Her knees buckled, and she sat down hard on the bench, her heart racing.

"How like us, Violet, to end up alone together at night."

As he came towards her, carrying the missing branch of candles, forgotten lessons from their time together surfaced. She knew the way he moved, even the way he came to a stop, and how it would feel to press her hand to his taut belly to hold him back, not that she had ever held him back for long. She knew he could lie at his ease, his limbs warm and sprawled as if in sleep and spring in a flash to catch her and pin her under him.

Us. Her poor heart beat overfast in her tight chest, making speech impossible. He stopped beside the trunk and dipped his branch of candles to light them from hers. "You want another look at Frank's trunk."

She found her voice. "And so do you." Her one thought was that they must not touch. That was all. No matter how many times in the past they had been mad to touch, if they did not touch now, Violet could manage the conversation. She would concentrate on Frank and get Blackstone to tell her what he knew.

He set his candles on the open trunk and took a place beside her on the bench, studying the trunk as she had done. "What do you think we overlooked earlier?"

We. Again he made a careless assumption of their being joined somehow, working together, having a common goal, which they did not. "I thought you'd gone."

"Leaving you to the potential murderers and the royal flatterer?"

She fixed her gaze on Frank's trunk. "There must be something. There was too little time earlier."

"I think we need more light." For a few minutes he moved about, collecting candlesticks and lamps and setting up a bright circle of illumination around them. Sitting down beside her again, he was so close she could smell the scent of his shaving soap, a fresh, clean scent that reminded her of the moment of breaking the skin of an orange. His shoulder was inches from hers. His long legs stretched out towards Frank's trunk.

"Where have you been?" She clasped her hands in her lap and twisted the ring on her finger. Her hands had done no wicked thing in five years, and now she wanted to touch him.

"Did you wonder?"

"I never thought of you."

"Liar. You were angry for months. You invented a thousand set-downs to give me. You burned all your keepsakes."

"I had none."

Undeterred by her denial, he went on. "You turned to your estimable friend Augusta Lowndes, who abused me thoroughly and told you that you were lucky to be rid of me and all such titled blackguards."

Violet glanced at his profile. His lids veiled his eyes. His dark hair fell slightly unruly over his collar.

He had exactly described her efforts to forget him. Except for the part where she berated herself and called herself an idiot a hundred times a day, and the part where she curled in a ball under piles of covers to muffle her sobs. After weeks Augusta had dragged her out of her fetid bed, combed the hopeless tangles from her hair, and set her on her feet again.

In the beginning, every step forward had felt as if she plowed into a gale, a howling wind of loss and humiliation and self-loathing. She'd kept at it, kept her head bent down pushing forward, kept herself endlessly occupied, turned her thoughts away from him, and now when she'd made such progress in forgetting, he had returned to say *us* and *we* and take away all the ground she'd gained. Well, she would not let him know he had cost her an ounce of effort.

She stood, pulling her shawl about her and moving to stand beyond the circle of light next to Frank's writing table. "Augusta suggested that I'd had a narrow escape and should count my blessings."

"I knew you could rely on her." He seemed to be regarding his black evening pumps with undivided attention.

"Ridiculous to have been so young," she told Frank's writing table.

"Unavoidable, however. So what have you been doing with yourself since those black days?"

Violet moved from the little table to the cold hearth. "Me? I am a formidable philanthropist. There is hardly a need for succor among the destitute of our great city to which I have not responded. I founded sewing schools for women where the silk trade declined and provided boats for fishermen. I promoted housing schemes for workers pouring into London and removed pauper boys from the prisons and workhouses to train for the merchant service. I am president of the British Beekeepers Association, as you shall see, because the prince is interested in my bee work."

Her catalogue of good works sounded paltry. What did it matter all the good she'd done, if he could come back and make her clasp her hands together to keep from touching him. What did it matter who she'd tried to save in London, if she had not saved herself. She wished she could say—*I fell in love and married*—that would have been an answer, but she could not claim such a complete recovery from their early attachment. She repositioned the pair of stone owls on the marble mantelpiece next to Frank's black and red Greek urn. Her hand lingered on the urn in which Frank collected pennies. He picked them up wherever he went, working girls, he called them. Blackstone's voice recalled her to the present.

"You've employed the time better than I have."

She turned to study his back. He was hardly being forthcoming. "You didn't answer my question about where you have been."

"Most recently? In Greece."

"Like Byron? Did you go to help them win their independence?"

"Most assuredly not; a fool's errand, that."

"You were ill there." She noticed again how thin he was, gaunt even, and how his skin had a look of parchment under a fading tan.

"No more than the ordinary complaints of travelers. It's a rough country. Bandits and warlords have more sway than any government."

"Have you been home yet?"

At the word *home* he stiffened almost imperceptibly. "No."

She blinked at the abruptness with which he closed the topic. "You've made yourself known in London."

"No more than before."

She thought she had achieved a nice symmetry with the owls, the urn, and Frank's bronze clock. "What induced you to work for the government?"

"I have some expertise they need, and the work is hardly facing cannon."

She returned to the bench, giving in to the pull of his presence. It was idiotic, but she still felt it, as if she'd waded into a swift stream whose current threatened her balance, dragging her inevitably towards him. "I should think you'd prefer the cannon."

"You would, I'm sure. What story shall we tell the world?" He reached over and stilled her fingers where she twisted the ring he'd given her. "We'll never convince the prince and his lot that we are betrothed if you twist my ring off your finger."

Blackstone did not pat as the prince did. He gripped with a firm, uncompromising hold. His touch jolted her. Violet's senses sputtered to life, like a fire catching in tinder and crackling, sending sparks cascading upward. Her fingers stilled under his touch. She did not do anything so foolish as to pull away. Cursed awareness streaked through her. She forced an answer past her tight throat.

"You should have informed your employer that we had a past history that makes you the wrong man for the job."

He released her hands. "Sadly for you, Violet, they know all and chose me for that very history. Resign yourself to tell the world that you changed your mind, discovered that we do suit after all, and have put the past behind you."

He stood, putting his back to her again.

Penelope would never forgive her. "Let's do nothing yet. For now we need only deceive the prince."

"No announcement in the papers then?" He glanced over his shoulder at her.

She shook her head.

"Very well." He moved to stand behind the bench.

"What does Frank's note say?"

"Frank didn't write it."

"It's not his hand?" She could hear at once that he found that detail significant, as did she.

"It's his hand, but the words are not his words." Violet pulled the little note from her sleeve. "Someone must have told him what to say."

Blackstone held the paper in the light. As he read, he seemed to forget her presence. "He always called you 'V.,' didn't he? Will you trust Preston to make a copy for me?"

Violet nodded. Blackstone tucked the note in his waistcoat pocket.

She returned her gaze to Frank's trunk.

"What's your impression of the prince?"

"When he isn't flattering me, he's flattering England."

"Did you get him to say anything about Frank?"

"Every mention of my brother led him to name some London wonder that Frank recommended his highness see. The prince can't wait to ride in the park, visit a gasworks and the menagerie, dance at a ball, and attend a balloon ascension. But he didn't act like a man with any guilty knowledge. He seems genuinely not to know where Frank went."

"Did he mention meeting the foreign secretary?"

"Never. That is the purpose of his visit, isn't it?" She remembered Frank telling her something like that.

"Yes, to report on his progress in building up the Moldovan army."

"Is Moldova supposed to hold Russia back from Turkey?"

"It seems improbable, unless miles of gold braid will frighten the tsar."

"Excessive, isn't he?"

"He gives new meaning to the term."

Blackstone's familiar voice was having an effect on her, and she tried to shake it off. She would gain nothing by staring longer at Frank's trunk. She rose again and returned to the hearth. No fire had been lit, and she felt the room's chill. Frank had been away for weeks, and the cold had settled in the room. "Is that what he bought with the government's money—miles of gold braid?"

"You think the money did not supply the prince's army?"

"I doubt it. Bankers always follow the money trail. We think what happens to money explains people's most desperate acts."

"In this case you think the money was misspent?"

"Almost certainly, and Frank caught on to it."

"Hence his report had to disappear."

"And Frank." Blackstone seemed to forget that point. She risked a direct look at him. He was so thin. "There's something you're not telling me."

"Surely, you didn't expect full disclosure from me." His closed face mocked her.

"This is not about us. This is about my brother."

"You rearranged his drawers. What were you hoping to see?"

He noticed. Blackstone noticed everything. It was one of the reasons Violet had liked him in the beginning. One did not need to explain the obvious to Blackstone. He'd seen it first.

Violet wished she knew what to look for. Whoever had searched Frank's trunk had undone Frank's message system. The rows of parallel lines did not match up in any of the ways Frank usually aligned them. She came back to the bench.

"Think, Violet. The trunk must tell us something. It sat in your brother's rooms in Gibraltar until porters removed it to a cart for a journey to the ship. Seamen brought it on board and put it in the cabin reserved for your brother. His trunk made the passage with or without him, and we need to know which. While everyone else went through customs, your brother's trunk sat in his room."

Blackstone stepped up to the trunk and pulled the cravat drawer from its slot. He turned, holding the drawer out to Violet. "Smell it."

"Smell it?"

"Preston told us that someone else rearranged the clothes. Does it smell like a man's hand passed through the clothes or a woman's hand?"

"You can tell?" She took the offered drawer onto her lap. He watched her with that heavy-lidded look of his. "Why is Frank's report of such importance to the government?"

"You said yourself that you think the prince has mismanaged the loan money."

"Yes, but that's not news. Princes are notorious spenders, as we know, and Frank would advise the prince openly if he saw him being taken in, you know."

"Suppose, however, that Frank found a truth that's uncomfortable for someone, dangerous even. Not mismanagement, but deception or fraud."

"It would have to be someone powerful, which I don't think the prince is, for all his extravagance, though I may be deceived by his manner."

"Smell the drawer, Violet."

She lifted the drawer to her nose. It smelled like Frank, of course, like the sandalwood soap he favored and his piney cologne. She stirred his cravats gently. Another smell came, fleeting and rose scented. Violet waited to catch the scent again. It was unmistakably feminine.

"A woman's hand." She met his gaze and realized he'd already come to the same conclusion. "You smelled the drawer earlier."

"I had a chance before you arrived, but I wanted to confirm my suspicion." He took the drawer from her and slid it back into its slot. Once more he sat beside her on the bench, this time on her left. Violet told herself he was not too close. It was merely that his shoulders took up a good bit of space. He took her cold, ring-bearing hand in his warm ones.

"The note is a good sign, Violet. It means that whoever has Frank has kept him alive so far, and whatever they want, they don't want it from you and your father."

"What do you mean?"

He didn't look at her, but at their linked hands. "They didn't ask for a ransom. If money is not their object, then they must want something from Frank."

"What could they want from him? They must have his report if all his bags are empty."

"Not if he anticipated them and sent the report by some other means or encoded its message in some way. They want to know what he knows. And they may want to know who his informants were."

"But by taking him, they have tipped their hand, haven't they?"

"Not necessarily. Frank may not know who has him or even where he is. He was likely unconscious or blindfolded when they took him." Blackstone was familiar with the abduction techniques of bandits and warlords.

"Why the note to us?" She couldn't help the plaintive question. He looked up then.

They were face-to-face on the little bench. How had she imagined him changed? The intensity of his gaze, the sharp edges of his face, the commanding line of his mouth. He tilted her chin up to meet his dark gaze. "They want you to think Frank is alive, and they want to keep you from setting up an alarm. Whoever they are, they do not want the government looking for Frank."

"And if they find out that the government is looking for him?"

"Frank's situation will not be a comfortable one. Hence our ruse, Violet." His gaze was steady, a reminder that she must play the role in which she had been cast.

"Then we must find him. Where do we begin looking?"

"You and I will be looking at the prince and his party. The government will be looking where the ship docked."

"You are not in charge of me."

"I am in charge of the government's investigation."

"You expect me to do nothing?"

"I expect you to act as if you believe your brother has been delayed and to pay sharp attention to the prince's party. One of them knows something. What was Frank's plan for the prince's entertainment tomorrow?"

"Blackstone, do not presume the rights of true fiancé."

"Only the rights of a government agent." His gaze was unyielding. In any test of wills between them, he would be a tough opponent.

Violet did not want to give in, but Frank was somewhere in the worst of circumstances, and whatever else she knew of Blackstone, she knew he could find Frank if anyone could.

"The prince wants to settle his horses properly. Later, my father is to show him the bank and the exchange, and tomorrow evening the prince has planned a dinner for the officers of the bank to express his gratitude for England's past support. His chef is to do all the cooking."

"It sounds like a day for you to play hostess and tend to your guests' comfort, Violet. Make sure their rooms suit them."

He gave her hands an indifferent parting squeeze, as if his mind were elsewhere, rose from the bench, and was gone. Violet began to shiver, which was just the room and the shock of the news about Frank.

The worst was over. She and Blackstone had met again. Such a meeting would have happened sometime. She could count herself fortunate that it had not happened in a public place. She'd survived two shocks, the news of Frank's disappearance, and the effect of Blackstone's return. She folded her shawl around her to keep off the chill and snagged the silk on Blackstone's diamond.

A score of candles burned, but she could hardly see anything clearly. With her free hand she pulled a delicate lilac thread from the brackets that held the false diamond. It made no sense Blackstone's working for the government, not going home. He loved Blackstone Court. He had not always been comfortable there, but for the brief time of their engagement, he had been full of how it would be for the two of them to live there. He had promised her miles of bookshelves and a bed big enough to hold a boxing match in. So why had he stayed in London?

Chapter Six

"How soon any other wishes introduced themselves I can hardly tell, but I believe in about half an hour after I had seen you."

—Jane Austen, *Pride and Prejudice*

Blackstone found the ways of Hammersley House as familiar as if he had not spent five years in exile from the easy intimacy he had once enjoyed with the house and its occupants. After midnight when he left Violet at the top of the ridiculous grand staircase, he had descended, then circled back through the servants' door and up another stair.

Now he passed from Frank's bedroom around the central courtyard towards the guest rooms at the rear of the house. He stood awhile in the dark looking down the hallway. No sign of light came from under the door of any of the rooms assigned to the prince's party. At the far corner of the courtyard, he spoke briefly to Stevens, the man Goldsworthy had added to the Hammersley staff.

"Anything to report?"

"A loud quarrel between the count and countess. Unfortunately, gibberish to me, Lord Blackstone. I don't speak a word o' any tongue but English."

"How long a quarrel?"

"Ten minutes, I'd say."

"And no attempt to hush it up?"

"No, sir. They seemed to enjoy going at it, like they wanted to be heard."

"A quarrel staged for public notice?"

Stevens nodded. "I'll be on duty, sir, until the other servants are up and about. The people here like Miss Hammersley and the young master. They'll keep a sharp eye out."

"Thanks, Stevens."

Blackstone left Stevens on watch and completed his circuit of the upper story passing through the oval drawing room and George Hammersley's study to stand outside Violet's bedroom. He leaned his shoulder against the wall. Last week he had felt too weary to follow the willing Lady Ravenhurst to her bedroom. Now he was awake, against his body's better judgment, in a state of sense-pricking awareness.

Violet, too, had put out her lights. That did not mean she slept. He imagined her restless mind working at the problem of Frank's disappearance through the night and considered how he was going to handle her need to act.

He should feel only bitterness at her mistrust and her willingness to judge him, but sharing a bench with her reminded his body of other feelings she stirred. When polite London turned on him, he should not have been surprised. London was fickle in her favor at best, but when Violet had turned on him, the one person who knew him better than his own family knew him, that had been the unforgivable thing.

He laughed at himself for standing on guard outside her door. There could be only one reason for it.

She was a walking summons to a man's most tireless soldier that he should stand and salute. Blackstone should know, he had begun having erections in her presence when he'd been a worldly seventeen and she, thirteen, plump as a partridge, with no breasts to speak of.

No one in his or her family had imagined there was any danger in their intimacy. He was older, her brother's friend, titled. She was outspoken, unpolished, and bookish, an annoying younger sibling. The first time he'd visited the house, she had been confined to her room for attending a lecture on economics in male dress.

Experience had not lessened her impact on him. The black eyes, alive with sharp intelligence and unholy curiosity, had acquired depths. Violet had grown into her eyes. With each of his youthful visits he had watched her grow into a slim beauty with lush ripe breasts and wondrous dark hair. Tonight her hair was up, coiled in some cunning way so that it hung in soft curls about her face, but he had seen it down, lying against the pearl white swell of a breast, thick lazy curls unwinding like smoke in a clear sky.

When he thought of the first time Violet had roused him, he understood that his reaction had less to do with her appearance than with Violet herself and her dangerous need to know things. It was an extreme need that went far beyond anything Pandora or Eve had ever contemplated, and that insatiable curiosity was accompanied by a singular unwillingness to take no for an answer. After that first experience he had tried to stay away from her, to reestablish some fitting distance.

For awhile he had succeeded. His real downfall as far as Violet was concerned began when he'd been in town between terms at his college. Coming from university, he had felt himself a man of the world. Still he'd been seventeen and incautious enough to have an erection in her presence.

"Show me," she had demanded.

He'd had no intention of showing her, but in the interest of satisfying her curiosity and ending the strange hold she seemed to have on him, he had yanked her hand and put it to his swollen shaft and told her to be boring. "Drone on with the dullest drivel you can manage, Violet, and you'll see the swelling go away."

Only it hadn't happened as he'd planned. Violet's hand on him had made him harder, and he had shifted so that aching part of his anatomy connected more fully with hers, and after that he couldn't say what happened as his brain had ceased to function. It had involved a great disordering of their garments. Only Augusta Lowndes, Violet's redoubtable governess, had saved them from disaster that time. She had interrupted and calmly suggested that in the future when Violet wished to know something, she choose her source of information more carefully.

Then at seventeen during the bullion crisis, Violet had wanted to know to an unholy degree how banks and stocks and money worked. As he was explaining, she had interrupted to observe that she supposed he had put his penis— she called it a penis—into any number of orifices. Female, of course, she assumed.

He had made his dry throat work to ask why she imagined such a thing. He could have asked why his particular penis had entered her thoughts at all, but of course, at the time he hadn't been thinking clearly.

She had told him she thought he was daring.

He assured her that he was quite conventional and asked her where she had got the idea that multiple orifices might be involved.

She confessed that she'd been looking at one of her father's books on the Greek vases and had come across a series of illustrations that suggested more possibilities than she herself had originally considered.

Blackstone reminded himself to be fair. Their youthful passion had hardly been Violet's fault alone. He was born to be a connoisseur of erections. He knew them all, the ones like slow bread dough rising, or those like wild Congreve rockets soaring, or others like a water douser's stick pointing straight at the source. When called upon to do his duty by a woman, he had taught himself to coax an erection out of the thinnest wisp of sexual stimulation. But that skill had come later after Violet had gone out of his life.

Still none of those was a Violet Hammersley erection. He hadn't recognized them at first as being uniquely inspired by her. He'd just assumed they were an inconvenience a young man had to endure at an awkward time of life. It was later he recognized the connection with her.

Tonight he did not mistake Violet's agreement to their ruse as a sign of docility or willingness to let him lead the investigation. The trouble with Violet's need to know was that now it was likely to get them both killed.

Chapter Seven

"I am quite sorry . . . that you should be forced
to have that disagreeable man all to yourself. But
I hope you will not mind it. . . . and there is no
occasion for talking to him, except just now and
then. So, do not put yourself to inconvenience."

—Jane Austen, *Pride and Prejudice*

Madame Girard's Hat Shop occupied a fashionable corner
off Leicester Square. A pair of tall double green doors with
elaborate glass panels led the way through an arch into the
interior. The showroom was divided between shelves that
held madame's creations, and mirrored alcoves, each with
a silk-covered bench, for patrons to try the wares.

As they entered, Violet leaned close to whisper in her
betrothed's ear, "Shopping! Frank is missing, and we are
shopping."

The prince's party had split in two with Papa taking the
men off to see those great monuments of commerce and
government—the Royal Exchange and Hammersley Bank,
while Blackstone and Violet took the countess shopping.

Violet hardly knew how the first half of the day had
passed. Blackstone appeared when she emerged from her
room. They'd left before her breakfast coffee cooled, accompanying the royal party to see the magnificent black horses

the prince insisted on stabling nearby. They made a circuit of the usual London sights, churches, squares, and monuments. The prince never failed to admire England's heroes when they appeared mounted. He seemed to view horsemanship as the chief quality of a monarch.

Blackstone was at her side every moment, to offer his arm as they crossed cobbles, or his hand as she climbed in or out of the barouche. His body seemed to anticipate hers, to move in relation to her. Her hand felt the weight of his ring with every move. Violet, who had been climbing in and out of carriages, passing through doorways, and managing packages with no more than the alert assistance of a well-trained and well-paid footman, was made to feel helpless.

The countess, on the other hand, seemed to relish Blackstone's interference. His gaze followed her, and she threw him appealing glances and becoming blushes whenever they met a curb. The countess could turn a simple curb into an impassable country stile that required a strong male arm. Violet did not think she had ever blushed, not even when she had said the most preposterous things. She knew now, of course, that they had been preposterous, but then it had seemed that she could say anything to him and he would not scold or look aghast at her.

The day seemed an endless dance in which she shared a reluctant partner with a more captivating woman. The music played on, and one was obliged to go through the figures over and over and never advance to the end of the ballroom. The government would no doubt commend Blackstone's devotion to duty.

In the hat shop the titled visitor roused the mercenary instincts of proprietress and staff alike. Madame turned to the countess and directed an assistant to help Violet with her coat, hat, and gloves. Violet allowed the countess to keep

Blackstone's arm and lead him about while she exclaimed over the cunning designs, madame's staff trailing in her wake. In no time, she was seated on a silk bench, trying to win Blackstone's approval for a youthful chip straw bonnet while the staff moved with quiet, swift efficiency to bring refreshments or new designs.

Just once Blackstone shot Violet a look that promised vengeance for her escape from the role of fond fiancé. His suffering look inexplicably cheered her as she turned to admire a high-crowned chocolate silk bonnet, its peaked brim embellished with a pair of dusky pink roses. It would suit her, she thought, simple and expensive. She nodded to the one clerk assisting her that she would like to try the piece.

An hour later as they made their purchases, Madame Girard's mouth grew tighter and tighter. The countess explained in a gush of girlish breathlessness that her bill must be sent to her husband the count at the Milvert's Hotel at the end of the week.

"Is it not done in England so?" she asked Blackstone.

The little shop bell tinkled, a lady stepped in, and Madame Girard abandoned them to greet her next customer. There was no mistaking the distinct countenance of Arabella Young, Lady Chalfont, friend of Penelope Frayne, and fellow patroness of Violet's ball. Arabella nodded to Violet, but her gaze went straight to Blackstone.

"Lady Chalfont." He strolled over to take her hand with an easy charm. "Your presence here confirms our good taste. Let me introduce my companions. You know Miss Hammersley? And her guest, the Countess Rezina of Moldova."

The encounter was over in minutes. Blackstone managed to charm Madame Girard back into good humor, escort the frail countess from the door, and bid Lady Chalfont farewell. Violet calculated the amount of time it would take for the news to reach Penelope. Women did not wager on the relative speed of raindrops down a window or the life expectancies of flies, but Violet was willing to wager that in less than thirty minutes the Duchess of Huntingdon would know that Violet and Blackstone had been seen together.

She should go home and toss the cards of invitation to her ball on the fire.

Nate Wilde was on assignment far from Goldsworthy's club passing through haunts he'd once known as a boy. At a corner where an old white church with pepper-pot turrets faced a sharp-edged brick charity school for girls, Nate turned and hunched his way down Nightingale Lane past opium dens to Wapping Highstreet in the center of London's docks. Some might say that Lord Blackstone had the better part of the case, riding around in a fine barouche with highborn nobs, but Nate saw the promise in his work. He might be the one to find Frank Hammersley.

In the perpetual shadow of the high dock walls, carts and wagons rumbled past, shaking the ground. Nate had left off the fashionable clothes of the club for a rough jacket and a tweed wool cap with a bill that concealed much of his face. His walk and manner changed to match his secondhand attire. A brisk breeze blew the stench of burning tobacco in his face. Near the Thames, condemned cargoes burned in furnaces day and night next to the acres of warehouses. Every shift of the breeze wafted a competing scent over him—coffee or spice or sulfurous ore or hides or the rank mud of the great river. A day in the docklands could exhaust a man's nose.

Goldsworthy's informants in the customs office said the ship that brought the prince to London had carried Spanish

wine and Ceylon tea. The barrels of wine had been off-
loaded and sent to the vast underground vaults of the London
Docks. The tea had followed a path to the merchant who
bought it, Waring & Sons Bonded Tea Merchants. Nate
picked out the route and followed it, noting lodging houses,
taprooms, and derelict buildings along the way. If someone
wanted to keep Frank Hammersley alive but out of the way
in London, the dockside warren of lanes and quays made
sense.

That was the best information they had so far. Someone
wanted Frank Hammersley's family to think he was larking
about on the Continent or doing some banking business in
Spain, and that someone did not know the government was
already on the case.

Feeling nearly invisible, Nate wove his way through men
and vehicles in the shadow of the dock's huge walls. Flaxen-
haired or brown-skinned sailors passed, speaking a medley
of tongues, and grimy shop windows displayed all the gear
a sailor could want, tins of meat and biscuits, brass sextants,
ropes and lines coated with tar. None of the hardened men
Nate passed would think twice to hear an odd accent or to
see a man half dragged as if the worse for drink. Some
would no doubt jump at the chance to knock a man senseless
for a bit of extra coin. Once Frank's captors had removed
him from the ship, he would be as secure as any cargo in
the locked warehouses or wine vaults of London.

How they had removed him under the nose of customs
officers was another question. And there was the darker
possibility that the government had in mind—that Frank
Hammersley had chosen to disappear and that he didn't want
to be found. No one had mentioned it openly, but Nate could
read Goldsworthy now after working with him for near a
year.

The warehouse of Waring & Sons Bonded Tea Merchants proved a dead end in a row of derelict buildings. The *Madagascar*'s cargo could not have been delivered there. The row of buildings had suffered a fire. Though the brick outer walls stood, charred rubbish lay in heaps against them. The doors were chained and locked and only two portions of the roof remained at either end of the building. Nate made a note of doors and windows to sketch for Blackstone.

Beyond the row of warehouses the river lapped the shore. Nate could see a narrow weedy path along the bank above the river. He declined to investigate that way. No sense in falling in the river if one couldn't swim. He would have to find another way to make a closer inspection. A burned-out building might make a good hiding place, and he looked for signs of recent entry.

Retracing his steps, he let himself slip back into his old ways. He'd once been a Bredsell boy. Before the Reverend Bredsell's arrest for fraud and manslaughter, the larcenous vicar had run a school for orphan boys that trained them in thievery and spying rather than in honest trades. In his three years with the school, Nate had learned to work a street. In those days it had been his ambition to become a high mobsman with a purple silk waistcoat and a gold watch the size of a turnip. Now that he had the finest coats to wear, that ambition seemed hollow. He didn't know yet how far he could go in his new profession, but he was sure he would beat the best mobsman all to pieces. He might even get a "Sir" to his name like Xander and Will Jones, men who had once been his enemies, but who had become steady friends.

Nate had come over to Goldsworthy's operation from Will Jones's employ. Sir William, as he was now called, was working with Peel on plans for a true Metropolitan Police Force, and when those plans hit a snag in parliament, Jones

had found a place for Nate with Goldsworthy. Nate knew he
would go back to straight police work in time, but for now
he could not complain—the clothes, the digs, and the close
proximity to Miranda Kirby—filled his days.

As he slouched along, he tried to put the pieces together
the way he'd learned from the copper Will Jones. Somewhere between the dock and Waring & Sons' ruined tea
warehouse, Frank Hammersley was confined. That meant
money had changed hands. A landlord or a watchman had
been paid to look the other way, to lock a door, keep a watch
on the prisoner, bring a plate of food. And someone had
to empty the prisoner's piss pot, the sort of someone who
wouldn't be above trying to make a little extra coin on the
side for his trouble. A familiar sign caught his eye up a narrow lane, as promisingly disreputable as any in London,
with the name Cat's Hole painted on the bricks at the corner.
Coming out of the lane was a small neat man in threadbare
finery whistling a shrill, sour tune. It was second nature to
Nate to notice others without being noticed, so he made
himself part of the scenery until the fellow passed. When
Nate looked back, the man had disappeared off the high.
Nate turned up Cat's Hole Lane to have a chat with the proprietor of the pawnshop. A friendly conversation today could
mean needed information tomorrow.

Violet took up her vigil in Frank's room at the end of the
second day of his absence, or the beginning of the third day,
depending on how one looked at it. Frank's trunk still stood
in the middle of the room next to his leather bench. Tonight
there was no danger that she and Blackstone would end
up on the bench again. She saw now how he meant to play
the role of fiancé—ever politely solicitous and close, while

flirting with the little countess. What she did not see was how his act helped them find Frank.

Papa had gone straight to bed after the prince's dinner for the officers of the bank. He did his best to appear hospitable before the prince, but when the prince said anything particularly thickheaded about Frank's absence, Papa's expression flickered between mild annoyance and naked rage. Earlier in the day he had tried to enlist Bow Street, and the magistrate had refused to help, claiming the matter was a foreign office affair.

From the door Violet surveyed Frank's room with care. She wanted to be sure Blackstone was not ahead of her, lurking in a dark corner. Last night when he had taken charge and acted like an investigator, she had hoped for Frank's immediate recovery. Whatever pain their past history might bring, she had been sure she could endure it to see Frank safely home. But during the day, that hope had slipped away. In Blackstone's manner she could detect no urgency, no concern for Frank. In all his interactions with the little countess he had seemed to be the man about whom Penelope Frayne and others would gossip—idle and carnal. Violet meant to take him to task about it as soon as he appeared. She took a stand by Frank's desk.

Blackstone appeared from wherever he'd gone after dinner, looking as unperturbed as ever, as if they had all the time in the world to find Frank and no unease about his circumstances.

"I do not see how we will find Frank in a hat shop."

"Good evening to you, Violet. I think we had a good day." He closed the door and reached up to undo the knot of his neckcloth.

She looked away. "What could we possibly gain with the purchase of a pair of hats?"

He crossed to the fireplace and lit the coals in the grate, taking time to stir the fire to crackling life as if he'd forgotten her presence. She thought she might leave without his observing it, and then he spoke.

"Your confidence in me astonishes, as always. No one in the prince's party got near Frank today. We kept them with us at all times. We appeared unsuspecting. We accepted their story of Frank's delay. Occasionally, we appeared to be properly betrothed. We might want to work on that bit some."

"If we failed to appear properly betrothed, it might have been because you flirted with the saucer-eyed countess at every turn."

"She plainly wants me to think she needs rescuing. Doesn't that rouse your curiosity, Violet?"

"Rescuing from what?"

He leaned an elbow on the mantelpiece. "A bad marriage, desperate circumstances? I don't know."

Violet thought about it. "Her helplessness hardly seems a threat."

"Violet, my job is to keep you and your father from harm. Other members of our . . . organization are looking for Frank."

"Did they find him today? Are you in communication with them?"

"Today someone questioned customs officials and everyone who was on board that ship. One of the *Madagascar*'s crew overheard a suspicious conversation and observed the countess in a part of the ship where he was surprised to see her. We have an idea that a distraction, created by the unloading of the prince's horses, allowed them to remove your brother before the inspectors came aboard."

"You think Frank was on the ship."

"Yes."

The plain certainty of the answer stopped her a moment, but then she looked at him, at the way he leaned an elbow on the mantel, his shirt open at the throat, his face a mask of indifference. She drew in a breath and began again. "The prince thinks—"

"The prince 'thinks' may be putting it too strongly."

"The prince thinks Frank took off in Spain in pursuit of a woman, and the countess implied that he went seeking a gypsy woman."

She thought some reaction registered in Blackstone's eyes, but he only gave a brief dry laugh. "Not like your brother to mix banking duties and women."

"It comes back to the countess then. Blackstone, you cannot think that peahen is in charge of some conspiracy."

"No, but you can see that the prince is not in charge."

She had to admit that she could.

"I'd say he's being managed, or he's having his strings pulled like a puppet or one of those French automata. He moves his limbs and speaks, but his head is empty." Again he looked at the fire, not at her, absorbed in some train of thought he did not wish to share.

"So, we go shopping?" She knew her voice sounded hollow.

"Not tomorrow. What did the prince say to you?"

"He wants to ride in the morning. He wants to show off his stallion, Oberon."

"Good, the park is a public place. You should come to no harm there." He pushed away from the mantelpiece and was gone. He didn't even offer her a bow.

He did leave the fire going, and she went to bank it. As she reviewed their conversation in her head, she realized how entirely professional he had been, an agent of the government, looking out for the interests of his majesty's loyal subjects. That was as it should be. It was Frank's situation, not Blackstone's professionalism, that weighed on her spirits.

Blackstone had to question his sanity as he settled himself for another watchful night in Hammersley House. He had spent the day in the company of two women, both with claims to beauty, one who hung on his arm, flattered him, and did everything in her power to suggest an absolute reliance on his manly strength, and the other who refused his assistance and questioned his character and competence at every turn. And the second woman, the one who doubted him, was a woman who had betrayed him, cast him off, and used him ill when he had most counted on her love.

When all of London believed him to be a shocking profligate with no sense of duty or honor, he had counted on Violet to know him better, to know who he was no matter what was said of him, or what that painting might suggest. His own lips had been sealed by a promise.

Five years had not changed Violet's opinion of him. She still believed the worst reports about his character.

Naturally, his mind fixed on the glow of her pale skin against her dark hair, the lively flash of her eyes, and the sweet pursing of her mouth, a preface to some barb of her wit.

Naturally he wanted to remove her clothes and expose the spare, elegant female architecture, chaste as marble, smooth and curved and unadorned, that was a naked Violet Hammersley.

Chapter Eight

"Do you suppose them to be in London?"

"Yes; where else can they be so well concealed?"

—Jane Austen, *Pride and Prejudice*

Over coffee and the club's excellent rolls, supplied by Wilde, Blackstone made another report to Goldsworthy. The situation was puzzling and irritating at once. Either the facts didn't add up or his brain didn't work in the face of Violet Hammersley. Yesterday he had touched her twoscore times. Whatever he told himself about her coldness, her betrayal, it was impossible for his body not to seek hers. In the clear light of day he tried to remember his Newton and the hours of university lessons about planets, suns, and moons, and the forces that spun them together and apart. There must be some law to explain his attraction to Violet. In the past, every touch between them had held the possibility of a conflagration, but that fire should have died. They should be no more to each other than a pair of lifeless rocks, circling each other in the vast reaches of the heavens, all that radiant energy of the past, spent.

Nothing he knew about carnal relations or physics

explained why he had not left Hammersley House until he
was sure she and her father were in no danger. He'd mocked
himself for staying so long, but he'd done it anyway. Time,
distance, other impressions should have dimmed the betrayal
of the past. Desire should not wake with such fire, like a
sleeping dragon.

Before dawn he'd returned to his room at the club. Now
he accepted a cup of Wilde's excellent coffee, and under its
influence he gathered his wits. The usual hammering and
muffled voices of workmen sounded from behind the canvas
curtain in Goldsworthy's office.

"Put an announcement of your engagement in the paper,
lad," Goldsworthy announced, settling behind his enormous
desk.

Blackstone narrowly avoided burning his tongue. He had
yet another reason to distrust Goldsworthy's amiable façade.
"Why did you? It's the usual custom for the parties involved
to announce their betrothal."

"No need to thank me, lad. I saw that you would be too
busy to make things official."

Goldsworthy's hands lay flat on his paper-covered desk
again, thick fingers spread. It was a sharper's trick, a sleight
of hand, the appearance of openness that concealed the big
man's grand scheme. Blackstone met the man's gaze and
watched a gleam of appreciation light there as if Goldsworthy were pleased with an apt pupil. "What do we know?"

"Frank Hammersley should be dead. If he had or has
information that led to the deaths of two British agents,
someone wants him stopped."

"But he's not dead."

"Whoever has him certainly wants his family to think
he's neither dead nor in danger, merely delayed."

Blackstone waited to see whether Goldsworthy would

volunteer any information. He knew both Goldsworthy and Wilde had been to the docklands, but the big man merely nodded for him to continue.

"The prince arrived with a letter for Hammersley's sister. She says the handwriting is Frank's, but the words aren't. He wouldn't address her in those terms or close the letter in the way he did. I had his valet make a copy." He handed Preston's work to Goldsworthy.

Goldsworthy looked over the note. "The prince gave it to her, you say. Where'd the prince get it? And when?"

"He claims it was left for him in Gibraltar." Blackstone had puzzled over those details as well. He couldn't picture the prince standing over Frank dictating that message.

"Convenient that note, from a man who went off to do his business without his luggage."

"It's safe to say that Frank and his luggage have been separated for days. His trunk has been thoroughly searched, linings slit, and his valise and satchel have been emptied."

"What's missing?"

"We don't know what was in the satchel. His valet says the valise had a gentleman's personal items, and that two coats, one blue, one green, a pair of gray trousers, and two waistcoats, burgundy and cream, are not in the trunk."

"Hammersley must be wearing one set of clothes, but not two."

Blackstone nodded grimly. He, too, had seen something amiss in the extra missing clothes. Kidnappers rarely provided their victims a change of attire.

"Did you note that, Wilde?"

"Got it, sir. Two coats, gray trousers, two waistcoats."

"So someone looked for Hammersley's report. The question is—did they find it?"

Blackstone could think of a half dozen other questions

about the missing report. "Wouldn't Hammersley be dead, if they had?"

Again he waited for Goldsworthy to volunteer information. The big man tapped his fingers together. "Hammersley had arranged to get a copy to our agent."

"But the agent, two agents, ended up dead. Why kill the agents? Why not kill Frank and take his report?" He watched Goldsworthy's face and got the clue he was looking for. "You think that if Frank Hammersley is alive, he's on the wrong side in this matter?"

"Frank Hammersley was empowered to provide Moldova with another hundred thousand pounds."

Blackstone's brain was not so sluggish that he didn't recognize that Goldsworthy had just altered the game substantially. "Where's the money?"

"Exactly the question that disturbs Lord Chartwell."

"The government thinks Hammersley took the funds? I beg your pardon." Blackstone shook his head and set his coffee on the edge of Goldsworthy's enormous desk. The government didn't know Frank. It was through Frank that he met Violet, and through Violet that he lost Frank's friendship. He hadn't thought of that piece of his loss in awhile. "Hammersley is a partner in his father's bank. He's worth forty thousand pounds a year. He doesn't need the government's money."

"Is the bank sound?"

"As any bank, I'd wager." Blackstone had been out of the country a year, but since his return, he'd heard nothing to indicate another bank crisis loomed. Goldsworthy's mild manner did not deceive him. Frank's situation was worse than he'd imagined. The government was Frank's only hope, and the government suspected Frank of murder and treason.

"Well, it's too soon to tell, lad, but two agents are dead

and Hammersley may have been the last person to see either of them alive." Goldsworthy's face wore its most cordial aspect. The canvas behind him bellied slightly with some shift of the air in the concealed room. Another uncomfortable realization struck Blackstone. The government expected Frank to contact his family. Goldsworthy had put Blackstone in place to catch any communication Frank might attempt. It was his job to betray Violet Hammersley. No wonder he'd been chosen for it. He had an unreasonable urge to slam his fist into Goldsworthy's solid, substantial person, but it would be exactly like taking a swing at an old oak. Instead he found himself defending Frank.

"If Hammersley arrived to find bodies, he might have prudently exited."

Goldsworthy rose to his imposing height and came round the desk to give Blackstone a hearty clap to his shoulder. "You've a fine grasp of the situation, lad. Stick with it. Where do you go today?"

"Riding. In the park."

Goldsworthy nodded and turned to Wilde. "You, my boy, must do some more scouting for us in the docklands. I'll have another chat with the customs official assigned to the prince's ship. Off with you both then."

Blackstone passed through the coffee room on his way out of the club, drawing the inevitable notice of Hazelwood and Clare.

"Where are you off to this morning?" Hazelwood seemed permanently molded to his sofa, but he never missed the others' movements or let anyone leave without an inquisition. Whatever plans Goldsworthy had for Blackstone's fellow spies had not developed. They were at the moment a pair of lucky sods.

"A ride in the park."

"Don't you have adventures! Let's see you off then. Club-men must stick together, right, Clare?" Hazelwood rolled to his feet, his wild hair and stained and rumpled clothing at odds with the sharp intelligence in his eyes.

Clare grinned. "Never let your fellow clubman down, I say."

Hazelwood and Clare followed Blackwood down the stairs to the club entrance. They stood in the portico under the scaffolding. A pair of workmen passed overhead on board pathways. It occurred to Blackstone that the scaffolding concealed the club's entrance and public rooms from view. A carriage could pull up to the entrance and a man could arrive or leave without being observed by passersby. As long as the scaffolding remained in place, the building would seem unoccupied.

The next moment Wilde appeared dressed in rough clothes, holding the reins of a pathetic creature that might once have passed for a horse. Blackstone took one look at the animal, and knew he was doomed to his fellows' abuse. He had not thought he missed having his own stables, till now. He couldn't make himself move forward to take the reins that Wilde held out.

Hazelwood shook his head slowly. "By the way, Wilde, never choose an animal for me. My reputation as a gentle-man wouldn't be able to take it."

Wilde cast Blackstone an abashed look. "Sorry, sir. Not my area. A fellow named Isaiah Tongue usually supplies our horses. Had no time to reach him this morning."

"Don't worry, Wilde. I'll survive. Just get yourself to Wap-ping." Blackstone took a deep breath, stepped out of the con-cealment of the portico, and mounted the old plug in front of him. He stroked the animal's neck, wondering if he could rouse a pulse in the beast.

"Well, Blackstone, if you're lucky, the nag will expire before you reach the park."

As the prince and his party turned, making their way back through the park, Violet began to calculate how much longer they would be exposed to public view. There was no sign of Blackstone yet. She had not told him the hour at which the prince intended to ride, but had let him assume.

Naturally the prince's glittering braid and his matching black horses had drawn stares but only from early morning walkers and grooms exercising their employers' mounts. The prince led the way, accompanied by his grim bodyguard, Cahul, a formidable figure in a blue uniform with a tall bearskin hat. Violet heard a pair of passing horse guards remark on his fanciful uniform.

"French? The King's Guard?"

"No, must be Russian. See the insignia. The Emperor's Marine Guard."

Behind the prince, the count and countess made a pair. Again Violet was struck by the apparent age difference between them. Blackstone believed the countess had some role in Frank's disappearance, and Violet meant to study the woman closely without Blackstone's distracting presence. This morning the countess hardly seemed helpless. Her horse was as spirited as any of the others, and she managed the animal easily. She never touched her husband or asked for his help as she did with Blackstone.

The prince's secretary, General Gustav Dubusari, and Violet brought up the rear of the party. The prince looked about, hoping for more notice. At intervals he liked to have Oberon perform a *pesade* with his front legs neatly tucked, as if the horse were a circus animal.

Violet had ignored his antics and set herself to question General Dubusari. The old man had a gentle look. He wore his coat loose on his wiry frame. His quaint powdered wig and his habit of steepling his fingers together suggested both the scholar and connoisseur. He had needed assistance to mount, but once on horseback he seemed to have no trouble controlling his horse. Like the prince he wore a jacket with a distinct military cut and the endless gold braid. Violet thought that perhaps making the braid might be the chief industry of Moldova. She tried to imagine the old general kidnapping Frank and failed. Frank was too smart, too strong.

"The prince designed our uniforms himself," General Dubusari told her. "Young as he is, he has genuine taste. He is a great patron of the arts. Perhaps you and Lord Blackstone can direct us to the studios of the principal artists in London. The prince will want to add to his collection."

They had nearly completed a circuit of the bridal path under the budding plane trees when Blackstone approached. Violet pulled thoughtlessly at her horse's head and had to soothe the animal, a bright bay mare with black mane and legs. She had turned to riding in the past few years. Neither her father nor her brother rode, but she had sought instruction and bettered her skills so that now she could handle her playful mare no matter what offenses London offered a horse's sensibilities. It was Blackstone whose mount stuck out. She wondered how he came to be riding a pathetic slug with a shuffle one would expect of an invalid taking the waters at Bath.

She could not imagine what had happened to his stable to reduce him to riding such an animal. Perhaps he had lost a wager. The prince brought the shocking contrast between horse and rider to everyone's attention.

"Lord Blackstone is the perfect English gentleman, but his horse is no worthy of him. Miss Hammersley, I think, has a finer horse, and she is what you call a commoner." He emphasized his point with a wide sweep of his arm between the two horses.

"There is nothing common about my betrothed, prince," Blackstone's tight smile, directed at Violet, might fool others but not her. "I'm sorry I'm late, my love."

"Yes, Lord Blackstone. It is too bad of you to be late. We could have raced." The prince turned to Violet. "Miss Hammersley, you will enjoy a race with me."

"Ladies do not gallop in the park, Prince," Blackstone pointed out, just as if he were in charge of her.

"I would not spoil your pleasure, Prince. Were my brother here to lend me countenance, I should like a gallop, but without him my spirits are not equal to it."

"Ah, Miss Hammersley, forgive me. I forget the brother's absence makes this difficulty. Lord Blackstone will oblige me."

Blackstone stroked the neck of his deplorable nag. "You can see, Prince, that I cannot offer you a challenge this morning."

"But my poor horse, my Oberon, he must show that he is a worthy opponent of the English horse."

"We can see that he is, Prince," Violet said. She caught the grim look on Blackstone's face. She did not know how he came to be riding such a slug, but she could see it did not suit him to be backed into a corner by the idiot prince. She tried to dissuade the prince. "You will spoil your magnificent uniform, Prince. The muddy track will throw up clods and splatter."

The prince glanced slyly at Blackstone. "I thought all English lords had two things on their great estates, you see, magnificent horses and dogs. I could not bring my dogs. Horses always find a place, but dogs are never at home in another's house."

A pair of guardsmen bearing down on them at a fast clip forced the party to move aside. The galloping horses threw up clods and sprays of brown water. The prince sighed heavily, and his horse danced under him.

"You may go for a gallop, Prince. You must not put that beast away with the fidgets in his legs," General Dubusari recommended.

The prince shrugged helplessly, and Violet glanced at Blackstone to see whether he, too, noted how easily the prince was led by his supposed underling.

"You see, Lord Blackstone," the prince insisted, "you must join me. You may ride Cahul's horse. We will have a friendly contest. Not a race. We do not need to put it in the betting book at your club." He signaled his bodyguard to dismount.

Cahul muttered something in his own language.

"Cahul agrees with me Oberon needs to run."

Violet saw how things were going. She glanced at the countess, who was arranging the veil on her riding hat. The count looked half-asleep on his mount. The prince would get his way. Sensing Blackstone's discomfort in riding a poor horse, the prince would take delight in keeping the horse's flaws at the front of the conversation. He was like a child, really.

The prince clapped his palm to his brow. "Ah, but I am being selfish. We must trade nags." He dismounted and gave the reins of Oberon to Cahul. "You, Blackstone, must choose. The horses must have their run."

There was a moment of confusion as the riders shifted, backing their mounts, rearranging the group. Oberon objected violently to the change. He reared, his front feet raking the air, his neigh near to a scream. All the horses stirred restlessly. Violet had to see to her uneasy mount. Only Blackstone's nag placidly hung its head. Cahul pulled sharply on Oberon's bridle to bring his head down.

The prince frowned. "I think Oberon does not like England. Yesterday an outburst on the docks, and now this. That is why we must have a run. Lord Blackstone, my horse."

"Prince, you are too kind," Violet said. "My fiancé will be happy to indulge you in the pleasure of a race. I will hold your mount for you, Blackstone."

Blackstone's gaze said he was anything but happy to indulge the prince, but he dismounted and led his bony animal to her. The poor beast immediately nosed the margin of the path for grass under the mud.

"I give you great honor, Lord Blackstone, and you wish to decline it?"

"Your horse feels less honored, Prince." Oberon still stirred uneasily, and Blackstone swept the animal's neck with soothing strokes. For a moment Blackstone simply acquainted himself with Oberon, letting the horse smell him and hear his voice. "Are you the only one who rides Oberon, Prince?"

"We were made for each other. Hah, he is just impatient to run. You will see. Give him his head, and he will outrun the wind. A quick down and back?"

"To the tenth plane tree," countered Blackstone. When Oberon stood quietly under his touch, only a slight tremor agitating the stallion's smooth flanks, Blackstone mounted. He shifted forward in the saddle to let Cahul adjust the stirrups.

The prince scanned the proposed distance. "Very well, but that is hardly enough for Oberon. Miss Hammersley, will you give us a signal?"

The men maneuvered their mounts into a line. Oberon immediately became agitated again, and Blackstone's attention turned to his wheeling mount, his face grim. Violet regretted pushing him into the absurd position. The best thing to do was to get it over with. The track was clear. The men's eyes swung to her. She lifted her arm and let her glove drop.

The prince's mount leapt forward. Blackstone's knees tightened around Oberon, and the horse bucked wildly. Blackstone lifted his seat but the horse continued its wild plunging, arching his back and spinning in the air, then rising up on his hind legs, his haunches lowered almost to the ground. If Blackstone hung on, they would go over backwards. Violet watched him release his hold and let the animal fling him off. For a brief instant he flew upward then landed in the path of the rearing horse. Violet held her breath. Blackstone rolled away as the horse's legs came down with a jarring thud. The trembling horse snorted and blew, muscles rippling under the smooth black skin as Blackstone came to his feet.

Dripping mud, he caught up Oberon's dragging reins and began soothing the distressed animal with his hands. As the prince cantered back along the Row, Violet urged the rest of the party to catch up to them.

The prince was splattered with mud from his toes to his thighs. His grin stretched his moustache even further. He dismounted and took over with Oberon, consoling the horse, saying, "You cannot win without me, can you, Oberon? Miss Hammersley, such a frown. Did you fear for us?"

She hardly knew what she answered. For a moment her whirling thoughts were consumed by Blackstone. He had let himself be thrown, and she had feared to see him crushed by Oberon's hooves. And now she was unreasonably happy to see him mud-caked and frowning. He stripped the ruined coat from his back. His hat had tumbled away. One cheek bore a dirt smudge. He looked absurdly young and utterly alive.

The prince supplied his own answer for the question she'd forgotten. "Ah, no, you are worried about your brother. But he is a trickster, you know, always disappearing on us and showing up to laugh at us when we do not expect him. He got away from us three times, you know. There is a lady, perhaps. In Spain, he went to see a lady."

Violet almost missed the remark with her gaze still on Blackstone. *Got away from us*. It was what the prince had said earlier, except for the one odd phrase.

"You gave us all a fright," she said to him as Blackstone came up to her. "What caused Oberon to spook that way?"

"Worried, my love?"

"I would hate to see that magnificent animal suffer a fall."

He took her gloved hand in his and opened it, dropping a kiss on her wrist. As he lifted his mouth from her hand, he closed her fist around a short sharp object. It pricked her palm through the leather. A thorn.

"From Oberon's saddlecloth."

She did not have to wonder any longer that Oberon had tried so desperately to throw his rider. As soon as Blackstone's weight had settled in the saddle, the thorn must have dug painfully into the horse's sensitive back.

Violet rode beside the prince on their return from the park. She could not say what the topic of conversation was. She had stopped thinking about Frank, her mind returning to the moment when it looked as if Blackstone would be crushed. When they reached the house, Blackstone excused himself and sought her father. That was when Violet first missed her glove. She thought Cahul had picked it up from the track. She still had the thorn, dark brown, thin, an inch long, round and straight as a needle. She did not recognize it as an English thorn.

Chapter Nine

"She is a handsome girl, about fifteen or sixteen,
and, I understand, highly accomplished."

—Jane Austen, *Pride and Prejudice*

Miranda Kirby smiled at the gentleman examining the jars
of ointments and salves. He was as fashionable as she could
wish. From the excellent cut and fine wool of his dove gray
coat, she could guess his tailor's name and the guineas he'd
spent. By her calculation the man was likely worth four
thousand a year. His lavender waistcoat had subtle gold
threads in the weave. Only the poorly tied neckcloth suggested a man in some distress. Well, that and the carefulness
with which he considered certain salves.

Miranda recognized the embarrassed scrutiny of a man
who had acquired an uncomfortable condition, which he did
not wish to disclose to anyone, but which needed immediate
relief. She drew a resigned breath. She much preferred to
help gentlemen select soaps and scents for their shaving
needs. She could stretch out her arm to offer a gentleman a
whiff of fragrant sandalwood soap in its porcelain bowl or

whip up a bit of foam with a badger-bristle brush and spread it on her palm to show how thick and rich it was.

Directing a gentleman to a remedy for his indiscretion would end the transaction quickly. The man would not be inclined to look twice at her and notice and admire. He wouldn't linger to exchange any banter. She wouldn't hear much of his toffy accent. She could listen all day to West End gentlemen talk. Sometimes when they asked about her, she told them about her mother, the young French lady who had fled the Terror in Paris, when to have a shoe buckle meant death, and come to London with nothing.

The shop bell tinkled again, and a low ruffian slouched in with a soiled jacket and a coarse cap over his face, the sort who had no business in a respectable shop. Miranda's fine gentleman shifted aside, immediately wary.

Miranda knew she must act quickly. "What are you doing here, boy? There's nothing here for the likes of you."

The rough youth thrust a grimy hand in front of the startled gentleman, and offered him a jar. "Here's the one you want, governor. Sloan's salve will clear up what ails you in a fortnight. She recommends it to all the gentlemen. Isn't that right, Miss Kirby?" The youth grinned at her with a full set of white teeth.

Miranda grabbed her broom and came round the counter in a move that set her skirts to rustling. "Oooh, it's you, Nate Wilde."

The gentleman backed away from the youth with the jar. "I say, miss, it's not the thing to let riffraff assault your customers." He eyed the door. "Be off, you."

The youth stood his ground. He even leaned towards the gentleman. "Don't forget, governor, Sloan's salve."

The bell jangled again with the man's hasty exit. Miranda

turned on the intruder. She would dearly love to whack him with her broom. His laughing eyes dared her to do it. But if she gave in to the unladylike impulse, he'd win. No lady would hit a man with a broom no matter how he provoked her, and Miranda was a lady. She knew it. She composed herself and returned to her place behind the counter, putting the broom away.

"Did you tell him about your mother and her shoe buckles?" he taunted.

"You delight in vexing me." She kept her back to him as she rearranged the display of shaving brushes and bowls.

"Vexing you? And here I think of myself as your champion, your knight." He put the jar of Sloan's on the shelf.

"My knight? That's rich. A cheeky devil, more like, sent to make misery for me, that's what you are." She sat on her work stool and took up the straw bonnet she had been trimming before her gentleman customer interrupted. She bent over the work again, applying a lavender ribbon to the brim. Nate Wilde didn't take the hint. He lingered as if he had not a care in the world. "Why are you dressed like that?"

"I had to go to Wapping about a case."

"A case? Not likely. As if you were a real copper."

"Close enough, but better paid, and usually, better dressed."

"Thanks to my father."

"Face it, Miranda, I'm as close to a gentleman as you are like to get." He hoisted himself up onto the mahogany counter. It was the sort of thing he did that she tried not to notice, but she'd seen his arms when he stood in his smalls for her father's measurements. He was not much above her in height, but his shoulders were broad and his arms had a lean iron strength.

She shuddered. "Spare me. I would throw myself in the Serpentine with rocks in my pockets first."

"The Thames would be better," he advised cordially. "As ladylike as it would be to drown yourself in the park, it takes a real river to be certain you'll get the job done."

"My mother did not bring me into this world for the likes of you."

"Shall I tell you your mother's true story? She was a beautiful Irish lass who came to London to work in a factory and listened to a honey-tongued rogue who got her in trouble and your father took her in." He did not say that her father had not married her mother. No need to rub salt in the wound.

"Hah! What do you know! Who was your mother? Who was your father?"

"You don't know anything about your mum, either. So we're even."

"I know I could have been a Nan or a Susan or a Molly, but I'm none of those. My mother knew things, and she named me to be someone. Miranda, a duke's daughter."

"A character in a play that anyone can see for a fistful of shillings."

"Well this Miranda will meet a prince's son, too. Not some flash cove that's gotten above himself."

"Not in London, you won't. Unless you meet a royal by-blow or plan to marry an infant. No prince's sons for that lot of brothers to King George."

Miranda stuck a pin through her bonnet with a savage jab. "Nate Wilde, you spoil everything."

"Where's Wilde?" Blackstone found his fellow members of Goldsworthy's exclusive club in their usual places. Hazelwood lay on his back on one of the long sofas tossing a tennis ball in the air. Captain Clare faced the carpet, his arms pumping his rigid body up and down, like a plank bobbing in a choppy sea. Neither man answered at once. Blackstone reached out and caught Hazelwood's tennis ball midair.

Hazelwood snatched at the ball, his reflexes quicker than Blackstone expected, but not quick enough. "We're having a contest, old boy. Unsporting of you to interrupt." There was no heat in the complaint. "One hundred, Clare!"

The captain lowered himself to the floor. "Wilde's around the corner at Kirby's shop."

"He's in love. It's the youth's one weakness," Hazelwood added.

Blackstone looked to Captain Clare for confirmation.

"Ah, you can't trust the sot, but you can trust the man in uniform." Hazelwood swung himself upright. He still wore his soiled eveningwear. "It's true, whether you believe me or not. The lad's deeply smitten. Clare and I have a wager on whether young Wilde can ever prevail with the fair Miranda. I say it's hopeless. The captain is not so certain."

Blackstone tossed the tennis ball back. He was familiar with the chemist's shop and the pretty young woman who handled the counter. Gold letters on the black paint at the brick front of the shop proclaimed that Kirby and Sons were "Purveyors to their Majesties the Kings of Hanover & Belgium & His Royal Highness & The Duke of Cambridge." There were no sons, only a daughter, and whatever the legitimate trade of the shop, its main business lay hidden from the public eye in the back rooms where Kirby himself labored to produce gentlemanly apparel for Goldworthy's lads. The shop's position directly behind the club, facing the next street, allowed for surreptitious coming and going as the club members were fitted for their new roles.

When Blackstone entered, he found Wilde transformed

into a street rat, sitting on the long mahogany counter, behind which Miranda Kirby bent her shining head over a chip straw bonnet, to which she was applying grosgrain ribbon in a lavender hue with sharp jabs of a needle. Wilde's fingers toyed with the end of the ribbon, and the girl jerked it out of his reach. Blackstone cleared his throat, and the youth looked up, disengaging himself from his rapt contemplation of the girl's beauty.

She was a beauty. Built on a bountiful scale, Miranda Kirby's pale skin was silky smooth and tinted dawn pink. Her blue eyes were fringed with dark red lashes, and her bow of a mouth drawn into a sweet pout. The boy looked like a starving man contemplating a dish of strawberry jam and cream.

"May I help you, Lord Blackstone?" Miranda liked to use the members' titles. She put aside her hat trimming and straightened so that her bosom had its full effect.

Wilde looked briefly dazed before he managed to tear his gaze from the girl's bounty. "I was just on my way to report, sir."

Miranda's glance took in Blackstone's coatless person and his muddied riding boots and breeches, and her mouth dropped open. "Oh, you've ruined your beautiful riding clothes."

"Did you get to the docks again, Wilde?"

"I did, sir, and found something of interest." Wilde dug into a pocket of his jacket and drew out six horn buttons from a man's jacket, each attached to a bit of fine blue wool cloth. "There's a pawnshop up Cat's Hole Lane where the proprietor is none too careful about the source of goods he accepts. For a couple of bob I purchased these from him. He only got them this morning."

Blackstone took one of the buttons. He could see what

had happened. Someone had pulled on the button and cut it free of the garment. "Wilde, you're a genius."

"You think it's Frank Hammersley's coat?"

Blackstone nodded. "What led you to the pawnshop?"

"Whoever took him has got to have someone local in on it. Someone who's not paid enough to do a dirty job. Only a local knows which fence to trust."

"If a man wants to profit, why not sell the whole coat?"

Wilde appeared to consider the question. "I'd say they're not so greedy yet. There's still money to be made out of the deal. If the detained gentleman were to die, then our man would strip the body, dump it in the river, and head somewhere to lie low. He'd sell the clothes later on Monmouth Street."

Blackstone turned over the button in his hand. "So our local jailer may not want to be a party to murder, but he still wants to make a profit? Where is that pawnshop? Can you show me on Goldsworthy's map? The prince said something this morning that fits your theory."

The girl looked up. "Lord Blackstone, would you like me to send over some fresh clothes?"

"Thank you, Miss Kirby."

In Goldsworthy's office they looked over the map of London. Wilde traced the route of the tea cargo, from ship to the derelict warehouse, and explained its ruined condition. Together they studied a rough sketch that Wilde had made of the building.

Blackstone shared the prince's remark that Oberon had caused a commotion while men were unloading the cargo. The morning's incident with the thorn showed how easy it was to deliberately provoke the high-strung horse. The drama of a squealing, air-pawing stallion probably created enough distraction to permit accomplices or hirelings to remove Frank Hammersley from the boat before the customs officers came on board, or for Frank himself to slip away if one accepted Goldsworthy's theory.

Blackstone considered the map again. Wilde pinpointed the fence's shop. The river, the tea warehouse, the dock, and the shop formed a rough rectangle crisscrossed by narrow lanes and alleys with hundreds of places in which a man could be kept out of the way. Frank Hammersely had known his report would cause trouble for someone. Twice he had been stopped from passing that report along to British agents. If he was alive, it would only be because his captors knew he had not reported his findings. Anyone suspected of receiving that report would be in danger. It was likely that the main role of the members of Prince Andre's gold-braided escort was to watch Violet and her father.

And there was the matter of the hundred thousand pounds. Where had Frank seen fit to stash that little inducement to villainy? Whatever the government suspected, Blackstone did not believe Frank guilty of theft or murder or treason. It was more likely that Frank, like his sister, had chosen to act independently.

"I'll take one of these buttons to his sister. She can confirm whether it's his."

Miranda Kirby knocked on the open office door with a brown paper package in her arms. "Oh, Lord Blackstone, they told me I'd find you here. I've a new batch of shirts and neckcloths." She tried ignoring Wilde without success. Her gaze took in the rough clothes that gave his appearance a dangerous edge.

Blackstone glanced from the girl to the youth. Wilde didn't try to hide the man he was—brash, competent, sure of himself. He seemed to be saying to the girl that he was not his clothes, not his appearance. He was who he was.

The girl turned up her nose.

Violet spent the afternoon confined to her rooms, which was history repeating itself. After the episode in the park, Blackstone had said something to alarm her father, and Papa insisted that Violet remain at home while he took the prince and his party to see Sir Alexander Jones's gasworks.

No one said anything about her own alarm, seeing Oberon rear and threaten to crush the man who was supposed to help them find Frank. She had since figured out the nature of the alarm she'd felt in that moment. It was concern for Frank. If Blackstone were killed, no one would help them find Frank. Chartwell and the government had no real concern for Frank, but Blackstone had once been Frank's friend. That must count for something. She did not believe Blackstone indifferent to Frank's well-being.

When Blackstone had first visited Hammersley House with Frank, Violet, thirteen, had been confined to her room for going alone to a lecture on economics in the city. In some odd way Blackstone's reappearance had set their old history in motion again. For three years she had been telling herself Blackstone was only a painful memory from her youth, like a broken limb that ached once in awhile. His return was like a cold frost that set the healed limb to aching once again. She simply had to ignore the ache and concentrate on finding Frank.

She had another problem to solve, as well, Penelope Frayne. Though she had asked Blackstone not to put an announcement in the paper, Violet could be sure that Arabella Young had spoken to Penelope. With their subscription ball only days away, a note to Penelope was imperative. Violet must thank her for her kindness and decline any further part in the ball. Only finding Frank mattered at the moment. In the long afternoon, she consulted her *Lady's Guide to Perfect Gentility*. Her former governess, Augusta Lowndes, had given her the little handbook as a parting gift. The book offered several models of polite notes declining various invitations, but Violet could find no sample letter offering another woman a crack at one's former lover.

Violet dipped her pen in ink and began by acknowledging the compliment of the duchess's support for the project and begging her grace to understand that a grave family matter now prevented Violet from continuing to play a part in the plan. She went on to say she hoped the duchess would continue her support of the ball, but would understand if she did not.

She put her pen down. It was no good. Penelope must know by now that Violet had been shopping with Blackstone. Nothing about the scene that Lady Chalfont witnessed could be construed as an accidental encounter. Gentlemen did not frequent ladies' hat shops. And once Penelope heard through whatever wagging tongue that Violet had engaged herself to Blackstone, any note, no matter how carefully worded, would appear false. Violet considered adding a postscript in which she disclaimed her interest in Blackstone. *I have no claim on Blackstone. He's yours if you want him,* hardly struck a tone of modesty and civility. Instead she wrote that if rumors surfaced linking her with Blackstone, Penelope should ignore them. Violet's intentions with regard to the man had not changed.

Chapter Ten

They were confined for the evening at different tables, and she had nothing to hope, but that his eyes were so often turned towards her side of the room, as to make him play as unsuccessfully as herself.

—Jane Austen, *Pride and Prejudice*

Blackstone entered the long narrow stateroom on the ground floor of Hammersley House, familiar to him because he and Frank used to pass through it on their way to George Hammersley's gunroom. The stateroom had an unexpected simplicity that was always a relief after the assault of the grand staircase. Though guests now filled the room, Violet, at the far end of the room, the prince's arm in hers, was impossible to miss.

He had not seen Violet for nearly eleven hours. He should not be counting the hours apart from her, but though her father was aware of the danger, George had never had any power to stop Violet from acting on her own. Blackstone did not know whether she had seen Goldsworthy's announcement in the paper.

He approached through the crowd, conscious of how few faces he recognized. As the daughter of a self-made man,

albeit a wealthy banker, Violet moved in different circles
from the titled circle in which he moved, where birth established one's position and relation to a familiar set of people.
One knew their faces and places in the same way one knew
one's sums. The mood of the evening gathering and the
absence of feathered headdresses struck him at once. Guests
engaged in earnest conversation, rather than flirtation, and
made polite way for him without any hint of recognition.
There would be none of Lady Ravenhurst's cronies in the
crowd. He could play the role of besotted fiancé without
rousing any gossip.

The snatches of talk he overheard as he angled his way
to Violet's side reminded him further of past visits he'd made
with Frank. Conversation in Hammersley House inevitably
revolved around London. It was no different now, he found,
than it had been when he first began joining the Hammer-
sleys for visits between terms at Cambridge. He saw Sir
Xander Jones again, and exchanged a nod with him. Jones,
a few years Blackstone's senior, was changing London with
gas lighting. At Jones's side a trim matron in green spoke
of necessary bank reforms, and a tall thin young man with
a head of thick brown curls openly advocated the merits of
cundums to an older gentleman. By the time Blackstone
reached his false fiancé, he could almost believe he'd stepped
back into his own past.

A shocked look flickered briefly in Violet's dark eyes as
she caught sight of him, as if she could not comprehend his
being there at all. He could read that passing look because
he knew the same jolt at seeing her. If he had died and begun
haunting her, she would have looked at him that way.
Dressed in silk the color of ripening berries, her skin glowed
like pearls. Her black hair was done up in soft ringlets that

framed her face. He was coming to know the current fashion of ladies' gowns, cut to show the slope of a woman's shoulders and the narrow span of her waist.

As he took his place beside her, she offered him a private glare of renewed hostilities. "You had no right to keep me confined this afternoon. I am no longer a green girl."

He lifted her palm to his lips and drew her close, inhaling a light floral scent. "Your father kept you confined."

"You scared him into it."

He leaned over, claiming a fiancé's privilege, to speak in her ear. Her posture had stiffened in his absence. There was a cold aloofness in her bearing that he did not remember. "Recall that someone put a thorn under Oberon's saddle this morning with intent to kill."

"I could have searched the royal guest rooms while they were out with my father."

"Their rooms have been searched."

She turned towards him, and her curls brushed his cheek. "By whom?"

He found it necessary to pull back, dizzied by the scent of her. "The two new members of your staff who received training from your housekeeper today. A sensible woman, your Mrs. Clark."

"What did they find?"

"Nothing that helps us."

She searched his face. "Nothing you're telling me."

"I do have something for you later."

"What?"

"Meet me in Frank's room at the end of the evening." He watched the little struggle on her face between outrage at his tone of command and her inevitable practicality.

"I've been thinking about the thorn under Oberon's saddle. It isn't an English thorn, is it?"

"We'll talk tonight."

Another guest claimed them, and for half an hour, they played at being betrothed, with the prince never failing to mention their engagement, Dubusari looking on with cordial politeness, and George Hammersley frozen in stiff formality. They accepted the surprise and the warmth of her friends, most of whom seemed not to know their history.

When a question about the dinner claimed Violet's attention, Blackstone moved away from close proximity to white arms and maddening womanly warmth and found himself the object of a furious stare from a young man with a head of close-cropped fawn-colored curls and a clerical collar that appeared to choke him. The collar and his rigid wide-legged stance set him awkwardly apart from the conversational knots about the room. He appeared to be maintaining his balance on a rolling ship's deck. He had youthful, softly handsome features, at odds with the cold disdain in his earnest gray eyes. He appeared offended, as if he'd encountered a scene of outright debauchery.

"Have we met? I'm Blackstone."

"Never. Arthur Rushbrooke, a friend to Miss Hammersley."

Blackstone lifted his wineglass to her friend. "How are you acquainted with her?"

"We share an interest in charitable works."

"Violet is active in charity, isn't she?"

"Miss Hammersley is a most remarkable woman, tireless in doing good for the poor. It would be a great loss to London if anything turned her from her devotion to good works."

Blackstone did not pretend to miss the man's meaning. "Such as a disreputable husband, perhaps."

Rushbrooke's chest puffed out. "I know I am beneath you

in rank, my lord, but I count myself gentleman enough to defend Miss Hammersley's good name."

"Which is hardly in danger from an honorable engagement."

"A man who returns to England with a harem . . ."

"Is unworthy of Miss Hammersley, to be sure, but then few men are truly worthy of the women to whom they aspire. I promise that when we're married I'll keep her in bed no more than eight in twenty-four hours of the day. She should then have sufficient time to continue her charitable work."

Blackstone saluted the gaping reverend and stepped into the courtyard where the dinner was to be served. Violet's staff moved about, laying out supper dishes and lighting candles on little tables. He drank his wine, finding himself unreasonably annoyed by Rushbrooke. He should not be. The man was a stranger to him and a prig. His judgment, while common and unthinking, was ignorant. *A harem, where had that one come from?*

He remembered a verse that had circulated about him during the worst of the scandal after his father died. His mother had begged him to buy up all the copies, but he had refused. It had been a page-long ditty about the trusty yard of young Lord Bl__kst_ne. He had not forgotten the damned refrain.

Lord Bl__kst_ne's yard it measures true
When ladies' locks love does bedew.
Thus London's ladies to him flock
To have their measure taken,
Lest by love they be forsaken.

Hazelwood's theory that Goldsworthy picked his spies for their notoriety made sense. Blackstone and his fellow spies could move in fashionable society, and society would see only the fallen hero, the wastrel, and the rakeshame. No one would guess that each had quite a different role to play in the game. Still he needed to talk with someone of sense. He put his wineglass on the tray of a passing footman and reentered the fray.

Violet's face hurt from smiling. She had been giving supper parties for three years and had never felt any strain in being a hostess till now. The informality of a supper party suited Hammersley House and her father's style of playing host. Mrs. Hill, Violet's cook, was adept at cheese puff pastries, tiny iced cakes, and all the delicacies in between. Her usual guests seemed to quite enjoy the greater freedom of sitting at supper tables in the open courtyard rather than enduring the formality of an endless dinner in the dining room. Tonight her guests were people from what Violet liked to call the sensible world rather than the fashionable world. Most of the gentlemen knew her father through his bank or his philanthropy. They were Londoners. They did not have vast country estates and three-hundred-year-old titles. They had businesses and political positions. Only Blackstone so obviously came from that other world. Everything about him proclaimed it. She had introduced him repeatedly to people, watching for the signs that they knew the scandal, knew the past connection between Violet and Blackstone.

At the time of those public revelations, she could not leave the house without feeling herself to be the object of curious, prying stares. It might not have been so, but she felt it nonetheless.

Violet recalled her unsent message to the duchess. She

must finish it in the morning. She had believed that asking
Blackstone to postpone the customary public announcement
would give them time to find Frank and dissolve their
engagement before the thing was widely known.

Now she could see that news of it would inevitably get
abroad, and it would not do to have Penelope hear indirectly
that Violet was engaged to Blackstone. There was little
danger from her current guests of any gossip reaching
past Violet's friends, but as she and Blackstone ventured
beyond Hammersley House together, they were bound to
stir more talk. Lady Chalfont's first report of seeing them
together would find confirmation and spur speculation. And
in London, speculation had a way of being taken for truth.

Blackstone hardly seemed aware of her as he mingled
with her guests, so much for the appearance of a betrothal.
At least the little countess had sought other admirers, while
Violet had Mr. Rushbrooke. He'd come to her side when
Blackstone disappeared. She could not remember a time
when she had enjoyed Rushbrooke's company less. He
frowned at everything she said and offered corrections to
her most commonplace observances. Abruptly he appealed
to her to explain her beekeeping project to Mrs. Pogue, and
she realized she had not been attending to him. The project
was dear to her heart, but as she tried to explain why it
seemed so promising, she found her account of it sounded
dull to her own ears. Mrs. Pogue's eyes looked positively
fixed like the eyes in a portrait.

A laugh distracted her. It was Blackstone's laugh, a low,
male sound, full of easy confidence, recognizable at once
to her ears. She felt the vibration of it in her stomach, a low
rumble that caused a swooping dip inside her. She turned
away from Mr. Rushbrooke just as he was explaining that
Bombus pascuorum was the common bumblebee. He was

fond of offering a bit of Latin, capping Violet's knowledge with his own erudition.

Blackstone was speaking with Lady Jones, a matron with three young children and a fiercely devoted husband. It was she who had made him laugh, and he made her laugh in turn. The intimate sound of their shared amusement made Violet feel that an abyss separated her from Blackstone instead of a few yards of carpet. From across the room Sir Alexander Jones heard the laugh and unerringly turned a proprietary glance at his wife. What had Violet's aborted note to the countess said? *There is a coolness between us, which cannot be overcome, in spite of public appearances to the contrary.*

She pulled her gaze away, and found that the company in the room had thinned. The prince was nowhere in sight, and the number of gentlemen had diminished. She had not yet given the signal to move to the courtyard for a light supper. The absence of so many guests puzzled her.

Mr. Rushbrooke spoke in her ear. "The gentlemen have gone to look at your father's gunroom."

"Thank you, Mr. Rushbrooke. Pardon me, I will see if I can move them towards the supper."

Her father, an avid duck hunter, had built Hammersley House near the last good duck hunting to be had in London. His gun collection lined the room's walnut-paneled walls, and it was not unusual for him to lure his male guests away from mixed company to see his prized possessions. In the doorway Violet smiled. It was just as she suspected. Papa had gathered a small group of gentlemen around an open case on the large worktable where he cleaned his guns. As she entered the room, he lifted one of his flintlock pistols from its velvet bed and placed it in the prince's open hands, commenting on the gun's features.

"You see, Prince," her father explained, "a properly tuned flintlock, with a good frizzen that sparks regularly, and a priming pan polished to a mirror finish, will fire every time."

The prince shifted his hold on the pistol, half cocking the hammer, not sighting, just pointing the gun idly down the room as five gentlemen watched. Papa's hand stretched out to push the barrel down when a rough hand snagged Violet and spun her into a close embrace. At the same time the gun discharged with an ear-splitting crack. Wood paneling to Violet's left exploded in splinters. Her ears rang. The smell of burned powder and grease stung her nose. In the next instant she became conscious of Blackstone's iron embrace, her face pressed to his linen, his chin resting on the top of her head.

Ordinary sensation stopped, as if time had taken a deep inhale, and waited to expel its next breath. Violet had a fleeting desire to stay closed in the suspended moment. Then the room erupted in male outrage.

"Damn! It was loaded." She recognized the prince's startled voice and the clatter of a pistol hitting the table in the jumble of noise that broke over her. Violet's eyes closed. Her body spasmed briefly against Blackstone's before she got control.

"Violet!"

Blackstone released her. She turned and Papa rushed forward, looking ashen. She moved to him and squeezed his hand. "No harm done, Papa, except to your wall."

The prince charged forward. "Miss Hammersley, a thousand apologies. Unforgivable of me. I never guessed. I am devastated. Please don't faint, dear lady."

"Thank you, Prince. I'm not going to faint." She was distracted momentarily by Blackstone pulling an ugly wood fragment from the back of his hand.

"I recommend, gentlemen, that we adjourn for supper."
She gestured towards French doors that opened from the
gunroom onto the courtyard.

Everyone continued speaking at once. Violet kept her
arm in her father's and her smile firmly in place, making
Papa move towards the courtyard. The prince stepped around
them and continued apologizing as he backed into the supper room.

Blackstone stood behind a potted palm as Violet led her
guests to the supper table. The prince continued to apologize.
As the story circulated in the room, other guests reacted
with disbelief and little shudders of alarm. Violet continued
talking to the prince and encouraging her guests to help
themselves to supper.

Blackstone waited for his own shaking to stop. It wasn't
a visible trembling. It was somewhere deep inside him. He
had stepped into the gunroom as the idiot prince idly lifted
one of Hammersley's old flintlocks. He had known by
instinct it seemed that the gun was loaded. Without a thought
he had spun Violet into his embrace out of the bullet's path.
He would have done the same for anyone.

She was alive. He could see her. In a few minutes he
would take a seat beside her, just as soon as the wood
stopped splintering next to them in his head.

He tried to make sense of the inner quaking. He had lain
with other women since they parted, not as many as his
reputation suggested, but enough. He had not returned to
England to find Violet Hammersley again, in spite of the
flash of memory he'd had on the *Redemption*. He simply
didn't want Violet dead. He certainly didn't want her killed
in a freakish accident.

He had returned to England to repair his fortune and restore his mother and sisters to their proper place in society. Once Blackstone Court was free and clear, he would withdraw in comfortable obscurity and let the world think what it would.

He saw her look about for him in her berries-and-cream dress. He had to step out of the shadows soon. He held out his right hand to judge his steadiness. Not yet.

At one, Violet found Blackstone contemplating Frank's open luggage. Ten candles burned in branches placed on top of the upended trunk. Light seemed to catch Blackstone's face giving her his profile in sharp relief. She couldn't get used to it, his being there. He was himself and not himself. She had heard him laugh tonight. He'd caught her in his arms and saved her from a bullet, but he had been distant throughout the meal. And now his cold profile as he stared into Frank's trunk reminded her of the other Blackstone, the stranger she had never known.

"What do you have to tell me about Frank?" Naturally he did not turn to her. She closed the door and came closer. Tonight he'd lit the coals in the grate, and the warmth drew her. She tried again. "The prince seems to be trying to kill us."

"We're meant to think so at any rate." He shot her a brief glance and returned to his contemplation of Frank's trunk.

"Generally, outside of Greek tragedy, I don't think guests murder their hosts, and, in fact, we're not dead, though we've each of us has had a close call. How is your hand?"

"A scratch." He stepped aside. "Come and sit, Violet."

She settled herself on the leather bench in front of the open trunk, which seemed to offer as little information as before. Blackstone sat next to her, and for a moment it was necessary to remain perfectly still. Just that, his sitting next to her, made it feel as if the elusive closeness of their old friendship had returned. She waited for him to speak.

"I think the accidents are meant to distract us. Or they're meant for the prince—he might have been riding Oberon this morning, you know. Your father's pistol might have misfired."

Violet felt that the important thing was not to look at him, not up close. She could feel his warmth, could see one wool-clad leg stretched out next to her. She straightened. "I grant you the horse, but one of Papa's guns would never misfire. He's obsessive about keeping his guns in good order."

"Unless someone tampered with them. The prince announced his interest in seeing the guns, didn't he?"

"Loudly, in front of his own retinue." She did look at him then. "Oh. You think one of the prince's own people might want him dead? Cahul, the bodyguard?"

"We can't rule him out. He's always nearest the prince, and as a bodyguard, he seems remiss. But I'd say that anyone in the prince's retinue might want him dead, and three of his servants were here during the day. One of them could have tampered with the gun."

Violet shook her head. "We, too, have servants about." As soon as she said it, she realized her mistake. She and Blackstone had become experts at evading the staff. The recollection warmed her more than the fire in the grate.

After a time he answered. "I know."

"What puzzles me is that as far as we know, neither the prince nor anyone in his party has actually read Frank's report."

"No one admits reading it, but we must assume that Frank's kidnapper has committed a crime that he or she thinks Frank's report will reveal."

"She? You suspect the dainty countess then?"

"I don't rule her out. For all her apparent helplessness, I'd say she's as delicate as an ice pick."

"So according to your theory someone has done something he or she does not want exposed by the report. If there had been a murder, that might make sense, but we don't know of any murders, do we? If Frank had witnessed a killing, the murderer would want to silence him."

Blackstone did not answer at once, as if her comment had started some train of thought. She glanced sharply at him. "Has there been a murder?"

He didn't answer.

Violet nudged him with her elbow and instantly regretted the touch and the sensation it stirred in her. "Blackstone, has there been a murder?"

He faced her then and spoke plainly. "Two, in fact, but we have a note in Frank's hand that suggests that he's alive."

He did not say *or was alive*. Violet blinked hard against the sting of oncoming tears. "What could Frank possibly know that's so dangerous?"

Blackstone offered her a plain male handkerchief, clean and warm from his body. She held it in her lap. "You suggested from the first that the money had gone astray. It's likely that Frank's report spells out where the money went."

"Where's the worst place the money could go?"

"To the Russians. If the money intended to build up the Moldovan army actually ended up in Russian hands, England would be financing her enemy."

"And if Frank discovered a plot to funnel the money to Russia, he would be in grave danger?" She pressed Blackstone's handkerchief into a ball between her palms.

"Are you going to tell me what you see in the trunk?"

"I wish that I did see something. As a precaution, Frank

worked out a system to communicate with us, me and Preston. He could make patterns with the design of the silk by altering the arrangement of the drawers. We would know a message was from him by the order of the contents. That order never changed. But whoever searched his trunk couldn't know that."

"If your brother is in the habit of anticipating danger, that's a good sign, Violet. He may manage his own escape. I have something for you."

"So you said."

"Open your hands."

Violet let the crushed handkerchief fall into her lap. Blackstone cupped her right hand in his and into her open palm he dropped a horn button about an inch in diameter attached to a bit of blue superfine wool. Her fist closed around it. Her throat ached. Her eyes stung again. Foolish drops filled them. The button was so small. It could not be all she would ever have of Frank again. She reached for Blackstone's crumpled handkerchief, but he was ahead of her. His hand captured and held her chin. He turned her face to his while he pressed the clean linen to her brimming eyes.

She stiffened but she had no strength to shake him off. She could only turn her face away.

"Is it Frank's?" He released her chin.

She nodded. "Where did you get it?" Her voice was thick, her throat tight.

"An associate found it in a pawnshop off the Wapping Highstreet."

"Does it mean that Frank is dead?"

Blackstone took hold of her shoulders and turned her to face him on the bench. Her skirts billowed over his leg. Her knee pressed against the muscle of his thigh. "Actually, we think it means that he's alive. If he were dead, they would

strip the body and sell the clothes. If he's alive, someone
has charge of him, someone who wants to profit from guarding him."

"I don't suppose we can just knock on every door in
Wapping." She brushed the moisture from her eyes.

"*You* can't."

She pulled back in his hold. "Where did the *we* and *us*
go, Blackstone?"

"You would be noticed in Wapping. We are searching,
Violet. If he's concealed there, we will find him."

He lifted a hand and pushed it into her curls, capturing
her head. He was looking at her with an absorbed look, a
purposeful male concentration that released a flood of memories.

"When did you change your hair?" His gaze on her
mouth seemed to have its own magnetic pull. A pause held
her suspended, as if she had pumped herself high on a swing
and hung in the air before the downward plunge.

I don't know. I . . . Don't look at me . . . she offered an
unspoken plea, but she knew that only her eyes protested.
Her throat was closed. Her foolish body was yielding, moving towards the pull of his attraction. But he did not kiss
her. Instead he drew her closer and pressed her head against
his chest and held her. And she let him, let his arms encircle
her, let herself breathe him in.

He smelled of wool and linen and soap, English things,
things taken from the fields and refined into plain elegance
that suited his person. There was no mistaking his strength
or his steadiness. There was no impatience in his hold. She
did not imagine that he offered forgiveness for the past. He
resented her. He was bitter still, but his quiet hold acknowl-
edged that Frank mattered to her.

They had met because of Frank. Frank and Blackstone

had met at university and liked each other, and when Blackstone had been reluctant to go home for a long vacation, Frank had invited his friend to Hammersley House. No one imagined that Blackstone would take an interest in plump, hoydenish Violet.

"You've lost an earring, Violet." His warm rough thumb stroked her lobe.

He pulled back, and she reached up to touch her ears. Her left ear was empty. In the moment of her confusion, he stood and crossed to the door.

She did not know whether she had wanted his kiss or not, but he had stopped, not she. She straightened on the bench. She had been the weak one, tempted to give in to their past.

He looked back, his hand on the doorknob. "Tomorrow we keep looking for Frank."

"And entertaining the prince."

"Did you promise him an outing?"

"I meet with Dubusari in the morning to make plans. The prince still has much of London he wishes to see."

Chapter Eleven

"You must learn some of my philosophy. Think
only of the past as its remembrance gives you
pleasure."

—Jane Austen, *Pride and Prejudice*

Violet sat at her desk in a rose silk wrapper, her morning
chocolate cooling into a chalky sludge in the bottom of the
cup. She was missing an earring, Frank, and her balance.
Blackstone could do that to a woman.

The earring would turn up she supposed, a thing of garnet and pearls. She had the mate. It would be easy enough
to have another made up if the missing one could not be
found, but most likely it would be found. Wembley, Violet's
excellent lady's maid, would make a diligent search of all
the places an earring could get itself to—the folds of a
shawl, the bottom of a wardrobe, even the inside of a slipper.
Finding a brother—that was more difficult. Recovering her
balance, she had to find a way.

A sharp rap on the door made her start, and as she turned,
Blackstone entered.

"You can't be here."

"You see that I am." He crossed the room before she

could gather her wrapper about her and attempt to rise. He put a hand on her shoulder to keep her in her seat. "Let's look at your calendar, Violet."

"My calendar?"

He brushed aside her failed attempts at a letter to Penelope. "A woman of your many engagements keeps a calendar, I'm sure." He found the black leather volume from Letts and opened it, leafing through the pages, making them flutter and rustle.

"What a number of ladies' societies you belong to, Violet. Are you president of all of them?"

"Of course not. Why are you doing this?" The closeness of the night before had vanished. Perhaps Blackstone had recovered his own balance.

He didn't answer. His hand, lean and brown and distinctly masculine, went on turning the pages, exposing her neat entries.

"Rushbrooke figures prominently here, I see. He thinks you a paragon of womanly virtue, Violet. Are you going to snatch him up?"

"I should be 'Miss Hammersley' to you."

His hand paused. "We've been naked together, Violet."

She could not speak. Her body reacted to the words with an instant flash of heat. He returned to turning the pages. "I don't remember."

"You can't forget." He let the book fall open. "Nor can I." The quiet admission shook her. Violet stared at the day of her life that he'd laid bare. She wanted to recover the sensible, well-regulated life on that page. That day she had attended two meetings with Mr. Rushbrooke, a meeting about her sewing schools project and another about a cricket team for poor boys sponsored by the bank. He stood next to her fully clothed in gray and brown layers of male elegance, but she remembered other times.

"You didn't tell Rushbrooke that." Her body, in its thin covering of cambric and silk, quickened and thrummed with awareness.

"Violet, you've never heard anyone accuse me of betraying a woman's secrets."

Except for showing the world a painting of your Spanish mistress. "Rushbrooke is a sensible man." She tried to mean it. She counted Rushbrooke as one of the better men of her acquaintance.

"He's a prig, and he's well aware of your fortune." He slid his lean brown fingers down the white page, a light grazing that made her skin expectant.

She didn't understand him. He had come back into her life to find Frank not to undo the order she had made in his absence. "Mr. Rushbrooke is a friend of mine. I won't have you being unkind to my friends."

"You need better friends."

"He's an avid beekeeper."

"Admirable."

"At least the . . . admirers that I attract are decent people."

"Ah, you've heard rumors about me." He lifted his hand from the book. "And you are always ready to listen to my detractors."

The accusation stung. Violet swung around. He had no right to be angry at her friends. "Not to your detractors, but to women who frankly admit they are curious about your carnal appetites and would welcome your attentions in bed."

Too late she realized her mistake. In her own hand was the notation of her morning call on Penelope Frayne. His knowing eyes understood too well that she had already heard the gossip.

"You have the advantage of such ladies, Violet, and can let them in on the truth."

"What do I know that other women don't know better?" She tried to make light of it.

"It's true. I might know a thing or two more now than I did at twenty-four. Curious?"

"Never." She lowered her gaze. She had kissed Blackstone a hundred times, a thousand times. She was not curious. She had no need to know what his lips would feel like against hers, how it would feel to be pressed against that lean, hard frame, how he would taste, how she could move him until he surged against her desperate for their union. That knowledge was part of her.

"Violet, you are more curious than Eve and Pandora combined."

"Not about you and your carnal practices." She managed to stand and move away from him, hugging her wrapper tightly around her. "The only thing I want from you is help finding Frank."

He pulled his watch from his waistcoat pocket and consulted it.

"That's what I'm here for, but you are going to have to put my name in your book, or our watchful Moldovan friends will not believe the fiction of our betrothal."

"How can my private calendar serve our fiction?"

"I left Dubusari at breakfast. He intends to confer with you this morning about your plans. I'd best appear more often than your friend Rushbrooke."

Violet studied a patch of the carpet where the sun through her window made a golden square. The hard brightness of the clear March morning made her blink back tears.

"Fine." She returned to her desk and took up her pen. For Frank she would put Blackstone on every page of her calendar. "I will put you in. You returned to London when?"

"A month ago." He came to stand behind her, again so

close that any incautious move would bring them in contact. She dipped her pen. Her hand shook a very little, scattering a few black drops on the fresh page.

"And we've been meeting where and when?"

"Here, of course, privately." His finger pointed to a day as if he could rewrite her life. "I came to see you as soon as I returned to England."

"Oh, that's helpful. This is a calendar, not a diary."

"Well then, we've been . . ." He flipped back through the pages, his arm brushing her shoulder. "Here you could squeeze me in between the Ladies Committee on Housing the Poor and your afternoon call to Augusta Lowndes."

"Where did we go?"

"To see the marbles, I think, appropriate for a Greek traveler, like me. I explained to you where they came from and how Elgin acquired them."

He was so close, so warm. If it were a past meeting between them, she would lean back, her head would collide with his belly, and his hands would drop to her shoulders, an acknowledgement of how helpless they were against desire.

"And you'd best put me into your plans for today, the beehive demonstration, and tonight and tomorrow and the day after that. What's this entry? *A worthy endeavor*?"

Violet tried to pass it off with a laugh. "It's a subscription ball to raise money to train former silk workers as seamstresses and *modistes*. Nothing could be worthier, you see?"

He flipped back through the book to the page that listed the dress fitting the patronesses would have at Penelope's house.

She brushed his hand aside. "If I put you in the book, I think we should agree to forget the past."

"To behave as strangers?"

"Think of the advantages. Strangers know nothing of each other. Words between them are just words. There's a reserve."

"Playing strangers would never do for you, Violet. You're too curious. You see too much."

"Then we should court amnesia. We should act like a pair of people who've fallen on their heads and have porridge for brains. We're lucky to remember our names and where we live. If I look at you in a dazed fashion it is because my brain has gone fuzzy."

"You think amnesia would spare you. There'd be no awareness of me? I could do this"—he leaned down and pressed his mouth to the place where her neck met the slope of her shoulder—"and you would not tremble as you do now."

Whatever he intended he did not stop. He slid the silken wrapper down her shoulder and found the thin strand of hair that secured her nighttime braid. He tugged to release her hair, using his fingers to part the strands and let them tumble over the shoulder he had bared.

Violet meant to twist away, but the twist turned into a stretch that gave him greater access. His hands slid down her arms. Her head fell back against him. He spun her around on the bench and hauled her up into his arms and his mouth descended on hers, and she was kissing Blackstone, opening her mouth, pressing up to meet him, tasting heat and need.

Blackstone kissed the dusky pink mouth he had watched for two days and two nights. Violet's mouth was haughty or generous, never prim. While he had her mouth occupied, he tugged at the tie of her wrapper so that it fell open, and he could press his whole aching self against the thin barrier of her chemise, not so much a barrier, as a sheer curtain. He knew the tips of her breasts would be the same dusky pink of her lips and just as ripe and ready for him, but at the moment he was preoccupied with her mouth.

She was responding to him, kissing him back with all the ardent fire of her nature, as if she, too, had stepped back into the past.

Violet was lost. She reveled in the sensation of being pressed, crushed against Blackstone's unyielding person. She knew how to tilt her head and press just so and open to him. He'd taught her years before, and the first touch of his mouth to hers had been like that joyous moment of a dance starting when musicians summoned a note out of the air and happiness itself claimed her as a partner.

Her body felt the imprint of his through linen and wool. Heat seemed to fuse them together. His hands slid down to cup her bottom and lift her to fit them together. He bent his knees and pressed his full erection against the apex of her thighs. But she was not nineteen. She knew where they were headed, and it was not towards happiness. She had learned that lesson, too, from him.

"Blackstone, stop."

That was a first. He heard it though, clear and plain. She flattened her palms against his ribs and shoved hard. He stumbled back a step.

He stepped back further. For a moment he'd been lost in the wonder and the joy of it. There was no concealing his state or hers. They stood breathing harshly. His cock, at full throbbing attention, strained against the civilized bounds of his trousers. Through her near-transparent chemise he watched the rapid rise and fall of her breasts. "Apparently, amnesia is not our disorder."

"No," she said, pulling her wrapper firmly around her and twisting her loose hair into a tight knot at the base of her head. She did not excuse herself. "No, we're simply bedlamites."

"You're right. Perfectly deranged."

"No more than half a brain between us. Maybe that's all we need, one person with sense enough to step back. Next time, it's your turn, Blackstone."

Next time. Blackstone could not stop the words from echoing in his head. He retreated to the inner courtyard and the uncensorious company of potted palms. He had not intended to kiss her. What rational man would willingly kiss a woman who thought so little of his honor that she believed the most idle report over the evidence of her own experience of his character? Last night he had congratulated himself for pulling back from temptation. At twenty-four he had believed he could endure the shock of discovering that his father had a second family, of discovering that he had a half brother, of whom his father was genuinely fond, on whom his father in fact doted, a boy he read to and laughed with. He had believed he could endure London's condemnation. But Violet had been his love and his friend. Violet should not have turned on him.

Now he'd done it. He'd let himself have a taste of Violet. And his groin ached to prove it. He needed a monastery, a frigid cell on a mountaintop, a spot on a polar expedition. Curse him.

And Goldsworthy and lost brothers.

What he wanted, had begun to want from the moment he saw Violet on the stairs, was to make love to her again in all the places he'd made love to her before in her father's ridiculous mansion. They'd made love in the room assigned to him as a guest, in the billiard room, in the long gallery, in one of the stillrooms below stairs among the jams and jellies, and in the old attic schoolroom. He had imagined in those days a future in which he would make love to her in a bed, his bed. He had told her about it, tempted her with a description of that bed.

He should not be thinking of where they could make love, since it was impossible that they ever would make love again. He had not been a schoolboy when he'd first made love to her, but close to it. He had thought about protecting her from the consequences of their affair only because Violet, with her usual curiosity, had made a careful study of cundums and knew where to get them. And he'd made love to her fully intending to marry her. He had proposed before they made love and almost immediately after and then had spent long naked hours persuading her that his offer was based on love not convention.

She had changed her room entirely since he had last seen it. It was plain and businesslike, stripped of the pretty green paper he remembered. She liked pretty things. Her black leather calendar was another change from her taste.

Those changes pained his conscience more than their interrupted embrace pained his groin. He'd read that calendar. It was plain from every page what she had been doing since she'd broken their engagement, making herself into a paragon of propriety, her days filled with meetings and good works. The only ball in that whole leather-bound wasteland of respectability had been listed as a "worthy endeavor." Rushbrooke might appear on every page, but the change had not been Rushbrooke's fault. It had been Blackstone's.

He remembered how fearless she'd been as a lover. Apparently, he'd not only killed that quality in her, he'd made her think herself so wicked that a lifetime of saving seamstresses and orphans would never make up for loving him. For a moment he thought they'd both remembered what that other time had been like, but she didn't want to remember, and he would be wise to follow her lead. He could give her back her brother—that's what he could do for her. He could not be the man to restore her to fearless love.

It was awhile before he found himself ready for public scrutiny.

Maybe when they found Frank, Blackstone would beg Lady Ravenhurst to dance naked before him and maybe then he would forget Violet Hammersley.

When Miss Wembley came to chide her and help her to dress, Violet submitted to her maid's scold and her ministrations. Blackstone's hungry kiss had made her forget who she was, but Miss Wembley quickly restored her proper self. Even as she allowed Miss Wembley to cinch and smooth and comb and brush her back to herself, the question that had come to her that first night occupied a part of her mind. After more than a year abroad Blackstone had not gone home to the place he loved. Violet wanted to know why. If he would not answer her questions, she would investigate on her own. She would start with his finances. It would be nothing, the work of a few hours to learn what his finances were. "Follow the money, and you'll find the truth," her father always said. In his person and manner Blackstone showed no want of wealth, but there had been that horse that never came from the sort of stable he was apt to keep. She puzzled over his working for the government and riding that pathetic nag.

She ended up writing two notes, one to Penelope, and the other, to a discreet employee of her father's bank who could be trusted to make the proper inquiries into Blackstone's financial situation. The next time she encountered her false fiancé, she would be armed with information.

Chapter Twelve

He wisely resolved . . . that no sign of admiration should now escape him, nothing that could elevate her with the hope of influencing his felicity . . .

—Jane Austen, *Pride and Prejudice*

Once Blackstone recovered from his encounter with Violet he recalled his intention. He wanted Wilde. The note he'd sent round for the youth much earlier asked Wilde to delay his daily exploration of the docklands. Someone in the prince's party must be taking messages to and from Frank's captors. Blackstone wanted Wilde to see the members of the prince's party so that the youth could recognize any messenger sent to Frank's guards.

Stevens had reported another argument between the count and countess and had followed the prince's valet twice to Milvert's Hotel, but he had not seen the man meet anyone other than the hotel staff. The management was still stalling the prince, claiming to make the extra preparations to the suite required for a royal visit. According to Stevens no one at Hammersley House had seen either the countess's maid or the prince's chef leave the house.

When he returned to the club, Blackstone found Wilde waiting for him in the coffee room. The sofas had been pushed aside to create a large open space in which Clare and Hazelwood were exchanging parries with the British cavalry's finest sabers.

The clang of metal meeting metal echoed in the room. Wilde sat in a brown leather wing chair drinking coffee and observing the match. He sprang out of the chair as Blackstone entered.

"You wanted me, sir?"

"Blackstone!" Hazelwood parried a thrust from Clare with more skill and energy than Blackstone supposed he possessed. "Settle a dispute for us."

"Not with a sword." Blackstone turned to Wilde. "I want you at Miss Hammersley's beekeeping demonstration. Can you get there?"

"Beekeeping? Where, sir?"

"Chelsea. I want you to be part of the crowd, so that you can get a good look at the prince and his party. One of them is likely sending or accepting messages from Frank's keepers. If you can spot the man in Wapping, he may lead you to Frank's keepers and to Frank."

"What disguise should I wear for this assignment, sir?" Blackstone studied the boy. He was dressed like a perfect gentleman, yet there was that in his features, in the breadth of the cheekbones, the outward turn of the ears, the freckles, that suggested an Englishman from the ranks of the bustling lower orders.

"Maybe a grocer . . ."

"Does he get to take the girl with him?" Hazelwood asked.

Instant hope sprang up in the boy's eyes.

"Miss Kirby would make the disguise perfect. See if you can talk her into it, Wilde."

Hazelwood gave him an approving nod.

Nate headed for Kirby's shop as soon as he dressed for his part.

The shop was empty. Miranda sat on a high stool behind her counter bent over a bit of sewing. Nate took in the fiery gleam of her hair, the neat white part across the top of her head, and the creamy wings of her collarbone above the lace at her bodice. She worked with quick neat jabs of her needle, attaching buttons to a silver-embroidered white silk waistcoat.

The sewing changed a bit when she noticed him and pretended not to.

"What are you up to?" he asked.

"You can see."

"Who's the waistcoat for?"

"Lord Hazelwood." She held it up and gave it a critical eye. "I wish Mr. Goldsworthy would not make him wear everything stained."

"It's his disguise."

Miranda rolled her eyes heavenward and jabbed her needle through the fabric again.

Nate was glad to see she wore a leather thimble on her middle finger. He waited. He knew she'd noticed his clothes, too. She was a tailor's daughter. She noticed every man's dress and could read the details of his bank statement in the cut of his lapels. "What are *you* dressed for? Cutting hay?"

"That case I'm on." He knew she would notice his open shirt and rolled up sleeves and the red braces.

"You're not headed for the docks dressed like that."

"You're a sharp one, Miranda Kirby."

"Well, where are you headed?" She cast him an annoyed glance.

"To see a prince."

"What a bouncer." She went back to jabbing her needle through the silk, but he knew he had her.

"It's the truth. Lord Blackstone asked me to go. He said I could invite you." "

"You're hoaxing me."

"It's a beautiful day. You could come. We'll go in a hackney there and back." Nate jingled the coins in his pocket from Goldsworthy's working funds.

She put down the sewing in her lap. "You think I would go anywhere with you looking like a farmer?"

"A grocer, a perfectly respectable trade. You'd have to dress your part, too."

"My part!"

"We're a pair of cottagers interested in beekeeping."

"Bees? You mean swarms of stinging insects." She shuddered.

"You've got bees all wrong, Miranda. They're honey makers, flower sippers, winged dancers. That's where Prince Andre Sturdzi is off to today, to see Miss Hammersley's beekeeping demonstration."

"Aren't you the honey-tongued rogue?"

"That's the spirit." He grinned at her pun. "Are you game?"

She was back in minutes, looking so pretty, in a white gown with bits of blue embroidery, he had a momentary loss of brain function. His body stood alert, like a good soldier awaiting orders, but no orders came from his befuddled brain. Then she spoke, and she was his Miranda again.

"No touching."

He nodded. "But you can touch me if you want to."

"Saint Peter will interview you first."

"We'll see." He held the shop door for her, and she sailed through.

Violet smiled at Mr. Rushbrooke, who greeted them at the door of the Tallants' cottage. He had donned a thick white cotton beekeeper's kit over his black clerical suit. His face was flushed, and bright beads of moisture dotted his brow in the heat.

"Prince, Miss Hammersley, welcome. You've come just in time. I've assembled the local people for the demonstration at the foot of the garden." To Blackstone and the others he gave a curt nod.

Blackstone merely quirked a brow. Violet turned to introduce the party to the Tallants. Mr. Tallant and his wife were among the more accomplished of the beekeepers in the organization. Their small cottage had a long narrow garden, protected by a border of hawthorn hedge with three damson trees to make a windbreak. A gravel path led around the outside of the garden and down the slope through beds of herbs and flowers and dark earthen rows of new-planted vegetables. The air was fragrant with turned earth and new green shoots of leeks. At the foot of the garden three hives stood in a clear space opposite a pair of apple trees about to bud. The faint drowsy buzz of bees and the warm fragrant air marked the garden apart from the streets they'd left behind.

Later in the season, on a visit to one of her beekeeping associates, Violet would also don a white cotton bee kit over her clothes with a hat and dark veil and stout leather gloves. Stepping into a garden as a keeper was like entering a stately dance after the mad reel of the day. When she listened to the bees and pumped the bellows on the tin smoker to send puffs of calming smoke over a hive, she found herself slow-

ing her movements, even her heartbeat. Under the influence
of the smoke the bees would seek the bottom layer of the
hive and fill themselves with honey.

Today she would not be working with the bees directly,
but she had dressed prudently in a long-sleeved, white muslin gown with lavender sprigs. Although she had recommended similar attire to her guests, the prince and his
companions wore their military blues and reds and gleaming gold braid. They gathered at the top of the garden by a
small shed where Mr. Tallant kept his tools and kits. General
Dubusari pronounced the garden charming. Cahul frowned
severely, and the countess plied her fan with gentle waves.
The count found a bench in the shade and leaned against
the rough shed, closing his eyes.

The countess clung to Blackstone's arm, her bosom pressing against him, and asked, "Are we safe in our gowns? Do
they attract bees?"

As Mr. Tallant helped Mr. Rushbrooke with his veiled
hat and gloves, he advised the other gentlemen to change.
"Now, my lords, and your majesty, you, too, best to remove
your jackets and waistcoats before we go down in the garden. Bees don't like dark colors. Reminds them of the bad-
gers that steal their honey."

Too late Violet tried to look away from Blackstone as he
shed his jacket. He handed the garment to Mrs. Tallant. A
chocolate silk waistcoat hugged his lean frame and showed
the breadth of his shoulders. When he unbuttoned the waistcoat, her throat went dry. The unseasonal heat made the fine
linen of his shirt cling to his chest and belly. He pulled the
fabric loose from his person. He was not naked. Violet
should hardly be distracted by him, but the fine fabric, like
a sheer curtain, blew against the hard shape under it. He
turned to hand his waistcoat to Mrs. Tallant, and Violet

found herself staring at the laces at the top of his breeches, taut across the narrow span of his waist. This morning she had pressed against him as if starved for contact with his ribs, his belly, his chest. It made no sense. If a woman craved contact with a hard surface, why could she not hug a fine marble column in her foyer and be done with it? Why did marble columns, hard and smooth as they were, not satisfy the silly urge to press oneself madly to a man?

Cahul helped the prince shed his military jacket. Without it, he looked like an overfed schoolboy, grown stout on treats sent from home. Next to Violet the countess studied Blackstone openly. "How warm it is! How lucky the gentlemen are to shed their clothes. Wouldn't you like to do the same, Miss Hammersley?"

Violet hardly knew what she said in reply. In the beginning she hadn't known precisely what she and Blackstone were doing. But, ignorant as she had been, she had known that clothes were distinctly in the way, that skin ached for the touch of skin. That first afternoon of discovery, Blackstone had shed his coat and waistcoat and pulled his linen shirt from his breeches so that her hands could roam his chest and ribs. Touching him had made her desperate to get closer, until she pressed her cheek to his chest to hear his heart pounding.

Blackstone's amused glance met hers. She'd been caught at her less than covert appraisal of his person. "Practicing amnesia?"

She dropped her wayward gaze and went to help Mr. Rushbrooke. Fully suited up, he was peering through the dark netting of his hat, looking for the smoker. Violet lifted it into his line of vision.

"Here you are, Mr. Rushbrooke." She could feel the burn of the sun on her neck and shoulders.

Rushbrooke's heated breath puffed his veil in and out.

"Ready?" he called. "I'll lead the way." He started down the path along the hedgerow, his pace deliberate. Violet followed. Behind them the prince talked excitedly and Mr. Tallant offered calm replies. Violet was coming to recognize the prince's erratic, impulsive movements. He seemed susceptible to suggestion. The smallest hint might set him off abruptly.

At the bottom of the garden, about ten guests of the Beekeepers Association had gathered under the dappled shade of two budding apple trees. Rushbrooke and Tallant approached one of the three hives in the clear area. Tallant's hives were constructed of boxes stacked on one another like the stories of a listing tenement. If they lacked the romance of the old-fashioned skeps, Violet admired the innovation because it meant Mr. Tallant could harvest his honey without disturbing the queen and her brood in the lower regions of the hive. Today, one of the earliest warm days of spring, Mr. Tallant would simply see whether his bees had honey enough to begin breeding. Sometimes the beekeeper had to offer a syrup of warm sugar water to tide them over until there were sufficient spring blooms.

Mr. Rushbrooke, lumbering like a dancing bear in his extra layers of clothing, pumped smoke from the smoker around the top edges of the hive. She had never noticed the awkwardness of his body before.

Mr. Tallant, following behind Rushbrooke, took up a short length of iron rod and began to pry up the lid of the top box. It stuck, and as he applied more pressure, Rushbrooke stood stiffly at his side, energetically pumping smoke from the smoker until the two men were enveloped in a cloud like soot from a chimney sweep's exertions.

"Wot's Tallant doing?" one of the neighbors asked in a loud whisper.

Violet turned to explain. "Sometimes the wax sticks the lid to the hive, and the keeper must pry it open."

Violet smiled at a pretty redheaded girl holding the arm of a straw-hatted young man with his sleeves rolled up to his elbows. An abrupt crack of wood splintering made the girl gasp and clutch her companion. Violet swung her gaze around to see what had alarmed the girl and saw Mr. Rushbrooke toppling like a tree felled by an ax. Before she could move, he hit the ground with a thud. He lay flat and still on the grass. The smoker rolled from his slack hand.

For a moment everyone simply stared.

"'as 'e been stung to 'is death?" someone wondered aloud.

The straw-hatted young man with his arm around the girl, spoke at once. "'e musta fainted in the 'eat."

"A man swooning? 'oo ever 'eard of such a thing," scoffed another.

Blackstone had already stepped forward. He knelt at the fallen man's side, lifting the veiled helmet from his head. "Mrs. Tallant. We need water!"

Mrs. Tallant hurried off.

Violet went to kneel at Rushbrooke's other side and remove his gloves. Blackstone opened the fallen man's bee suit and loosened his collar. Rushbrooke's eyes remained closed, his face scarlet. When Mrs. Tallant returned with her bucket, Blackstone stripped off his own neckcloth and handed it to Violet. "Bathe his neck and temples. Tallant, help me get this suit off of him." For a few minutes the three worked in silence to cool the overheated man.

Violet dipped Blackstone's linen in the bucket a third time when she became aware of a distinct change in the drone of the bees. She saw Mr. Tallant lift his head, a look of alarm spreading across his countenance. He sprang up, and she turned to follow his gaze.

The prince held a length of dripping honeycomb in his bare hands while bees poured out of the opened hive and swarmed about his head. Several clung to his moustache, doing a dance of tails and wings, signaling more bees to come. Instead of helping, Cahul backed away from the prince, waving his arms furiously, inciting the swarming bees to more aggression.

As Mr. Tallant sprinted for the hive, Violet tossed Blackstone the damp cloth, snatched up the fallen smoker, and sprang to her feet. She shook the smoker back to life, and began to pump its bellows, wreathing the prince's head in smoke. Bees circled her hat. "Close your mouth and your eyes, your majesty, and stay still."

In a minute Mr. Tallant was at her side, offering her a soft bristled brush. Violet passed him the smoker. She could hear the bees' drone growing calm again. She began brushing bees from the prince's face and hair. The prince winced and trembled, and Violet knew he'd been stung.

"Just be patient a few more minutes, your majesty." She could hear Blackstone speaking to Rushbrooke, and General Dubusari scolding Cahul in a language she did not recognize. Mrs. Tallant was speaking calmly to the visitors huddled under the apple tree.

A short silence followed before she heard Rushbrooke speak, and Mrs. Tallant say, "There, you see, he's not dead."

Half an hour later, when they had all been inspected by Mrs. Tallant and pronounced free of lingering bees, the gentlemen donned their waistcoats and jackets again. The neighbors left, shaking their heads, likely convinced of the danger of bees. Violet brought Rushbrooke a draught of Mr. Tallant's cider from the cellar and watched as his color gradually returned to normal. He said he was not yet up to a carriage ride, so Violet arranged for the barouche to return for him after her driver delivered the prince and his party to Hammersley House. As the barouche drove off she could see Cahul and the countess break into rapid speech and the prince lean back with his arms folded across his chest.

Blackstone remained talking with Tallant and the straw-hatted young man with the pretty girl. Something Blackstone said made them all laugh. Violet felt an absurd stab of envy that he should make strangers laugh so easily. She told herself not to be foolish. She did not want to laugh with Blackstone. She wanted to find her brother and go back to her beekeeping and her good works. Then Blackstone was coming her way. He took her arm and turned her towards him, plucking a bee from the flower arrangement on her bonnet. "You're coming with me."

She should protest. Things would not have gone so horribly awry had she not been distracted by Blackstone's presence, but he was already in motion, hurrying her along to his carriage, a smart curricle.

Blackstone gave his own horses, no nags today, the command to go. "I had no idea that your efforts to do good in the world were so fraught with peril. Were you stung?"

"No, but I'm afraid the prince must have received three or four stings on his upper lip. He's going to be most uncomfortable tonight."

"You're not sympathetic, are you?"

"I'm amazed he doesn't get himself killed. He behaves like a child with no sense of caution."

"You did notice that none of his people came to his aid."

"Most people are unreasonably afraid of bees."

"Cahul is. Terrified of them, apparently, but the others simply watched the episode unfold."

Violet thought about it. Blackstone was right. For the second time she had cause to reproach herself for the turn of events. If she had paid less attention to the way Blackstone's shirt clung to his person, she might have noticed. "As if the prince were an embarrassment or an inconvenience."

"A useful embarrassment as long as our government gives him money."

"At least no one tried to kill him or us."

"I don't know. Can you have Preston get some of that pomade the prince uses on his moustache? I'd like to have a chemist look at its composition."

"You think someone put a bee attractant in his pomade?"

"It had a suspiciously floral scent, and it did draw all the bees."

"I hadn't thought of that."

"What did you and Dubusari put in your calendar for tonight?" Blackstone guided his pair in a neat turn into Park Lane, where fashionable equipages passed in a parade. He seemed able to mention her calendar with no recollection of the kiss that ended their conversation. He was fully clothed, his hands cased in driving gloves. Their bodies did not touch on the carriage seat. Violet ducked her chin and clung to the side of the vehicle. She had not posted her letter to the duchess, and to ride openly with Blackstone along the most fashionable street in London, past Penelope's very door, was to invite notice and talk. "Oh dear."

"Oh dear?"

"Tonight we have a box at the theater."

"Do you expect assassins to be lurking in the audience?" The carriage rattled down the wide lane, passing oncoming traffic of various sorts, drawing appreciation from drivers and passengers.

"Not at all." Violet wished for invisibility, but they were not invisible. Blackstone could never be invisible. There was nothing embarrassing about his horses or his rig today, but Blackstone himself drew people's notice. The angle of his hat, the ease with which he managed his horses. "I'm sorry. I just remembered something. You interrupted me, and I forgot."

"The perils of amnesia."

"Or the blessings."

She folded her hands in her lap. Even now it might not be too late. People would notice Blackstone, not the lady with him. She would send her letter directly upon her return to Hammersley House.

Chapter Thirteen

"I can readily believe . . . that reports may vary
greatly with respect to me; and I could wish . . .
that you were not to sketch my character at the
present moment . . ."

—Jane Austen, *Pride and Prejudice*

As they entered the theater box, the prince's party showed
no sign of their earlier irritation with one another. For a
moment they looked like neither kidnappers nor murderers,
but a party of travelers weary of unfamiliar surroundings
and over-familiar companions. Frank had often made Violet laugh describing that moment in every journey when he'd
been amiable to the point of eating some mysterious dish of
great national importance served in his honor. Afterward
his stomach twitched while words in his hosts' tongue failed
him. General Dubusari seemed to be the only member of
the prince's party who traveled well. He was speaking his
own tongue, at ease, settling the company in the narrow box
and making them smile a little.

As much as Violet wanted to believe the picture of polite
guests they presented, she couldn't forget Frank's note or
that button. A situation in which someone was cutting the
buttons from Frank's coat was not a comfortable one for her

brother, and someone in the group before her had put him there. While Blackstone assisted the countess, Violet took a seat beside the prince.

"You survived the bees, your majesty?" His face was puffy and mottled with red blotches.

"A few stings, Miss Hammersley. I don't regard them. A leader is prepared to suffer for his people, you know. Or his men won't follow him."

"How many men do you have, your majesty?"

"In my guard, you mean?"

Violet nodded. "The ones for whom you've designed the uniform."

"Ah, my royal guard." A pleased smile lifted his moustache. "They began as a small unit, but we have been growing. With England's help, I have been recruiting and training new officers. I believe we now have two full battalions. Dubusari, would you say that's right?"

Dubusari, overhearing, joined in. "Quite right, your majesty."

"My brother must have been impressed then. When he left for your country, he was eager to see what you had accomplished."

The prince frowned in puzzlement for a moment. "But Miss Hammersley, your brother never saw my men."

"Oh? I misunderstood. I thought he went to see your army."

"Yes, but you see, the training grounds are in Tiraspol. Isn't that right, Dubusari?" The prince patted Violet's gloved hand. "The next time he visits, we will have to have a full military review."

Violet watched his countenance for signs of alarm or consciousness, but there were none. Just the prince's happy inability to question anything he was told. He turned to

Cahul and spoke to him in their language. Cahul shook his head. The two of them shrugged as if they hadn't any idea how odd it was that Frank had not seen the troops English money had funded.

Dubusari seemed more alert. "Miss Hammersley, have you heard from your brother? Is he a good correspondent? The English are great letter writers I hear."

Dubusari looked as polite and quaint as ever in his gold-braided military coat and powdered wig, but his interest in Frank's correspondence was hardly the mere politeness of guest to host. Dubusari waited for her reply while over his blue and gold shoulder Violet saw the countess tilt her head towards them.

Dubusari's comment made a pocket of silence into which Violet tried to slip her thoughts without his notice. Frank traveled for weeks at a time on his tours of their European banking interests. Because his work often involved loans from the British government to various allies, he sent his weekly messages in the foreign office's sealed red dispatch boxes. Violet could see now that Frank's practice of relying on the government to carry his letters could make him appear to be a dangerous spy. Her thoughts had reached that point in mere seconds, even as Dubusari's smile became a trifle stiff.

She let her small beaded evening bag slide off her lap to fall at her feet in the crowded theater box.

A quick frown crossed Dubusari's face. Violet started to rise to retrieve her bag when Dubusari put a surprisingly firm hand on hers, holding her in her seat. "Allow me, Miss Hammersley."

He reached for his cane and snagged the braided silk cord of her bag, lifting it within reach. She offered him her sweetest smile. "Thank you. Frank is a good correspondent. I can count on hearing from him every Sunday, regular as a sermon."

She tried to read some reaction in Dubusari's face, but two young men entered the box, hailing Blackstone. Everyone turned to them. Blackstone rose from his conversation with the countess. Her gloved hand slipped from his sleeve. The little chairs were pushed aside and everyone shifted positions, so that the newcomers might crowd into the box.

The taller of the two, a long-faced gentleman with golden hair, spoke first. "Blackstone, we're here to accuse you of dullness. Where's that harem of yours tonight?"

His shorter, stouter friend joined in. "Didn't see you in the greenroom. Thought you'd be after that little actress with the legs. Lady R. wouldn't like it, though, would she?"

"Gentlemen, you've not met my party, I think." Blackstone named the prince and his companions to his friends Lord Slindon and the Honorable Charles Fothergill.

Slindon, the golden-haired man, catching sight of the countess, bowed deeply with a look of sly comprehension on his face as if the fair beauty in the box explained Blackstone's presence.

When Blackstone turned to introduce Violet, lifting her hand in his, she realized what must happen, even as she was powerless to stop it. Before the prince and his cohort, Blackstone must name her as his fiancée.

His friends' expressions faltered. "I say, you can't have a—" began Fothergill, the short gentleman, when Slindon elbowed him sharply.

"Blackstone, we've not come to rake up your scandalous past, but to get you to tell Fothergill the story of Vasiladi and the goats. He's not heard it."

Blackstone lifted a brow. "Surely everyone has heard that story. I dined out on it for weeks."

"Not Fothergill. He's been waiting on his dying aunt in Bath."

Fothergill nodded. "Met your sister Elena there, Blackstone. She says she can't reach you by post. Asked me to hunt you down with some letters that have been returned to her. Didn't bring them tonight, of course."

A change in the music from the pit ended their talk, alerting the crowd to the opening ceremonies. Blackstone's friends took their leave.

"You owe us, Blackstone." Slindon wagged a finger at Blackstone.

The conductor looked up to their box, and Violet rose with the prince on her left. Blackstone took a place to her right, and the orchestra below struck up the Moldovan anthem. The prince beamed and waved to the crowd in his gold-braided blue coat. His eyes, sunk in the red puffiness of his face, did not seem to sparkle less at his enjoyment of the attention. To her right Blackstone held her gloved hand in his. She could feel the hard press of his unmistakable signet ring.

She smiled blindly while contrary images of him clashed in her mind. His friends' casual mention of his harem, and their desire to hear amusing anecdotes, made his travels seem as scandalous as his youth had been. But if she thought about her hand in his lean one and his altered looks, she must conclude that he'd endured more than he'd told her in his time abroad. She did not know how to reconcile the two pictures in her mind, his reputation for extravagance and profligacy and his courage and kindness.

Tonight she had learned shocking details of his finances. She could scarce believe what her father's friend had discovered. According to the bank's information, Blackstone had no fortune left. No one knew exactly what he had done with it. It was a matter of public record that he had mort-gaged the unentailed portions of Blackstone Court to the fullest extent possible, and leased the house itself to a wealthy manufacturer of crockery. His last act before leaving for Greece had been to withdraw an enormous fortune from his bank. There the money trail ended. How and where he had spent a fortune she could not know. He had certainly not restored the missing money.

Violet didn't know how he lived or where his bachelor quarters were. Her informant had driven by the Blackstone townhouse and found it occupied by tenants. Plainly his friends were unaware of any change in his circumstances.

It did not help that he looked briefly bleak and withdrawn at the mention of his sister.

In the next moment he leaned down with no sense of propriety, his lips almost touching her ear, to say, "You may have more enemies here tonight than the prince. Have you particularly offended the Duchess of Huntingdon? She's looking green daggers at you from across the way."

Violet lifted her gaze and spotted Penelope. There was no going back. Blackstone's friends would already be spreading the word of his betrothal. She must preserve a look of indifference, as if his nearness had no effect on her, and above all not look at Penelope. In a few minutes the play would begin. They would still be on display, but at least some of the crowd's attention would be directed to the action on the stage. She did not expect to hear from or to see Penelope again. She could imagine how her public intimacy with Blackstone must look and how it must seem that she had misled Penelope. She hoped she had not offended her. Without Penelope's support, Violet could scratch her *worthy endeavor* out of her calendar. There would be no ball to support the seamstresses of Spitalfields in their new work.

Violet sat in the middle of the prince's party. Blackstone did not know which of them he distrusted more—the idiot prince, his hulking bodyguard, the polite general, the clinging countess, or her claret-swilling husband. It was his duty to keep Violet in sight. With a slight adjustment to the position of his seat he found he could watch her perfectly. Tonight she wore another gown as dark and rich as wine, against which her skin glowed. She held her head high, but he could see the tension in the taut cords of her neck. A marble obelisk would be more yielding.

He had not missed the fleeting alarm in her expression when she realized he must introduce her as his betrothed. He was surprised that such a thing could still bother him after his time in Greece. He wondered at it. She had broken their true engagement. She should have no trouble breaking a false one, but he was no longer sure that he knew who she was.

While he was away she had somehow become this cold sophisticated woman in the fashionable gown with its black figured lace and bold color. Only a dusting of pale freckles across her cheeks and nose reminded him of her younger self, of the trusting girl she'd been. It had been a mistake to kiss her, a mistake he had repeated so often in the past that he ought now to have avoided it. In the past, kissing Violet had led them to the folly of an engagement.

At the time, he had believed himself free of his family. His father and mother and sisters seemed to lead separate lives from his, so he had imagined himself free to marry Violet whatever disapproval his family might express. He believed he had carefully considered everything that could be said or done against their marriage. He knew his father would likely cut off his allowance, but he had savings and George Hammersley would look out for him, and in time

Blackstone Court would be his whether his father approved of his bride or not. He never foresaw that he would have to choose his family over Violet, just as he never doubted her commitment to their union.

But summoned to his dying father's side, he had seen only that he must make his father's unexpected death bearable to those who would suffer from it most. He gave the promise his father asked of him. *You are Blackstone, now*, his father had said.

It had been days before he could return to Hammersley House and Violet. By then the scandal had broken. All of fashionable London had seen the painting. He had gone to Hammersley House to find comfort in Violet's arms. Instead he'd found her hurt and unreachable. He still did not know whether he or she had blundered more that night, in that moment of decision when he waited for her to choose him and to let the world say what it would. Instead she had ended their engagement and returned his ring.

This morning it had been a mistake to kiss her, not because it summoned the past, but because he wanted to kiss her again and change the future.

During the first act Violet sat between Dubusari and the prince while the count stared out over the theater. On the stage, the actors strained valiantly to make their lines heard and relied on the broad comedy of exaggerated gestures. Violet studied the count and countess, who did not fit any idea she had formed of how married couples behaved, neither those with a warm attachment towards one another, nor those whose familiarity with each other rendered them apt to snap and pick at one another even in company. She had to admit to herself that she might not have seen all the possibilities of the married state. Her mother's early death had given her no opportunity to watch her own parents' marriage, an opportunity which might have given her more insight, but she felt there was something missing in the count and countess's relationship, some connective tissue whether of affection or irritation, that would show that they belonged together.

The prince leaned forward, entranced by the play until the first half ended. He turned to Violet to declare that the young actress who played the lost slave girl was remarkable. He dabbed his eyes at her father's grief over their parting.

In the next moment, the interval brought another guest to their box, Penelope Frayne, the Duchess of Huntington. They shifted chairs and persons again at the duchess's arrival. She smiled at Violet and dropped a gracious curtsy to the prince, who, on being informed of her grace's rank, raised her up. Penelope thanked him for his kindness and begged to be acquainted with his party. The prince performed the introductions admirably, ending with Blackstone and Violet.

"Is each English lady more beautiful than the last?" The prince executed a sweeping bow. "You will break my heart if you have a fiancé like Miss Hammersley, Duchess."

Violet did not miss the quick stiffening in Penelope's spine, the faint contraction of her smile. Her grace recovered at once. "I have a husband, your majesty."

"Oh a husband." The prince waved away the husband. "A husband must always make way for his wife's admirers. You must allow me to become one of your *cavalier servente*, Duchess, for I am sure you have many."

"How very Italian sounding, your majesty."

When the prince begged everyone to be seated again, Blackstone sat with the royal party, and Penelope sat next to Violet.

"What happened to the prince?" Penelope circled her own lips with one gloved finger. "Is it a state secret, or are you at liberty to say?" Penelope's question was about the prince, but her gaze was on Blackstone. Violet watched her watch him.

"Bee stings."

"What?" Penelope's laugh was bright and genuine. She looked directly at Violet. "Did you take him to one of your projects?"

"I did."

"I must say, he bears it well." Again, Penelope's gaze returned to the royal party, to Blackstone and not the prince.

When she turned back to Violet, she observed, "The prince doesn't seem to quite understand the way of things here, does he?"

Violet agreed. She tried to see what the other woman saw in Blackstone. To her he was both Blackstone and not Blackstone. He had seemed so much older than Violet when they had been lovers, but she realized now that when she'd first met him he had been but seventeen. She had believed him to know infinitely more than she did because he could ride and shoot and hold his own in conversations about money and politics with her father and brother. In those first months of knowing him she had feared above all that he would find her ignorant and silly like other girls.

Penelope watched her closely. Violet tried to keep a bright indifferent face.

"Now my dear Violet, I came to condole with you as you knew I must. You must find Blackstone's return at this moment of your own triumph quite awkward."

Violet studied her gloved hands.

"But what does the prince mean by calling him your fiancé? Is the announcement in the papers true?"

Her gaze flew up. He had agreed not to make an

announcement and yet he had. "I beg you, do not misunder-stand our situation. My brother was to play host to the prince, you know, but business has delayed Frank's return to London, and the ministry sent Blackstone to us because of his knowledge of that part of the world."

"Ah, so Blackstone has been inflicted upon you by an indifferent or ill-informed government." Penelope cast a quick glance at Blackstone.

"I hoped you would understand."

Penelope rose. "I think I do. Perfectly. I simply tore up your letter, Violet. We must still give our ball, my dear. I insist."

Penelope's rising, signaled the others that the interval was ending, and there was a general shuffling of limbs and chairs to form a path for her. Blackstone rose, extending a hand to help her move through the disordered chairs. He meant no pointed attention. It was natural to him to offer courtesies. It was only that his smile made a woman want more from him, want something his sinful body seemed to promise. Violet understood that the duchess made the most of her momentary contact with him. When she thanked him, there was a subtle invitation in those green eyes. The count-ess saw it, too, and her face briefly lost its doll-like sweetness.

The play resumed. In her perturbed state of mind Violet saw nothing of the slave girl's travails or her touching reunion with her dying father. She realized that she had fallen in love with Blackstone as a girl, without ever seeing him in the company of other women. He was her brother's friend. He had seemed to belong to them, to their family, and to her in particular. She knew that he had a mother and sisters, but she had not imagined his female acquaintance, had not considered how other women would see him. Nor had she seen his behavior towards them. It was something more than civility. His body seemed designed to awaken sensual awareness in any woman he met.

His friends saw it. The duchess saw it, but Violet had not seen it until now because she had only known him at Hammersley House. In those early days they could not have been more alone if they had been cast ashore on some barren island in a distant sea like Crusoe. The folly of it struck her forcibly. All the rules for female behavior existed so that impressionable girls like herself would not be subject to the stirring effect of a man's presence. She had made the mistake of thinking herself different from those other girls. She had known herself to have a good mind and steady nerves. She'd never been silly, and she'd felt fearless. She'd been wrong. The only right thing, the only hardheaded, sensible thing she'd done in her whole connection with Blackstone had been to end their engagement.

And she would do well to remember that fact. His hand still bore the signet ring, the most famous signet in England perhaps, with its unmistakable bold masculine *B* on the black face and its gold acanthus leaves on the band. The ring appeared prominently in the infamous painting with the man's fingers splayed possessively down across the naked collarbone of a reclining beauty, claiming her as his own.

Violet's humiliation had taught her not only about men but about her true friends. The school friends to whom she had announced her engagement, dropped her at once when her humiliation became known. Since that time, she had learned better how to judge a prospective friend. The satisfaction in knowing that she had been wise, and that the more she knew of him the wiser she appeared, was a peculiarly dull satisfaction. Being wise didn't quicken one's steps or make one laugh or shout aloud. It simply meant you wouldn't trip and break your shin. Violet supposed in time, and with Frank's safe return, she would take off Blackstone's false diamond and begin again.

Hours later Blackstone sauntered into Frank's room with the easy authority he always showed. "What did you learn tonight?"

Violet had a dozen candles burning, anything to reduce the intimacy of their meeting. She wanted no repetition of the morning's kiss. She had wrapped herself in a warm wool shawl and taken a wing chair by the window. "Frank never saw the prince's regiments. The fact seemed to puzzle the prince, as if he couldn't figure out how he'd managed not to show them off to his English visitor."

"How did Frank miss them?"

"Apparently, they're billeted away from the capital in a place called Tiraspol. I thought Dubusari rather quick to divert his highness's mind from the subject."

"Dubusari manages them all. And he's not as frail as he looks." Blackstone watched her from across the room, a preoccupied look on his face. After their morning encounter, he seemed as determined as she was to hold himself aloof.

"You're right. He doesn't tire, and Cahul watches Dubusari as much as he watches the prince."

"So what do we make of that? Does it help us find your brother?"

He was distracting her with "we" and "us." They were not an "us," and to let herself think they were would be a dangerous relaxing of her guard against the memories, which kept massing like troops ready for an attack. "The count and countess don't behave like married people."

"You're right there. She'd do away with him if she could." He seemed to see her then, and moved towards her, reaching up to pull the end of his cravat, undoing the fashionable knot. He pulled the linen free of his neck and undid the button at his throat so that the points of his collar fell away.

She swallowed, watching him toss the discarded linen over the back of a chair. She wanted him to stop being familiar and at ease as if they'd taken up where they left off. "Murder him? She looks seventeen and talks about gowns and hats. She's never said anything to me that indicates she's other than a peahen, and she bats her eyelashes at you with enough force to blow the leaves off a garden path."

Blackstone leaned an elbow on the mantelpiece. "She's an odd sort of seductress, I agree. She doesn't bat, however; she widens her eyes." He widened his own eyes in mimicry.

"Seductress?" He would recognize such a thing she supposed.

"Have you noticed? She's more intentional than a mere flirt. She has quite a repertoire of helpless gestures—the trembling hand on the sleeve, the helpless shrug—nothing accidental, nothing spontaneous, and she's always watching the effect, but she's not affected herself. Not like your friend, the duchess."

"*Friend* overstates the degree of connection between Penelope Frayne and me."

"Yet, she's paid you calls, which you've returned, and you are working together on your 'worthy endeavor,' a ball."

His gaze was shrewd and knowing. He had noticed more about her calendar than she liked, but even he didn't see what was now so plain—Penelope's interest in Violet's charities had begun only after Blackstone's return. Penelope had sought her acquaintance, not out of common interest in charity, but out of interest in Blackstone.

"Violet, are you with me? We're trying to understand the enemy."

She looked up to find his blue gaze fixed on her. She had to make him stop saying *we*. "Who is Vasiladi?"

He pushed away from the mantelpiece and moved to Frank's writing desk. "A Greek patriot with whom I spent some time."

"You need not lie to me about him. I can look at you and see that his hospitality did not include sufficient food. Is Vasiladi the reason you mortgaged Blackstone Court?"

"I thought you were keen to investigate the people who have taken your brother."

Violet took a steadying breath. "I had a banker investigate you."

"Did you?" He flattened his palm against Frank's desk. Light gleamed on the gold of his ring. "Are you worried that I'm after your fortune with our false engagement?"

"You put an announcement in the papers after we agreed not to."

"I didn't in fact. My employer did."

"The government? Why?"

He did not answer.

"Blackstone." Violet plunged ahead. "My investigator found that your entire estate, everything that is not entailed, is mortgaged. The townhouse is closed. Blackstone Court is leased to a crockery maker. A man who makes knick-knacks with scenes on them."

"He's quite prosperous."

Her hands fisted in the folds of her shawl. She wanted to hit him to shatter that imperturbable calm. "And your mother and sisters are living in Bath, and not in the most elegant of addresses."

"Yes, Elena, has not hesitated to point out to me the

disadvantages of their situation, comfortable, but obscure. I expect to restore them to a better situation within a year."

"I couldn't discover where you are living. You don't keep your own stable, apparently, but today, you were . . ." He regarded her over his shoulder with a look she'd seen before, when she'd broken their engagement, his face barren of expression, as if he'd gone away somewhere and left a mask behind. But he was changed, too. In the candlelight she saw the hollows in his gaunt face. His face with its lean edges was nothing like the sleek faces of his friends. Her mind, her busy, unstoppable mind that wanted to know things, went on putting the bits and pieces together. She pushed herself up out of the chair.

"Your year in Greece was not about goats and harems. It was about ransom. You paid Vasiladi money." Her mind raced on calculating, connecting the little she knew. He didn't blink or change. "How much you must have paid!" Almost, she wanted to reach out to him, but she kept her hands knotted in her shawl. "What did you ransom, Blackstone?"

"Your investigation has been quite thorough, madame." He came towards her, his mouth a taut line. She titled her chin up to meet his dark rigid look. He reached down and disengaged her hands from the wool.

"You seem to be wearing a lap dog, Violet." The edges of the woolen shawl fell open. She felt it slip and cool air settle around her.

He took her left hand in his and closed his fingers around the false betrothal ring he'd given her. "Violet, this is paste on your finger. Your large fortune is in no danger from my lack of fortune." He turned away.

"You could have told me," she told his back. She did not understand him. He risked public censure for becoming engaged to her with no fortune of his own. He would be named a gazetted fortune hunter and endure more public scandal. She could not think what could possibly make him do it. She opened her mouth to ask, but he cast her a dark glance over his shoulder.

"I'd rather, as always, that my private concerns not be so wholly available to public scrutiny."

Violet was stunned. Here was an end to *we* and *us*.

"You said the prince's royal guard is quartered at Tiraspol."

She nodded.

"That's on the Russian border. Interesting." His voice had regained its ordinary tone. "I wonder who decided to train the army there."

Violet made herself stand tall and steady. Blackstone had recovered. He was in control of himself. He could come into Hammersley House and flip the pages of her calendar and unsettle her life, but she was not permitted to know the first thing about his life.

And Frank was still missing.

Chapter Fourteen

"... you should take it into further consideration, that in spite of your manifold attractions, it is by no means certain that another offer of marriage may ever be made you."

—Jane Austen, *Pride and Prejudice*

Violet found Mr. Rushbrooke in her straw-colored drawing room at an exceptionally early hour. Together they had worked to sponsor a cricket match between a group of town boys and some collegians. Violet had dressed for the day's excursion in a chocolate jaconet dress with a corded band around the waist and a square collar of worked muslin. Not a single unnecessary inch of her person would be exposed to Blackstone's scrutiny.

When Granthem greeted the visitor and asked if Mr. Rushbrooke would be accompanying Miss Hammersley to the cricket match, Mr. Rushbrooke turned quite somber and regretted that he would not. The night had restored his natural color, except for two red splotches in his cheeks, like bright flares above his sober clerical black.

He fixed Violet with a stern look and announced that he would take no more than a minute of her time.

"Mr. Rushbrooke, do sit down, and let us offer tea and marmalade cakes."

"If you insist, Miss Hammersley."

"I do. The effects of the sun are not to be trifled with. I hope you will take care until you feel fully recovered." Violet nodded to Granthem who turned at once. He had probably already ordered a refreshment tray.

She sat, and Mr. Rushbrooke did the same with obvious reluctance. He regarded her with an expression of sullen petulance as if he were offended, and he seemed to be gathering himself to make a speech.

Granthem returned with a footman bearing a tray of tea and cakes. As he placed it on the table before her, he smiled at her. "Your lads have their match today, don't they, miss?"

Violet nodded.

"Good luck then. I'll be putting my money on them."

Granthem cleared his throat, and the footman retreated into proper anonymity. With their leaving, Violet could feel the heaviness of Rushbrooke's disapproval settle in the room. She poured and served and waited.

After far too long, her guest brushed cake crumbs from his fingers. "I own I am disappointed, Miss Hammersley. I did not understand that you intended to bring Lord Blackstone with you yesterday." He frowned at Violet's hands.

She stopped twisting Blackstone's paste diamond on her finger. What a ridiculous situation. She could not blame Rushbrooke for misunderstanding her true circumstances. "We are much together at this stage of our betrothal."

"So I see, but I can't think that betrothal to a man like Blackstone suits you, Miss Hammersley."

Violet felt herself stiffen. The diamond and the pretense it represented had betrayed Mr. Rushbrooke into being impertinent. She wanted to remind him that though he was a friend, he was not in a position to advise her on such a personal decision. "A woman must decide which man suits her." She spoke as gently as she could. If he would take the hint, they could get past the awkward moment. "More tea?"

He shook his head and leaned forward, speaking earnestly. She hardly recognized him as her old friend. "My dear Miss Hammersley, a woman may mistake the basis of her attachment. Blackstone is a man who represents an affront to all that we've been working for among the poor and the destitute. He's turned your head. You can't think properly. You've abandoned all our work."

Violet felt the first prick of resentment and an utterly unreasonable desire to defend Blackstone.

"Mr. Rusbrooke, I am temporarily obliged to entertain the prince, but once the royal visit ends, I will continue my usual interests."

"How can you—betrothed to such a man—the enemy of all we work for."

"You must acknowledge that yesterday Lord Blackstone acted with quick and kind competence when you fell ill." It was true. Blackstone was equally kind to silly clergymen and to distempered horses that tried to kill him.

The drawing room door closed quietly behind her. She put down her teacup, and prepared to rise as soon as Granthem announced that the carriage was ready. She would be glad of an end to the awkward encounter.

But Granthem did not speak, and Rushbrooke carried on. "Nevertheless, a man of Blackstone's habits of idleness and excess should not have been present at a demonstration intended to promote industry and honest work."

It was now necessary for Violet to stop her guest before

his certainty, his insistence that he knew her, created an irreparable rift between them. "Mr. Rushbrooke, I think . . ."

She got no further. A pair of warm strong hands clasped her shoulders. *Blackstone.*

His voice, quiet and cold, sounded so sure and calm after Rushbrooke's effusions. "You've said enough, Rushbrooke."

Rushbrooke flushed an alarming shade of pink. He jerked to his feet and pointed a shaking finger over Violet's head at Blackstone. "You, you have ruined a good woman."

Blackstone's hands remained unmoved on Violet's shoulders, his fingers pressed against her collarbone. "You mistake her character, Rushbrooke, if you imagine that I or anyone can corrupt Miss Hammersley. I would leave now if I were you."

"Are you—"

"Now, Rushbrooke. With your dignity intact." Blackstone's hands kept Violet from rising to see her guest off.

Rushbrooke stepped forward, colliding with the tea table and rattling the cups in their saucers. He steadied himself, executed an abrupt turn, and stalked off. He did not quite slam the door but closed it as firmly as he dared.

Violet sat still under Blackstone's hands. She could not decide whether to thank him for coming to her defense or to hit him for interfering. He had driven off one of her friends, scratched him out of her life, like a dance partner scratched off a dance card. But she had not realized quite how Mr. Rushbrooke had been thinking about her or how he was less a friend than a man who thought he could take charge of her life.

"I've made things awkward for you apparently."

"Yes. I think one of us, Mr. Rushbrooke or myself, must resign from the Beekeepers Association."

"You won't have to. He will."

Violet realized Blackstone was right. He had been in company with Mr. Rushbrooke three times and understood him perfectly. "I expect I'll receive a letter from him later today."

"He would not have made you a good husband, Violet." He lifted his hands, and Violet shivered in their absence. His hands had been warm and unexpectedly comforting on her shoulders. She had never associated Blackstone with comfort.

"I see that. I'll remove him from the list of hopeful applicants for my hand. Thank you. I had not thought of him in quite the same light as that in which he apparently thought of me."

"No, I'm sure you did not. He thought of you as a way to fulfill his ambition for a bishop's miter."

"You don't flatter, do you?" Violet dropped her gaze to her clasped hands in her lap.

"Did you think that he saw you as a beautiful, desirable woman he had to have in his bed?"

Bed. Violet had not put bed and Mr. Rushbrooke together in the same thought. The possibility made her shudder, and she knew that Blackstone saw the betraying tremor. She hated to give him the satisfaction. What did she know of bed after all, but being in bed with him?

"Imagine it, Violet. Yourself as Rushbrooke's bride, returning here to Hammersley House to live, while that earnest, rising man of the cloth serves a modest church and waits for the more important appointment to come. There will be the usual congratulations and wedding cake and friends, though I think your papa and Frank will hardly smile. Mr. Rushbrooke will be quite pink with pride and happiness. He will swell a bit and squeeze your hand, and say 'my dear' and 'my wife,' as often as he can. He will describe the great projects that the two of you will do together as you scold the poor into propriety and thrift. With elaborate courtesy and formality he will come to you in your bedroom, modestly covered from his shins to his chin in a nightshirt and wrapper, uneasy but stoutly determined to do his duty as a husband and clergyman."

"Stop it. You don't know how it would be between me and my chosen husband."

"But I know how it could be, Violet." He dropped a kiss on the top of her head and left.

Blackstone took Violet's hand to steady her as she descended from the open barouche. What a joke that firm grasp was. Nothing could steady her less than the touch of his gloved hand holding hers, lifting her down to the ground. With the kiss in her bedroom and the banishing of Rushbrooke, Blackstone was back in her life, but this time, she told herself, she was not a green girl. This time she knew how to resist him.

Clouds piled up in the blue sky overhead, turning from dazzling white to sullen gray. Somewhere the prince rattled on about the upcoming match, spectators gathered under a red-striped awning, and a cool breeze ruffled the cricket whites of two teams of boys gathered on the green expanse of the pitch. Dubusari, the count and countess, and Cahul descended from a second vehicle, but Violet could not attend to those distant events. Her world was the narrow realm of touch where she and Blackstone connected. She tried to turn off her awareness of him. One could blow out a candle, shut a door, lift one's fingers from the pianoforte and stop the sense impression of the moment in an instant, but the sensation of Blackstone's touch marked her in some way, made her skin tighter, more sensitive where his hand had been.

He had first touched her when she was thirteen and learning to ride. The plan had been to teach Frank so that when Frank visited Blackstone Court, he and Blackstone could wander the estate on their own. Violet had tagged along for Frank's lessons. She had missed dozens of Blackstone's touches before she learned to attend to them. He had fitted her foot to the stirrup or positioned her hands on the reins or caught her by the waist as she descended. Then one day he'd given her a queer look and backed away. She had puzzled over that look for weeks before she saw him again. Much later she understood it. She had definitely not seen that look for years. It was one of the things she'd lost.

When her feet were firmly on the grassy verge of the field, she withdrew her hand from his.

"Ah, Miss Hammersley, a perfect day, a perfect spot." The prince wore a top hat and a splendid set of cricket whites. Over one shoulder he carried a pristine, untouched bat, its polished wood surface unscratched by play. "Your brother gave me this bat. He told me I could not understand your countrymen if I did not understand the game cricket."

Violet could imagine the scene. Giving his Moldovan host a cricket bat was just like Frank, a way he had of making diplomacy a bit playful, and not so deadly earnest. Violet had had something of the same idea when she had proposed a cricket match between the Knightsbridge team and the boys from Camden Town.

In the carriage, Violet and Blackstone had agreed that his highness could play. The dangerous episodes of the past two days were accidents or they were acts of the prince's own people. The public nature of the cricket match should guarantee a measure of safety. As Violet looked about she saw only the two teams, the group of schoolboys from Knightsbridge and her own team from Camden Town, and their families, gathered to watch them. She doubted any enemies, except perhaps the prince's own countrymen, lurked in the small crowd.

The prince tapped his bat against the ground. "I'll take a few practice swings, if I may. I've not had a chance, since your brother visited me, Miss Hammersley. No one in my country understands the science of bowling."

The prince took a batsman's stance when the sound of another carriage arriving made them turn. Violet recognized the livery of the outriders at once, the Duchess of Huntingdon's servants. She did not think she had ever mentioned the match to Penelope, nor that the duchess had any interest in a charity game between schoolboys. If Penelope had troubled herself to come this far on a blustery day, it was for Blackstone, not for a group of nameless boys.

"You do not mind that I invited other guests, Miss Hammersley?" The prince tossed his bat to Cahul and took hold of Violet's hand. He had the grace to look like a schoolboy who had overstepped. "The duchess assured me that she would be quite honored to attend one of your charities, Miss Hammersley. You and she are working together for some seamstresses, are you not?"

"We are, Prince."

He smiled broadly, delighted to have his way. He patted Violet's shoulder and hurried over to welcome his guest. Violet was conscious of Blackstone at her elbow.

"I wonder who put the idea of inviting the duchess into his head."

"You don't think it was his idea?"

"I don't think he has the capacity to have an idea." Blackstone palmed a red leather ball in his hand with the ease of familiarity.

The prince returned with Penelope and the rest of his

party, and once all the greetings had been exchanged, he began expressing his enthusiasm for the event.

"It's a dangerous game, Prince," Blackstone offered with a faint smile on his lips. "They say a cricket ball killed Frederick, the Prince of Wales, near here not long ago."

"Seventy years ago." Violet shot Blackstone a sharp glance. "I doubt our young bowlers, for all their expertise, will throw with such lethal power. We'll have each team choose a bowler to pitch to you, your majesty. It will be an honor for them."

Blackstone nodded, an amused gleam in his dark eyes. "Prince, and your grace, I'm going to see how Miss Hammersley's lads are doing, shall we?" Blackstone led them out onto the pitch headed for Violet's team on the opposite side of the field. Violet wanted to know how he had recognized which team was hers, but she wasn't going to call him back.

She turned to her own duties, greeting the team from Knightsbridge. They were sure of a win and aware of conferring a favor on lesser mortals. She supposed they were not so different from her brother at that age, but their certainty of victory irked her, and her smiles felt strained again. That was the result of having Blackstone back in her life. Things she had been doing for years now seemed irksome. It didn't matter. She must do them anyway, and keep doing them after he left again.

She tried to pay attention to her guests, but she could see Blackstone in the midst of her boys while Penelope and the prince looked on. The boys seemed to consume Blackstone's entire attention. He led them to the center of the field, to the strip between the stumps, and had them rub their hands in the grass. He shed his jacket and tossed it carelessly aside, so that his white sleeves billowed, and his gray silk waistcoat hugged his lean torso. She watched appalled as he made the boys wipe their hands on their new white flannel trousers. They grinned at each other and exchanged shoves and slaps. Then Blackstone turned them to look at the field. They spread out, looking over the field and gesturing to different parts of it. He shook hands with each of them and made his way back to her with his easy stride. The prince and the duchess and Cahul remained on the field while the prince took practice swings with his bat.

"How did you know that the blue caps were my team?" Violet wondered what the duchess made of Blackstone's walking away from her.

"New uniforms, right?"

"I wanted them to have all the proper gear. They are not inferior players just because they don't attend a public school."

"I'm sure they're not."

"Then why did you have them dirty their new whites?"

"Do you want them to win?" He accepted a pot of ale from a waiter.

"Yes."

"Then thank me, Violet. They weren't going to play fearlessly if they were afraid of getting a bit of grass on their finery." He reached up and tucked a strand of her hair behind her ear under her bonnet, the chocolate silk she'd purchased from Madame Girard. And she thought, *Don't make me love you again.*

"And why did you tell the prince that piece of ancient history about Frederick's death? Do you want to terrify him?"

"It popped into my head. The past is on my mind, and the prince needs a better sense of caution. He has none." He downed his ale and strode back to the field.

The count, countess, and Dubusari returned to the spectators' awning to watch the match with Violet. She should be questioning them, trying to get at the mystery of Frank's absence, but she could not while Blackstone stood in the field with the duchess.

First Blackstone, and then the prince, gave the duchess lessons in holding a cricket bat. The prince showed Blackstone his bat, and then Blackstone tested the bat with some bowls from one of Violet's boys. He pointed out something about the bat to the prince, and then a tall boy from the Knightsbridge team offered the prince his bat. Blackstone handed Cahul the rejected bat and took a position behind the wickets to cheer the prince on. After hitting a ball over the boundary without a bounce, his majesty escorted Penelope from the field, flushed with triumph. He mopped his brow and accepted a glass of cold ale at Violet's side. "Miss Hammersley, I must thank your brother. He taught me well."

The officials signaled the boys to begin play. By two the sky was leaden with overcast. The Knightsbridge schoolboys had had quite a run, and as Violet's team took the field, it was clear they would have to play extraordinarily well to match their opponents. Blackstone moved from boy to boy, offering advice or a steadying hand on a shoulder. The Knightsbridge bowler and fielders quickly eliminated the first of the Violet's team's batsmen while the spectators retreated more and more under the awning, except the supporters of Violet's boys. She excused herself from the royal party, and went to urge them all under the flapping tent. Blackstone stayed on the field. Penelope took up a position next to Violet.

"He's a pleasure to watch, isn't he?"

"He's a great example to the boys."

"You never saw that painting of him, did you?"

Violet shook her head. There was no question of which painting Penelope referred to and no reason for Violet to pretend she had seen it.

"You would be vastly reassured if you had," Penelope remarked. "It's obvious from the painting that he's so wrong for you."

"You think I should see the painting? Now?"

"It can be arranged, you know."

"What need is there? I told you I know his true character." She said it to be contradicted. She wanted someone to say—*Violet, dear, you have it wrong. Blackstone has no harem, no lost fortune. He's a man of honor and principle.*

But Penelope made no contradiction. She continued in a calm voice.

"You should see it for your own peace of mind, Violet. He's a game player, and you"—she shrugged—"are not. You are one of life's earnest, sensible people. You're straightforward and honest. You're never idle. You don't strategize and you don't risk. You tick things off your list. You don't do frivolous things—like playing a game—just for the pleasure, just to be alive and enjoying doing something."

"I stand condemned of dull respectability. Apparently, it's the Rushbrookes of the world for me." She felt her cheeks flame with humiliation.

Penelope laughed. "My dear, I sincerely hope not. But you will not be happy with Blackstone. It's natural for him to charm. He's a man who enjoys women. A woman cannot expect fidelity or even sustained interest from such a man. He's simply made for pleasure."

Penelope drifted back to the prince and his party. Violet watched the action on the field. What did she really know of Blackstone? He was right in front of her, but every moment she was reminded that she didn't know him. Except one thing, the thing that was right in front of her. He was instinctively kind.

She remembered the day she'd borrowed Frank's robes and gone in male dress to hear Ricardo lecture on economics. She'd sat apart from the young collegians in the lecture hall, but not so far apart that she could not overhear conversations around her. They talked of sports and drink and abused each other about debts not paid, and she'd felt superior in her intellect. Then two of them near her had joked about a friend of theirs and his Master Bates, a conversation she knew instinctively to be sexual and bawdy, but that she could not understand. It caused the others to howl at a conclusion she never saw coming.

The economics lecture she'd grasped with no difficulty, but her lack of understanding of the joke stayed with her, humiliating proof of her ignorance. She had not even asked Frank to explain.

The painting of Blackstone and his mistress, that was the other grand joke on her. Everyone else had seen it and understood it, while she remained an ignorant, helpless girl. Everyone else knew the joke she didn't know.

With a distant flash and a low rumble of thunder, the rain arrived and drove the players from the field. For half an hour, everyone huddled under the awning, the boys in two groups at opposite ends of the tent, glumly watching the field.

The sky was clearing when Dubusari sought Violet's attention. "I beg your pardon, Miss Hammersley, but his majesty is missing one of his medals, the Order of Saint Stephen. Could you ask your boys to look about them in the tent? I am sure it has fallen off somewhere."

Violet did not miss the implication that her boys would know where to find the missing jewelry. Blackstone was at her side at once. "The prince likely dislodged the pin when he batted." Blackstone's hair was wind ruffled, and rain stuck the thin lawn of his sleeves to his arms, outlining the lean muscle and sinew there. His face wore rivulets of water, and the dark spikes of his lashes sparkled with drops.

For a moment Dubusari looked anything but gentle and polite. He looked menacing. Then Cahul dashed out into the downpour. They watched the bodyguard search the ground, and hold up his arm in triumph. He returned to the awning thoroughly soaked, the perfect loyal servant.

Nate made Kirby's shop bell ring merrily as he entered. He couldn't help a bit of a swagger. His trip to the neighborhood of the docks had paid off. He not yet spotted one of the prince's people in Wapping, but today he had found an unlikely prize and tucked it in his pocket. He was on his way to Blackstone, but first he meant to show the thing to Miranda Kirby, just so that she'd know his work was important to the case.

As he entered, Viscount Hazelwood pushed away from leaning over Miranda's counter. She looked up, consciousness of the intimacy of the moment with Hazelwood bright in her cheeks. She straightened and flicked Nate a cold glance. The shop was fragrant with the scent of the sandalwood shaving soap Miranda liked to show her customers.

"Young Wilde, you must have something to report."

"I do, my lord."

"Don't 'my lord' me, Wilde. I think Goldsworthy has the two of us mixed up. It's you he should be sending to dance at Almack's while I take my disreputable self off to the lowest dives in Covent Garden."

Miranda's gaze grew icicles. "Don't say so, Lord Hazelwood. You were not born for such disgraces. Nate Wilde knows his way around low places because he came from them."

"My family would quite agree with you, Miss Kirby, nonetheless, I've courted disgrace, and she's a willing mistress. Pardon me, I'll take myself back to the club."

Hazelwood was telling the truth whether Miranda believed him or not. He could dazzle her just by being a viscount, even in the rumpled, soiled clothes they had him wear. Goldsworthy's uniform for Hazelwood was deliberately made of stained fabrics. Though the viscount had been sober for nearly a month, Goldsworthy didn't want the world to know it. He wanted everyone to see the same man he'd plucked from a sponging house. Hazelwood had apparently had his first affair at eighteen and had drunk or gambled away all of his fortune except for the funds he'd put aside for his by-blows. His father, the Earl of Vange, had taken his son to court to ensure that Hazelwood would be a life tenant of his estate, and that the property would pass to his legitimate heir if he lived to have one.

But Miranda refused to credit any story about him that contradicted her idea of a gentleman to the manner born. She firmly insisted that Viscount Hazelwood could not have done the things said of him.

The shop door closed behind the viscount, and Nate took a moment to shake off any thoughts of his rival. Fate had cruelly put Miranda Kirby in his path just when he was making the most of opportunities that had come his way through the copper, Will Jones. She was exactly the sort of beauty he could not ignore. He hadn't known, couldn't have known at thirteen, as one of Bredsell's boys, that a woman could have such a hold on a man. It was a curious but true fact that a certain tilt of a head, or the way that a chestnut curl bounced, or a bit of creamy softness under a chin or an arm, could stop a man in his path, make his mouth go dry and his brain turn to mush.

Now he had his work cut out for him to convince his fair Miranda that deeds, not birth, made the man. It was a campaign. Like a war, it could take years to win. At near twenty he was in no hurry. He had once met the great man, Lord Wellington, and he knew that Wellington had taken all of Spain and France from Napoleon one city at a time.

Nate's current work put him at a bit of a disadvantage because he had to wear the rough clothes of the docks. Miranda liked her gentlemen with all the fine trimmings—wool coats and silk waistcoats and lace cuffs—he could manage those as well as any man in London, and it hadn't been so hard. A man simply had to pay attention, to notice. Goldsworthy understood. A man of fashion made a good spy, after all, because he had a habit of noticing details. Being a Bredsell boy had trained Nate to notice looks and voices and a dozen gestures that gave away a man's intentions. Will Jones had freed him from Bredsell and taught him to organize and analyze what he saw. And Goldsworthy had given him a new language to master, full of idiom—fashion.

Winning Miranda Kirby would take all his skills.

"Sorry I scared your admirer off." He moved closer to Miranda's counter.

"Lord Hazelwood doesn't scare, and he's not my admirer. We were just talking is all." She fussed with the jars and bottles on the shelf behind the counter.

"I saw. It must get lonely in the shop."

"Nate Wilde, are you trying to turn me up sweet?"

"Never. I was just thinking you might like to do more than whip up shaving lather. Maybe you'd like to take part in the work." He leaned back with his elbows on Miranda's counter.

"You mean the cases?"

He nodded, not looking at her. It was better not to let himself be distracted at the moment.

"Like going to be stung by bees? A lady can never go the places you go. It wouldn't be right."

"No bees. Just a chance to use your loaf." He risked a glance at her.

She rolled her eyes. "My loaf! How you talk!"

"Do you want to?"

"Use my brain? As if I don't every day." She looked at him then. "What are you suggesting?"

"I have something that's likely got a bearing on Lord Blackstone's case. I thought you might like to take a look at it." He waited. It was unfair to mention Blackstone, but he wasn't going to play fair in this game.

"What is it?"

"Do you want to have a look?"

"You're putting me on."

"I'm not. You could help me figure out what to make of it." He reached into his pocket for the prize he had tucked there, a Spanish banknote.

When the proprietor of the King Edward, a low drinking establishment, where Nate was keeping an eye on the dock neighborhood, had complained about the useless note, Nate had offered to take it off his hands. The fellow had been suspicious, but real money had made him willing to make the deal. Nate knew at once that a Spanish banknote was an odd possession for a local dockhand. Like the buttons, the note came from someone other than a common sailor, someone like Frank Hammersley. "Do you want to take a look?"

Miranda put aside the brush she was cleaning. "Very well then. I'll help you."

"Most gracious of you." He grinned at her grand lady tone.

"What?"

"I found this particular item, so I get to say who sees it and under what terms."

"What do you mean 'terms'?"

"Terms." He watched her, weighing the balance of curiosity and suspicion in her frown. "Say, if you were to let me touch you."

He'd rendered her speechless. A rich red blush flooded her cheeks. Rude parts of him that could claim no gentlemanly manners at all responded instantly. He steadied himself. If she said no, she said no. A battle was not the whole campaign.

"If you touch me, you're no gentleman." That stung a little.

"Depends on where I touch you. I didn't say yet." His hand was still in his pocket, on the item she couldn't see. "A gentleman's gloved hand touches a lady's gloved hand in a dance or when he helps her into a carriage."

She had stiffened, and she relaxed a little. The small change made her bosom shift in interesting ways.

"Is that what you meant—a touch of hands, gloved hands?"

He shook his head. He certainly wasn't going to settle for something as tame as glove to glove. He'd get that anyway, some day. "What I have in my pocket is worth more than that."

"Well, what do you want then?"

"I want to touch your face with my ungloved hand." He tried to make his voice light and careless, but it sounded a bit rough.

Her bosom swelled with a quick intake of breath. She was looking down, contemplating her options. Nate knew enough to wait. He could watch the thin white part on the top of her burnished head for hours.

"All right. What is it?"

"First the touch."

She gave him a cool haughty look with a lift of her chin. Her smooth throat disappearing into the white lace of her collar made him swallow hard.

"Perfect. Stay just like that. Close your eyes."

"Why?"

"I won't know what you're thinking if you close your eyes."

"Yes, you will. I won't like it."

"Close your eyes."

"Well then. You have to be brief, you know."

"You have to wait until I finish. It won't be long."

She gave him one more suspicious glance and closed her eyes.

The temptation of that mouth drawn in a stubborn, shut line was almost too much. Nate reminded himself that he wanted the final victory, that this was only one step. He'd been a thief, but now he was a strategist. He raised his hand and let his knuckles graze the underside of her chin. She was as smooth and soft as he'd imagined. He steadied his hand. If he broke contact now, she'd open her eyes and pull away. Girls had instincts, too. Even a motherless girl like Miranda had mysterious girl knowledge. He drew the back of his hand up over her chin and turned it so that he could stroke her lips with his thumb. She didn't open to his touch, but he felt her react. She was fully alert, conscious of him. It made him a little dizzy.

He withdrew his hand. "You can look now," he said.

She opened her eyes and pressed her lips together.

He allowed himself a brief grin before he pulled out the banknote and spread it on the counter. "What do you see?"

"A banknote."

"From?"

She looked again. "Spain, I think."

"*Le Banco Espanola de Madrid.*"

"Why does it matter that it's from Spain?"

"Because it turned up in a taproom in Wapping where it doesn't belong, not three days after Frank Hammersley was supposed to arrive in London from Spain. What do you see when you look at it?"

He smoothed the paper on the counter.

Miranda leaned over to look at it. "Well, I see the number one hundred and some fellow whose clothing looks medieval. Does he have a name?"

The bill was printed in two inks, one dark blue and the other faint red. The figure on the right looked like a portrait of one of the old kings with a stiff white ruff around his neck, a long face, and an inverted V of a moustache. "I don't know. Must be one of their old kings."

She gave him one of her disdainful looks, and he turned the bill over. The other side had a shield with a coat of arms between two pillars.

"What's this?" She pointed to a line of darker blue ink. She rubbed it, and held up her finger to show him a faint blue smudge. "Someone wrote something on the note."

Nate looked where her finger had been. What he had not seen in the dark taproom were lines of script hidden between the printed lines of the note. The script looked like no language he knew, which didn't help his theory that the bill came from Frank Hammersley, but it was another oddity that needed to be examined. Someone had used the spaces in the design to write on the bill, and recently if the ink still smudged.

He snatched it from under Miranda's pretty nose. "Thanks, Miranda." He slipped behind the counter and headed for the back door of the shop. "You know what I like best about you, don't you?"

She glared at him.

"Your brains."

It was near dusk when the game finally ended in a great splashing of mud as the teams gathered to cheer one another. The blustery storm had passed, and sunlight streamed through broken clouds in long slanting afternoon rays that made gleaming patches on the wet grass. When the defeated Knightsbridge team moved off the field, Violet's triumphant boys swarmed about Blackstone. By the end, he had mud in his ears. They trudged off the field in spattered whites and made a ceremony of presenting Violet with a team sweater.

The moment proved his undoing. She smiled at him, a smile like the winter sun. And then, because she looked so pleased and grateful, hugging the sweater to her chest, he kissed her. Surrounded by the cheering, mud-splattered boys, it had been a kiss with nothing of desire in it, just joy and recognition, a moment of shared happiness, as fleeting as one of the shifting patches of light on the grass. She looked at him for a moment as if she truly saw him. That look induced a moment of dangerous distraction in which he missed the departure of the two carriages with the duchess's and the prince's companions. He didn't like the separation of their party. As a precaution, he directed their coachman to take a different route back to London.

"We'll talk tonight," he told Violet as he handed her into the vehicle. Once again he was muddied and damp. He chose to ride back on the coachman's box, wrapped in a carriage rug, while the prince scrambled happily into the carriage, babbling in English and his own tongue, pouring flattery over Blackstone's betrothed.

Chapter Fifteen

... she went boldly on with him alone.

—Jane Austen, *Pride and Prejudice*

Blackstone stripped off his ruined clothes. He was going through Kirby's finery as fast as the club could supply it. Being involved with Violet Hammersley was hard on both a man's dignity and his wardrobe. Twickler, the competent valet who tended the three members of Goldsworthy's club, had laid out new clothes and left two buckets of hot water. Blackstone poured a pitcher over his head. The mud he could wash away, the foolish kiss lingered.

A knock interrupted him, and he shrugged into a wrapper. "Enter."

It was Wilde. His glance took in the pile of ruined clothes. "Brought you something of interest, sir." He held up a Spanish banknote.

Blackstone took the note, a hundred Spanish pesetas. "Where did this turn up, Wilde?"

"In a taproom in Wapping. Not the usual place for a Spanish note, is it, sir?"

Blackstone didn't like it. If it came from Frank, it tended to support Goldsworthy's theory of a disappearance not a kidnapping, a man in hiding rather than in captivity.

"Someone's written on it. Ink's still fresh."

"Written on it?" Blackstone laid it on his bureau, drawing a branch of candles close. Wilde showed him the looping lines of some unreadable script in the spaces of the printed design. The hand was unrecognizable as Frank Hammersley's, he was pretty sure, but it should be possible to compare the ink to that used to write the note to Violet. The writing changed everything.

"What do you think, sir? A message?"

"One that his captors can't read. How did he get it to the taproom?" Blackstone was sticking to his theory that Frank was a captive. Certainly, if he were free, Frank would not be so foolish as to walk into a public house and flash a Spanish banknote.

"I'd wager Hammersley offered one of them a bribe."

"Makes sense. He needed something. What did he get in exchange?"

"Pen and ink?" Wilde suggested.

"He has the pen and ink already. He wanted something else." Blackstone thought of Vasiladi's cave. If he could have bribed any of his captors, what would he have asked for? He had been intent on freedom for his fellow captives, most of them young and helpless. If he could have, he would have bargained for them to be spared, but to signal to Vasiladi that he cared about the sufferings of the others would have been to increase them. Vasiladi would have enjoyed tormenting some helpless child just to watch Blackstone endure it. Above all he had had to be careful to show no feeling for his young half brother, taken in one of Vasiladi's raids on the youthful idealists who had gone to free Greece from the Turks and found themselves mired in mud and quarrels. So he had made it seem a rich man's whim, his ransoming of twelve captives. He had told Vasiladi he wanted a harem of his own.

"Does Hammersley need food and drink?"

Blackstone shook his head. Frank's guards were probably feeding him even if the kidnappers meant to kill him in the end. They would not want to signal their intention to their henchmen.

Wilde voiced the question Blackstone had already asked himself. "Why would kidnappers provide a man pen and ink?"

"They want him to write something. They tested him with that note to Violet to see whether he would follow orders. Now he's testing them. He wanted to see if he could get a message out."

"It worked, didn't it?"

Blackstone nodded. "It did. Whoever got the note off of Hammersley took it straight to the nearest taproom without detecting the message. Where is this taproom?"

"It's on the high street, not far from the pawnshop where I found the buttons."

Blackstone could see the layout in his mind, the river, the warehouse, and the warren of lanes off the high street. "So not far from the burned-out tea warehouse where the *Madagascar*'s cargo was headed. But you've seen no sign of anyone in the place?"

"Goldsworthy's night man thought he saw lights last night in the southwest corner. Easy enough to keep my eye on the taproom, sir, to see if one of the prince's people shows up there."

Blackstone nodded. "Wilde, keep the banknote between us for now. Not a word to Goldsworthy."

"Sir? Yes, sir."

As Violet descended for dinner Granthem handed her a message that Blackstone had news of Frank. Violet was aware of the wording—*news* did not mean that Frank was found. Dinner became an unbearable interval. She wished she had told Mrs. Hill to cut the menu in half. Their guests, a pair of bankers and their ladies, sat quietly awed by the presence of royalty. To Violet's right the prince offered repeated congratulations on her team's success. Flushed and bouncing in his seat, he delighted in recounting the cricket match bowl by bowl, getting tangled in his account of the scoring. To her left the count drank sullenly. Across the table the countess leaned towards Blackstone, and Papa engaged his fellow bankers and Dubusari in a discussion of wheat price fluctuation and its effect on the value of the pound. She was impatient for the dinner to be over, and then impatient for the interval between dinner and coffee to end.

Her female guests easily followed the countess's lead, taking up the topic of Violet's benefit ball. Violet was obliged to explain in some detail the arrangements she and Penelope had made. She was relieved that the men lingered a shorter time than usual over their port. Blackstone gave her the briefest of greetings and no hint of his news when she offered him a coffee. He returned to the countesses' side.

Violet straightened over the tea tray and smiled at the banker in front of her. Blackstone's withdrawal was probably wise. They had forgotten the barriers that should separate them already twice in one day. Acting like partners was more dangerous than acting like a betrothed pair.

When Violet entered Frank's room, a candle burned dimly on the trunk next to their bench. Blackstone had not waited. Maybe there was no news after all. They had been together most of the day, and no one had attempted to kill them or the prince. A twinge of disappointment made her cheeks warm. She had wanted to see him, and she could not lie to herself that the disappointment she felt was for Frank's sake.

She crossed to the trunk to see whether he had left a note and found none. For a moment she stood absorbing that second disappointment. He had withdrawn not only from the past, but from the partnership they had entered into to find Frank. Well, he would be back in the morning. He might let her down, but not the government. Whoever Blackstone worked for, he would complete his mission.

She leaned to blow out the candle he'd left. She should be grateful that he had thought the better of meeting her at night. He had ridden back on the carriage box, soaked and dirty, avoiding her, she suspected, because they had kissed again, and most unwisely.

All the way home, in the carriage that smelled of wet wool and the prince's cologne, she'd pondered what Blackstone meant by that kiss. Jolted along uneven roads that brought her knees against the prince's, she felt that happy kiss. It was unlike the kiss in her bedroom. She thought it tasted of friendship, if not of love. At the same time, that kiss had made her realize something she had long ignored. As a girl she had envied his freedom, to come and go from Hammersley House to his other life among London's titled families, where she could not follow. She had imagined that when they parted he had simply stepped out of her life into that other life, but now she knew he had not. He had left her behind, but he had not been free to enter the drawing rooms

and ballrooms of London as he had before. His name had
been sullied as if there, too, he had been covered in the mud
of a soggy cricket field.

She blew out the candle on the trunk. As she straightened
and turned, her light picked out his form through the curling
smoke of the snuffed candle. He lay on Frank's bed, leaning
back against the bolster as if he'd just meant to close his
eyes for a moment, but the evenness of his breathing and
the slackness of his hand against the counterpane told her
he was deeply asleep.

She approached slowly, quieting the rustle of her skirts
and holding her candle to one side. His long legs stretched
nearly the length of the bed, legs that had often been
entwined with hers when they lay together. He had shed his
neckcloth again, and undone the collar of his shirt. His dark
hair fell back from the peak at the center of his brow.

She should wake him at once. The thought was immediately replaced by a sense of the advantage of the moment.
Blackstone awake was a formidable noticer of detail. Where
the prince and Rushbrooke stumbled or charged down narrow paths, Blackstone moved at ease taking in everyone and
everything around him. For once since his return, she could
look at him without being observed and work at the puzzle
of who he had become.

She stood at the edge of the bed and let herself look.
There could be no danger in it as long as she held back in
mere contemplation, studying her adversary.

The candle's golden light gilded one side of his face, all
bones and hollows, his mouth defined by a sharp valley
above his lips. He had a Greek nose, straight and symmet-
rical as a sculptor's dream. His brows were dark slashes
across his forehead. Again the leanness of his face struck
her. His Adam's apple made a sharp ridge in his throat. His

cheek and jaw had unfashionable edges and angles rather than the smooth curves of the polite male face. Byron, celebrated for his sensuality, had had a rounded fullness of face that Blackstone lacked.

Blackstone's sensuality was a wiry sensuality of taut bowstrings vibrating deeply, of curving stone or hammered steel. His long lean fingers curled lightly against the counterpane, but corded veins stood out on the backs of his hands.

At times since his return, he looked like a starving man. The pallor of his skin added to the impression. Tonight a rosy band of sun-warmed color crossed his cheeks and nose. Below the dark lines of his lashes, he looked boyish. In sleep he looked as young as he had been when she'd first known him. She told herself it wasn't so. He was a jaded rogue who had returned to England with a harem, but on the cricket pitch, he had moved with bursts of speed, quick turns, and deft tosses of the ball as if he had been a boy himself. He had been unafraid of mud on his clothes or in his ears.

She had thought herself modern and rational when she had announced to him at nineteen that she would not marry a man without knowing what intimacy with him would be like. They had been lying on their backs on the floor of the attic schoolroom looking at a waning moon. He had immediately rolled on top of her and advised—*Then you'd better lie with me, Violet, because you are going to marry me.*

His words had changed everything. She'd gone still, knowing that her future had been decided. Marriage, which had seemed as distant as the yellow half moon from the window, had suddenly been as close as the roof next door behind which that heavy-lidded moon was setting. She would marry not some stranger waiting in her future but the man in her arms. Weeks later she had accepted his ring. A brief period of giddy joy passed until he came to her wearing that other ring with its distinctive capital, and she had ended their engagement.

She looked at his beautiful sleeping face.

Today she had seen joy in his eyes and kindness in his acts. He had known instinctively what her boys needed. Without Rushbrooke at her side, she had seen them differently. It was Rushbrooke who had insisted that they be neat and proper, while Blackstone understood that they needed to dirty their uniforms to win the match. She saw now that Rushbrooke's insistence on fine uniforms for the boys had not been charity at all, but disapproval. He didn't really like poor children as they were. He needed to disguise them and clean them up and make them respectable before he could support them. He had tried to clean Violet up, as well.

She reached out to touch Blackstone's shoulder, and the candlelight fell on his face. He started and his dark eyes flew open, blue as the night sky. In that unguarded waking moment she might have thought his eyes full of love.

He caught her wrist in his grip. She pulled back, and the candle trembled in her hand, spilling wax into the brass pan. A drop ran over the edge and splashed on the back of his hand where the splinter had left its jagged mark. Her heart pounded. She had come too close. She'd let herself linger and enjoy looking at him instead of getting straight to the business of finding Frank. She steadied the candlestick and brushed the cooling wax from his hand. At her touch he stilled.

"Violet, you are living dangerously." He shifted upright and swung his feet to the floor. Neither moved. The candle flickered and sent up acrid curls of smoke and hot wax. In the past at this hour, alone, so close, they would have fallen into the available bed, helpless in the grip of mad desire. Tonight she reminded herself to think of Frank.

"How long have I been napping?"

She shrugged. She would not admit to studying him. "You wanted to tell me something about Frank?"

"Your brother may be trying to get a message out." Blackstone's eyes were still the color of longing.

A carriage rattled by in the street.

He released her hand and stepped around her. "Right. Your brother's message. We need someplace with more light and a magnifying glass."

"My father keeps a glass in the gunroom."

"The gunroom it is."

He strode to the door, and held it open for her to pass. In silence they made their way down through the darkened house. Violet waited inside the gunroom with her candle while Blackstone lit a pair of table lamps to make a bright space. "Sit." He handed her a banknote. "You can see that this is a Spanish note."

"Yes. I've seen them before. Hammersley Bank has dealings with the *Banco Espanola de Madrid*."

"It turned up today in the Wapping neighborhood where we found your brother's coat buttons."

She turned to look up at him. He sounded grim when the clue seemed helpful. "So, he's in Wapping? It should be easy to find him then."

"Turn it over."

Violet did as he suggested. He leaned over her, his coat sleeve brushing her shoulder, to point at the central image of a coat of arms flanked by a pair of columns. "If you look in the spaces between the pillars and the shield, there's script. The ink came off on one of our associate's hands."

Violet touched her finger to her tongue and to the bill and got a smudge of blue ink. "Do you think it's the same ink as Frank's note?"

"I do. Can you read the script?"

Violet took up the glass to study the mysterious ink lines. The added script looked like no words she knew. She shifted the glass back and forth over the strange writing. Then a little shiver of recognition passed over her.

Blackstone noticed. "You know what it is?"

"It's upside down and backwards. I used to write like that when I was trying to be cleverer than Frank, but he could do it, too."

"Can you make it out?"

"Let me make a copy."

Blackstone rummaged through her father's drawers for ink, paper, and pen with his usual command of her house. He and Frank had spent hours in the gunroom. She rolled up her sheer sleeve and set herself to extract the hidden lines from the printed image on the note.

Blackstone watched Violet work. He told himself there was nothing remarkable about Violet Hammersley to make him kiss her at cricket matches or catch and hold her wrist. His youthful infatuation with her should have no power over him now. He should not care if she supported poor boys or seamstresses or beggars or dogs. He should not care that she loved her brother. Nothing was so common as family affection.

She wore a burgundy shawl over an evening gown of pewter silk with sheer sleeves gathered at her wrists. Candlelight lit her forehead, slid down her straight serious nose, and caught her firm chin, making of her clean profile a bright edge against the darkness.

He had watched her at work before, on a night long ago

in the midst of the bullion crisis. She had been barred from the nightly meetings of bankers and cabinet men who gathered around George Hammersley to determine a way through the crisis. In her room at her desk she'd spread out newspapers and notes and was deep in thought when he'd entered. The men downstairs had forgotten a girl of seventeen, but he had felt his friend's absence from the urgent conferences of men.

He had thought to divert her mind from the crisis that consumed the household and the nation, but she wanted to understand everything to help her papa and her brother. For half an hour she had pummeled Blackstone with questions. Her dark eyes had flashed with curiosity and determination to understand the workings of money. He hadn't known it at the time but he knew now that Violet, in quest of understanding, came passionately alive.

At the time he'd been conscious only of her new more grown-up form, of her dark hair curling against the pale tops of her breasts. Her clothing had been simpler then. The energy of her thinking seemed to warm them both, so that her scent invaded his senses. Before he could summon any of his defenses, he found his trousers lifted in a blatant display of his interest in her person, and before he could make any excuses and take himself out of her presence, she'd noticed and made her comment about his penis.

Within minutes they had been tearing at each other's clothes, trying to connect wholly and completely, until Augusta Lowndes found them, tangled in each other's arms on Violet's bed. He had managed an unconvincing apology for forcing himself upon her, which Violet had spoiled by announcing that she was fully as much to blame as he was.

Tonight when he'd wakened, he had caught her look of concentration directed at him, and something inside him had given a glad leap in answer to that scrutiny before he brought it to heel. Now in a colder waking moment, he was using her, getting her to betray her brother. And he must not forget that she was smart, and that he had to distract her from where the evidence of the banknote would inevitably lead. Her next question when it came was not the one he expected.

"Why does the countess take such an interest in you?"

"I suspect that she wants to get me alone."

An amused smile played on her lips. "Blackstone, you cannot believe that every woman succumbs equally to your charms."

"I think our countess succumbs to no man."

"Then why does she want to get you alone? Suppose her helpless act induced you to follow her down the proverbial garden path, what would she do—betray you in some embarrassing or compromising situation? Get information from you?"

"She might murder me."

"Really?" Her hand paused, and she looked up. "I understand the sentiment, but is it possible? She's inches shorter, pounds lighter, and a woman. Does she carry a weapon? It's hard to imagine where she could conceal a pistol or a knife in those gauzy frocks of hers."

He didn't answer. The fall of light revealed the wintry landscape of her white throat against her dusky curls. The tops of her breasts glowed above the dark pewter of her gown. Then she bent to her work again. He listened to the careful scratch of her pen and thought he heard something else, something like slippers on the flagstones of the courtyard. He didn't turn. In the lighted gunroom they were perfectly visible through the French doors from almost anywhere in the darkened courtyard. He himself had used its potted palms for concealment.

In the end, Violet could make out two words. Because the bill had been folded, part of the message had been smeared beyond recognition. Only two words emerged clearly from the smudges. She looked at the copy she'd made.

"What does it say?"

She passed him the written note. "Leave England."

Blackstone looked at it and laughed. "Just our luck. Your brother offers travel advice."

"What did you expect?"

He shifted closer to her, speaking lightly as if he jested. "I had hoped he would say—'Come to number seven Cat's Hole Lane. They've got me in a back room on the ground floor.' "

Violet stared at the two words. Her shoulders slumped. She had taken care. She was sure she had decoded them properly. She had no doubt they were from Frank. She and he had played at scripts as children, and he always kept banknotes hidden on his person. She had worked carefully in the hope that the hidden script would solve the mystery of Frank's disappearance before it was too late to save him.

Blackstone watched her from the end of the table, his left hand resting on it, behind him the French doors of the dark courtyard. There was some tension in him, something alert and wary in the way he held himself that triggered an answering wariness in her. The light caught the gleam of his ring.

She thought about what she had just done, and her stomach clenched with a sudden uneasy feeling. A sick feeling. Her knees went limp, and she slid off the stool and only caught herself by grabbing hold of the table. He could kiss her in the morning or in the moment of dizzy victory for her boys and stand there now, dark and cool and treacherous. He'd tricked her, misled her, deceived her again.

The weakness passed, and anger, hot and bracing, surged through her and lifted her. "Three days you and I have played this cruel farce. Three days have passed. You hold my hand with its false ring and whisper in my ear. You give me buttons and banknotes, but only to make me betray my brother."

She lunged for him in a swirl of skirts and rage, lifting her hands to strike him. He seized her wrists stretching her arms wide, bringing them face-to-face.

She leaned in. "You are not looking for Frank's kidnappers. You are looking for Frank. That's why Bow Street wouldn't help Papa."

He tightened his hold and marched her backwards along the length of the table, their strides matching in an angry dance.

"Are you mad!" She twisted against him while he pinned her between his hips and the edge of her father's book-topped cabinet.

Violet's writhing woke the clamoring part of Blackstone that should have no say in their conversation. "Look at me, Violet. Keep your voice low. We're lovers, remember."

"Lovers. Hah. *We* are not working together. *You* are using me. You think Frank's hiding from the government. I see it now. Our engagement, the announcement in the papers, is a lure to draw him out."

Her eyes flashed with the rapid flow of her thoughts. She twisted in his hold, one step from figuring out the whole, ready to bolt.

"Violet, we have a spy. Behind me in the courtyard, who must not hear your suspicions."

The words stopped her. She stared at his shadowed face. He lengthened the stretch of his arms, bringing their bodies closer, silk brushing wool. Violet sucked in a breath as her breasts flattened against his chest, no escape for either of them.

Fashion, Blackstone thought, was every rational man's enemy. Fashion bared Violet's neck and shoulders, her collarbone and the tops of her trembling breasts flushed a shell-like pink. The friction of their bodies meeting shot arrows of glad sensation straight to his groin. He was supposed to betray her, so that he could win back everything he had lost to scandal and treachery. He was supposed to use her, but his body throbbed in answer to the angry pulse that rocked her against him, while to his back a spy looked on. Of course, Violet's unstoppable brain went on asking questions. His stalled as her scent rose up to beguile him.

"Who is spying on us?"

"Someone in the prince's retinue." He kept his arms extended, holding himself between her and whoever watched them. He had not forgotten that a bullet had nearly missed her in this very room.

"Why? What do they suspect?"

"They think Frank will try to give you something they want."

What? Her eyes asked it.

"A hundred thousand pounds."

"You're mad."

"The government, Violet, thinks Frank took a hundred thousand pounds and murdered two agents."

"No." Her quiet voice was firm and unwavering, but bright betraying drops welled up in her eyes.

The tears distracted him. They were in the shadows, and he kept himself between her and the spy in the courtyard, but he could not track the spy's position or determine what the spy might have heard or read on Violet's lips earlier.

Violet pressed up against him, her mouth close to his.

"My brother did not steal a hundred thousand pounds or betray his country or murder anyone. How can you believe it of Frank? You *know* him."

As soon as she said it, her face changed. Her eyes went hollow, and the fight went out of her. He could feel her slump in his hold. He pressed her against the cabinet, holding her steady with his outstretched arms.

"That's the unforgivable thing, isn't it, that someone who knows you has no faith in you."

She closed her eyes, and the bright liquid burned in shining tracks down her smooth cheeks, a glittering snow melt. And damn him, he wanted to comfort her. He wanted to kiss her and burn away the pain. What did it matter that he understood that pain precisely because she had once inflicted it on him. What did it matter that this moment was a just repayment, a betrayal for a betrayal.

"I'm going to kiss you, Violet." It was the only warning he gave. He caught her waist and lifted her up onto the low cabinet, nudging her knees apart and making a place where he could press the ache she made him feel against her warm, womanly center. Through wool and silk and linen, he could feel the heat of her.

With one arm he anchored her to him. With the other he captured her head and held it so that he could take her mouth. Her spine was straight, unbending, but she tilted her head and opened her mouth under his and let him in.

He kissed her because he had missed kissing her for so long, because in that time he had not been living exactly, and he was alive right now, as she was alive, for him.

She stopped trying to push him away. Her hands gripped his head, sliding into his hair. Her gown billowed between them like the foam of stormy waves. He freed one hand to brush aside her insubstantial gossamer skirts and slide his palm over her silk-clad knee, feeling the muscled contour of her thigh until his fingers passed over the gathers of her satin garter and met skin. The softness of it dizzied him momentarily.

He reached the apex and traced the crease where thigh and hip joined. She shivered and clung to him more tightly. He slid his open palm then to cup her, his palm pressing down, his fingers curving up to play lightly, until he felt her body bloom for him, opening, spreading under his touch, and he could slide his fingers into her slick warmth and feel her ready for him.

Remember, his lips said, trailing along her throat. *Remember,* his hand said, warm and strong sliding over her knee, stopping to quake like her at meeting her flesh. *Remember,* his fingers said sliding into her cleft, opening her.

Then, because she was Violet, daughter of Eve and Pandora, curious and questing, she slid her own palm between their fused bodies. Her fingers, sure and swift, released the fall of his wool trousers and the closure of his linen smalls, and closed around the smooth hot shaft of him, and did to him what he did to her.

Blackstone's consciousness flickered like a candle in a draft. He flexed his hips up, sliding into her touch, and thought that he had come home for this, for Violet Hammersley's hand on him, he had stayed alive for this, that Violet Hammersley would once again love him.

He pulled her hand free of his cock and shifted so that he might push into her, but she shuddered at his first touch, pulsing around him even as he came into her. A cascade of books fell from the cabinet, hitting the floor with a clatter, recalling him to reason.

He drew back as she quaked in his arms. He lifted his

mouth from hers and kissed her forehead. Their ragged
breathing filled his ears. His back was to the courtyard. He
and Violet appeared to be no more than impatient lovers,
but he did not know how close the spy had come or what he
or she might have heard of their conversation.

He helped her from the cabinet. They had hardly disordered their clothes. She did not look at him as she shook her
skirts and twisted her hair into a neat knot. He fastened his
trousers concealing his aching arousal.

He made her leave the books on the floor. He did not
know whether she realized how he had betrayed his
employer. Maybe he had already decided he could not play
the government's game when he'd asked Wilde to keep the
Spanish banknote between them. Not that Violet would
accept him back, but now he had to make his own plans to
find Frank Hammersley before Goldsworthy did.

Outside her bedroom door, he stopped her briefly.

"It's time to move your guests out of the house. I will
make sure the hotel is ready for them tomorrow."

"I won't let you betray Frank to the government."

"I know."

Chapter Sixteen

"... I have always observed, that they who are good-natured when children, are good-natured when they grow up; and he was always the sweetest-tempered, most generous-hearted boy in the world."

—Jane Austen, *Pride and Prejudice*

The five patronesses of the Spitalfields Seamstresses' Benefit Ball and the five women who had produced their gowns gathered in Penelope Frayne's back drawing room overlooking her garden. Penelope was her husband's second duchess, the comfort of his old age. His heir, her stepson, was away at university. Violet had actually seen the duke just once, a tall strikingly handsome man, whose age she guessed to be seventy.

Gauzy curtains drawn to shield the room from sun and prying eyes billowed in a slight breeze. Silks and female voices rustled with a constant sound. Ross, Penelope's lady's maid, an austerely elegant woman of fifty, oversaw lesser servants who moved cheval glasses and provided refreshments and supplied pins and tape and extra hands as each lady ascended a small sturdy box for adjustments to her hem or stood in front of the glass to admire her silhouette.

Violet smiled and nodded mechanically, one part of her

mind consumed with the mortifying awareness that she had responded to Blackstone's kiss and touch, another part of her mind thinking of Frank. This second betrayal of Blackstone's, treating Frank as a thief and a murderer, went far beyond the first. Today Blackstone was to accompany the prince to meet the foreign secretary, and the prince's entourage was to move into Milvert's Hotel. By afternoon Violet should be free of spies and duties, free to think how she might find Frank without Blackstone's interference.

In between fittings, the ladies lounged in wrappers sipping tea, eating lemon cakes, and commenting. Violet had known from the moment she entered the room that her connection with Blackstone, not her gown, would be under scrutiny. Her ring drew sly and open stares.

Arabella Young was the first to comment. "The joke will be on Lady Ravenhurst. One wonders whether she will ever find a lover. I thought Blackstone was her last hope. What was that rhyme about him? You remember, Victoria?"

"Oh, it was something about his yard, I believe."

"I remember, 'London's ladies flock to him—'"

Penelope glanced at Violet and spoke. "Enough, ladies. Miss Hammersley is an unmarried girl yet. You must not embarrass her with such frank talk."

"Now, Penelope, you know we are not being truly frank." Arabella smiled wickedly.

"Don't worry, dear Miss Hammersley, Blackstone will want his heir, of course, then you'll be free to do as you please."

"Penelope, you haven't taken her to see the painting, have you?"

"I have not."

They all grew quiet. Charlotte, who had not spoken earlier looked quite earnest. "She should see the painting. She should not become Blackstone's bride without knowing what everyone else has known for years."

All eyes turned to Violet. She could see in their faces not malice, but pity. They pitied her ignorance. They knew more of Blackstone than she did. Only Penelope's gaze differed. Penelope's gaze dared Violet to face the whole truth, to let go of any illusions about him. She had only one, really: the illusion that he had once loved her.

"Very well, if Violet is willing, I will take her to see the painting. Her royal visitor is quite eager to see some artists' studios, I believe."

The patronesses agreed. Violet should go at once before she lost her nerve.

Blackstone had to admire the prince's outrage. He strode from the secretary's office in full military splendor, his boots ringing on the marble flagstones. "Lord Blackstone, I don't think your Mr. Secretary understands Moldova at all. An army such as mine, such as my imperial guard, costs money. I have spent no more than I was required to do by the needs of my country."

Blackstone fell into step beside the prince, and the others scrambled after them. "What did the secretary say, Prince?"

"He told me his majesty's government will no longer be of assistance. I brought him my fine report, everything exact, the way Miss Hammersley's brother likes."

Blackstone shot a quick glance back at the rest of the party. They were out of earshot. "You had a copy of Frank's report?"

The prince looked offended. "Of course. No longer of assistance? All my money goes to the army. I keep nothing for myself. But your secretary will see. He may read. It is all there." The prince stopped and shook a fist back at the closed door. "You will see. Not a penny for me."

"Did the secretary explain his refusal to offer more aid?"

"He tells me to retrench. Retrench? I do not understand the term. I would live in a field tent for the sake of my country. Perhaps the secretary has a tent to spare, eh? I will set it up in your Regent's Park, see if I don't." He turned to Blackstone. "After Miss Hammersley's ball, of course. I must not miss that."

Violet returned from the fitting in Penelope's carriage, intent to set off once again as soon as she could change. She found Blackstone's additional housemaid waiting for her.

"Miss Hammersley, I came direct to you." The girl held out a smoke-discolored bit of paper with a charred edge.

When Violet took it, she saw that it was Frank's writing again. It was an accounts page, lined and divided by red columns, with dates and items listed on the left and amounts on the right.

"I found it in the countess's room when I went to clean the fireplace. It had settled in a corner."

"Thank you. There were no other pages?"

The girl shook her head. "None that survived the burning."

"No one saw you?"

"No, miss. They'd all gone."

"Of course. To the hotel."

The girl nodded, bobbed a curtsy, and let herself out. Violet took the charred paper to her desk. The fire had consumed the lower right side of the page. The upper left showed that the page had been ripped from the middle of a ledger book, a right-hand page. She laid the paper down gently. The burnt edges crumbled, leaving black flakes of ash on her desk. The dates spanned a month of the previous year, and the items listed were expenditures for such goods as an army might need—canvas tents, wagons, hay, cords of wood, cooking pots. The costs did not seem unreasonable to Violet. Each line had the cost of a single item and the cost of the total number of items purchased. The math seemed sound enough for the entries that had survived the fire. The suppliers from whom the items were purchased would have appeared on the facing page. She looked again. The page had an odd lopsided appearance even though the columns were perfectly aligned in Frank's careful hand. When she ran her finger down the page, she saw what it was. One letter in each entry was slightly darker than its neighbors, as if Frank had traced over the letter a second time. The result was a faint line of darker letters that ran in a diagonal down the page.

Violet took a fresh sheet of paper and a pen and wrote out the sequence of the darker letters—"prince leave engl." There it was again, her brother's incomplete message. She was sure that the ledger was meant to be part of the documents the prince presented to the foreign secretary. Frank knew exactly who would read them. But someone had read them first and decided to destroy them.

And now the prince's party was removed from her reach. This morning Violet had welcomed the change. Blackstone was not a friend or a partner, but an agent of a suspicious government. She had wanted him gone so that she might find Frank herself, but now she needed to know what Blackstone had learned this morning. She would not mistake his intentions or be distracted by his kindness. She would use him to get to Frank before he did. Going with Penelope to see the famous painting would ensure that Violet made no

further mistake of Blackstone's feelings, and it would allow
her to see the prince and his party without Blackstone's
distracting presence.

She summoned her own maid, changed her dress, and
sent for the footman who could be trusted to convey a message to Blackstone about the burnt ledger pages. Then she
descended to meet Penelope's carriage. When she next saw
Blackstone, there would be no danger or confusion. She
would know the truth about him that had eluded her for
so long.

The last artist on the duchess's hastily arranged tour was no
member of the Royal Academy like the others they had
visited. The elegant carriage with its ducal coronet roused
rude comments from a brawny, big-bellied knife sharpener
as they passed his barrow in the crowded street. They
encountered cattle bound for a nearby slaughterhouse and
active bustling citizens, more inclined to use their own two
feet than to rely on liveried coachmen.

Violet knew the raffish neighborhood well. It lay to the
east of Regent Street, that bit of city planning designed to
cut rich Mayfair off from its less affluent neighbors. Still
the neighborhood was a thriving one, businesses jammed
up against one another—a grocer next to a bonnet maker,
an engraver next to a pub, a dressmaker next to a baker,
round bow windows next to columns and arches. Violet
passed along the same crowded streets to visit St. Luke's
workhouse two blocks away. Her Committee for the Welfare
of Widows and Orphans of Servicemen often found positions for the women of St. Luke's.

In all her visits Violet had not imagined that the artist
Reynolds Royce kept his studio at Number 33 Compton

Street. She had apparently passed the place dozens of times, unaware that the painter whose scandalous painting had separated her from Blackstone was happily pursuing his profession so close to her. Penelope set two stout footmen to guard the carriage.

Royce's studio took up the top floor of what had once been a grand home for a family and its servants before the neighborhood changed. Now Royce had the original servants' bedrooms converted into a single stretch of space with dormers and skylights letting in light. At one end of the long room were his domestic arrangements, a sink, a bed, and a sitting area. At the other end the walls were crowded with paintings of nudes in gauzy drapery that exposed creamy, rounded limbs. Each bore the name of some lofty virtue or aspiration. Violet recognized the style made popular by Emma Hamilton's "Attitudes." Royce's paintings had rather a smirk to them than earnestness. *Chastity* with raised arms and bared breasts wore the most clothing of the lot.

Violet felt a twinge of sympathy for the man with the coarse, misshapen face, who painted so much smooth-skinned beauty. But his crooked mouth twisted in a sneer, and she turned away.

The brief formalities of greeting barely held the prince's attention. He strode to the wall of nudes and began to gesture excitedly. His party followed, Cahul frowning, Dubusari lifting his glass, and the countess looking disdainful. The prince spread his arms wide encompassing the whole wall. "Ah, I see, we've come to the right place."

Royce bowed to the duchess and turned to Violet. "Miss Hammersley, have we met?"

"Never."

"You look away from my work. Are you offended by the human body?"

Violet smiled politely, aware of the countess's attention shifting to her. "Oh no, Mr. Royce. I'm rather fond of the human body. Where would a woman be without one?"

"Ah, but displays of the human form—the female form— in all its glory—these alarm you?"

"Not at all. I am perfectly equal to seeing what my sisters are willing to display in the service of art."

Penelope laughed and slipped her arm through Violet's. "You must not attempt to discompose my friend, Royce. It's the prince who most wants to see your work. He's been to see all the members of the Royal Academy and purchased nothing."

"Bah, cowards the lot of them. You'll find my work quite different, Prince."

The prince picked up a canvas, which Royce snatched from his hand. "I beg your pardon, majesty, but you must not touch what you are not willing to buy."

"But I am willing to buy. That is why I have come. They say that you have painted the most beautiful women in England. My taste is excellent. You will benefit when it is known that I, Moldova, buy your work."

Royce perked up at once. "In that case, your majesty, come this way." He rummaged through a pile of canvases and picked one that showed a woman in a scarlet coat of military cut standing with a brown horse before a grand country house.

The prince gave the painting a quick dismissive scrutiny. "No, no, no, too much landscape and a horse not as good as my Oberon. You are famous, Mr. Royce, for more attention to the form than the clothes of a woman."

Royce drew their attention to a velvet curtain covering a portion of the wall. "No one draws that curtain except me, your majesty, and only for those who appreciate my work."

Royce rubbed his thumb across the tips of his fingers, like a street vendor demanding to see coins.

The prince laughed. "Ah, like everything in England, there is a price to be paid, even for a few minutes enjoyment of beauty."

"Especially, for beauty."

"But you do not offer the painting behind the curtain for sale?" Dubusari asked.

Royce shook his head. "I did once, but the man to whom I offered it would not meet my price. I keep it to teach a lesson to those who think they can refuse to pay a true artist."

"But also to make the public curious."

Royce laughed. He reminded Violet of the touts at side-shows with their taunting dares to spectators to step inside and see some poor creature made freakish by deformity.

The prince, of course, wanted to see what was behind the curtain.

Penelope watched Violet. She tried to brace herself for the revelation. It was what Penelope wanted her to see. It was the reason they had come to Royce's studio to see the portrait of Blackstone's mistress, the cause of the scandal associated with his name. She had sought the truth about him, and now she felt unready for it, uneasy about it. There was something wrong even with the desire to see the woman with whom Blackstone had once been intimate. She didn't understand herself.

The prince turned to Dubusari. "Dubusari, Royce drives a hard bargain. It appears we must buy something. What do you recommend?" The two men strolled to the far wall of the studio to study the nudes.

Royce followed and soon began to lift up canvases at the prince's request. Penelope took Violet by the arm and led her away from the curtained painting to look at Royce's paintings of street vendors. Violet liked his street scenes better than his other work. He had captured the energy and eccentricities of a group of men gathered around the brawny knife sharpener with his cart. Here were all the faults of face and form celebrated. People swarmed the street around them, and a barefoot boy with a pint pot in his hand stopped to watch the man work. The painting had a naturalness Royce's other work lacked.

"Violet, you're not losing your nerve, are you?"

"Not at all."

"The affair was years ago. Blackstone no longer has any connection with the woman, I'm sure."

Violet thought how easy it was for Penelope to use the word *affair* as if such a betrayal were an everyday occurrence, the daily fare of the scandal sheets. Penelope had sources of information, gossip, others would call it, that Violet would never have. Penelope would know, as would the titled half of London, whether Blackstone was a faithful husband while his bride, whoever she turned out to be, might never know. Violet had come to face Blackstone's real nature. She could not hide from it or pretend that he was the person she'd once thought him to be. She had to know finally for whom or for what he had betrayed their love.

She steeled herself to meet the test. She would not flinch. Looking at the painting behind the curtain would be like listening to some ancient prophet speak truth. She believed herself to be less given to extremes than those old Greeks. She could see whatever lay behind the curtain, and not stab her eyes out with her hatpins.

Royce returned with the prince and Dubusari. Money had obviously changed hands for Royce's coarse lips wore a smirk. "Now, ladies, gentlemen, majesty, do arrange your-

selves for a viewing." He motioned them into a loose half
circle facing the velvet curtain and went to stand against the
wall beside the curtain. He waited until they had settled into
position looking expectantly at him. "You won't have long,
because I like to keep her protected from the light."

Then he pulled the dangling golden cord, and the curtains
parted. Violet did not look at the others, only at the painting.
She could hear them sigh or swear or murmur, but she
couldn't look away from the reclining woman. It was like
nothing she had expected, like nothing else Royce himself
had painted.

Royce had chosen to paint the two figures in an extreme
close-up. Violet could think of no painting she had ever seen
that suggested such a shocking intimacy between a painter
and his subjects. Always in her experience the painter kept
himself at a distance, but Royce had not. He had stood so
close that he painted neither of the lovers' faces, only the
woman's inviting smile.

She lay on her side on a velvet sofa in a shade of gray so
deep it was near purple, with a high curving back like the
curve of the woman's hips. The light captured the glitter of
the sofa's gilded frame and the shining pearl luster of the
woman's flesh. She turned, as if waking at the touch of her
lover's hand on her shoulder, looking up at him, her breasts
arching up to him, her lips breaking into an inviting smile.
Her lover's right hand with its distinctive Blackstone signet
rested, long fingers spread, on the ridge of her collarbone,
strikingly masculine and possessive, laying claim to the
smooth golden curves of the woman's body. The distinctive
black and gold ring with the bold *B* had been captured in
exact detail.

Violet turned away. She understood why the piece had
created a scandal, but she felt dirty, as if Royce had invited

them all to look through a peephole at a woman in her most vulnerable moment. Looking behind Royce's curtain violated the mystery woman's heart more than her body. She was not like Royce's other nudes, both abstract and vulgar. Instead she had been caught freely bestowing her love. The painting showed how genuinely she had loved Blackstone. His powerful hand was so different from her warm smile. That was part of the picture's cruel exposure of the woman. She had loved more than she had been loved. The man's hand expressed a certainty of possession and dominance, not love.

Violet heard the rustle of Penelope's skirts. "My dear, I'm sure that was painful, but now that you know the truth, you can judge how you wish to act."

"Yes." Violet turned and lifted her head. She didn't have a choice really. Her second engagement was as false as the first. It would end as soon as they discovered Frank. But now she knew what to believe. Blackstone had never loved her, Violet, while she had loved him, as hopelessly, apparently, as the woman in Royce's portrait.

As the prince and Dubusari discussed arrangements for shipping the prince's purchase home to Moldova, the ladies descended the stairs. The afternoon turned cool with a threat of rain, though the street seemed busy as ever. They endured several moments of standing in the cold, as the prince expressed his gratitude, before Dubusari announced, "We have kept you long enough. Now we return to our hotel and not your kind house, but tomorrow we will see you at your ball."

Blackstone sauntered into Violet's room just when Violet was close to giving up on him.

She was at her desk puzzling over the fragment of Frank's writing. "How did the meeting with the foreign secretary go?"

"As well as could be expected. The prince was outraged by British deafness to the merits of his case. He turned in a report, by the way."

"He did?"

"He claimed it was all in order the way your brother likes it."

Violet showed him the bit of charred paper. "But then what is this? And if the prince had Frank's report all along, why did he wait to see the secretary?"

Blackstone frowned. "Where did you get this?"

"The government's maid brought it to me when I returned from the fitting this morning." She didn't quite meet his eye.

Blackstone was reading the document. "Your brother is determined to get a message out, isn't he? I think he has less regard for his own safety than I gave him credit for."

"Why did they burn it?"

"Because your brother has been using his accounts to communicate with the foreign office. He knows exactly who reads them. I wonder how long he's been doing that?"

He set the charred fragment on Violet's writing desk, looking down at it with a grave air. "I think this explains why your brother is missing."

"Last night you were ready to have him arrested for murder and treason."

He moved away from her to stand at her window looking out into the street. "The Moldovans needed a report from your brother—facts and figures—to show that England's funds had been properly spent. That report would secure them a new loan. But your brother's report worried them. They suspected that his report revealed discrepancies or, as you thought, something more than mere fraud."

"So they took my brother?"

"They've kept him to rewrite the report. That's why he's not dead."

"You think he would do that? Cover up some fraud?"

"They would pressure him to do it."

"How?"

"By letting Frank know they were close enough to harm you. Frank knows they are capable of murder."

"So this bit of his report is a fake to suit them?"

He shook his head. "Either it is part of the original report, or it's a draft they didn't like. They may have spotted your brother's code."

" 'Leave England' does not seem to be a message about missing funds."

"No. It's about the prince. Your brother likes the prince, and he's likely realized that the prince's loyal countrymen won't need him after today. He's an obstacle or an inconvenience. Whoever really has the power in Moldova has used Prince Andre as a front, a harmless smiling cartoon prince, easily guided by England."

"Did it work?"

"Not today. Apparently Canning hinted none too gently that the prince might retrench, and the prince vowed to set up a tent in Regent's Park to demonstrate his frugality and willingness to sacrifice every personal comfort for Moldova—after your ball."

"Oh dear. If he is in danger, he really is absurdly unaware of it. Will Dubusari and the crew let him pitch his tent?" Violet looked away. The quick alertness in Blackstone's eyes signaled his mind at work, puzzling over the details, making sense of them.

"Never. They won't let him out of their sight. But the prince talked of nothing else on the way back to the hotel, and it gave me an idea. You and I must get him out of their hands immediately after your ball."

"You think the accidents and the attacks were meant for him?"

"I think if he leaves England with them, he's a dead man. That's what your brother's message is trying to tell us."

"So what do we do? We have no proof. I don't imagine that the government wants to send an armed guard into Milvert's Hotel. And what happens to Frank if we go after the prince's people?"

Blackstone did not answer at once. The evening traffic in the street below seemed to absorb all his attention.

Then he turned back to her. "What's on your calendar for the day after your ball?"

"Nothing."

"Let's change that. I've a friend who can help us, a Captain Rodriguez. He's a balloonist from Barcelona, a charming rogue. You'll like him. The prince wanted to see a balloon ascension. I think he'll enjoy a ride, don't you?"

"If he doesn't fall out of the basket."

"If I'm right, the prince's people are looking for an opportunity to act against him. Let's get the prince out of their reach. We'll get the captain to take the prince up, and put him down where the government can protect him. While his people hunt for the prince, we find Frank."

"Thank you." For the moment he seemed her old friend who would save Frank not betray him. She wished she knew whose side he was truly on. She twisted the ring on her finger.

"Something's bothering you."

"I have a confession to make."

"What?"

"I saw Royce's painting today."

He didn't move, but she felt him change, close himself off to her. "Did seeing it change anything?"

"No! But hear me out."

"You wanted to know, and now you know."

"When have I ever not wanted to know something, to understand. You find that foolish, I know."

"Mostly admirable, Violet, but apt to land you in the soup."

"Well, I won't deny it. I wanted to know. I have wanted to know forever it seems, who it was that you loved so much that you would endure scandal and disgrace for her sake."

"Now you know."

"I think I do. So why does it feel as if I'm the one who has committed an unpardonable act, not against you, but against that woman. It was wrong of me to go. I cannot speak to her, but I can apologize to you for intruding on a private moment."

"I believe Royce's presence made the moment distinctly unprivate."

"You are a better judge of that than I. I thought it was a painting of woman's love. I thought a woman should be free to look at her lover without the whole of society censuring the moment."

"In that we agree." His gaze did not meet hers. "Anything else? We have a plan."

"I do not require that you attend the ball tomorrow."

His head came up. He fixed her with his mocking gaze. "Oh, you do not have a choice in that, my love. Until we have your brother safe, you have a fiancé, however false."

Chapter Seventeen

He had followed them purposely to town . . .

—Jane Austen, *Pride and Prejudice*

Nate was back in the docklands, his collar up, his hat low, and his hands shoved deep in his pocket, one hand around a knife. This time Blackstone had sent him, and he was acting alone. Neither Goldsworthy, nor Goldsworthy's other scouts knew where Nate was. It was a chance, following Blackstone's lead, but Nate had taken chances before. To his way of thinking, Blackstone meant to give Frank Hammersley a chance, too.

The hour was late, and the great daytime bustle of moving ships and cargo had been replaced by nighttime activities of seeking comfort or oblivion of various sorts. The target of Nate's vigilance was the taproom of the King Edward public house where the Spanish banknote had turned up. For the neighborhood, the King Edward offered the relatively tame amusements of getting roaring drunk, breaking the heads of one's rivals or detractors, or finding a willing woman to pay for a different sort of sport.

Nate had found a place in the shadows from which he could see the public house's two doors. They stood on either side of a central window from which a good bit of light shone out into the street. The face of a man leaving by either door would be briefly illuminated as he stepped outside. Nate felt himself close to a breakthrough in the case, and he knew it mattered. They needed to know with certainty where Frank Hammersley was if they meant to save him.

As the evening wore on, the prospect of Nate's success dimmed. Face after face emerged from the public house with all the marks of a seaman's life and no sign of anyone connected to the prince. Most of the patrons leaving the King Edward lurched or staggered up towards the high street. Nate shifted his feet to keep off the cold of the evening and the damp of the river. Then a man emerged who didn't lurch. He stopped in the doorway and glanced up and down the street, giving Nate a thorough look at a face he knew, the prince's valet.

Nate felt his pulse pick up and cautioned himself not to move. The valet let the door close behind him and turned up the street with a steady, purposeful stride. Nate listened to the footsteps, waiting for the moment when it would be safe to follow. The King Edward's other door opened, a second sober man stepped out, glanced after the first and turned the opposite way. The second man took a couple of steps before he commenced to whistle in a jarringly off-key way. A lovesick cat sounded more tuneful, but Nate recognized the sour whistle from his first trip to the docklands.

In another minute he realized the whistler must be headed for Frank Hammersley, and Nate decided to follow.

Late as it was, Frank knew it was the hour when fashionable London came alive with music and the rustle of silks and the flutter of fans. The silence around him reminded him as sharply as any other circumstance that he was far from Hammersley House. He sat at the battered desk with fresh pages and mended his pen. He believed he had satisfied his captors with his latest effort, which meant that they could now dispose of him. He might never know whether his messages had gone through.

The river was quiet. The street below his prison, if it was street, was dead. Only the sound of some animal rummaging about came through the grate. A distant church bell sounded faintly the passing quarter of an hour. Frank knew his keepers' treads on the steep narrow stairs. Sackett, a broken-down pugilist with a spongy red nose, eyes sunk in rolls of fat, and fists that didn't close, made the stairs quake and the door rattle in its frame when he came to relieve Glover, his former trainer. Glover, a short, spry fellow, daily slipped in and out of Frank's prison whistling a sour off-key tune. Glover, who had known all the great fighters and shaken the king's own hand, felt his fall in the world.

"You had Cribb on the ropes," he liked to remind his former charge. "If you'd a done 'im, like I told you, we'd be in bloody Leicester Square instead of this hole. But you had to have your drink and your doxies. The ruin of us both."

"Being paid, now, ain't we?"

Frank had heard that exchange or some variation of it at every passing between the two men. If his count was accurate, he'd come to in the rough, windowless room five days ago under the watchful eye of Glover. Even before Glover opened his mouth, Frank realized he was in England and not far from the Thames where the *Madagascar* must have docked. He'd made the crossing trussed up in darkness and unconscious, except for brief moments when he heard voices speaking Russian.

In his present room he'd wakened to a headache as if an
army of smiths had taken over his brain and begun hammering out their wares. Glover had stood him on his
unsteady feet and led him to a rough table, assuring him
that he was pretty well fixed where he was until he did as
he was told. He pointed Frank to a supply of paper, pens,
and ink and told him he had a job to do or else. Frank briefly
considered stabbing Glover in the eye with the pen, but his
own fuzzy head and weakened body vetoed the plan.

A note was given to him to copy in his own hand. The
words swam before him. He was to promise his dear sister
that he had been delayed, but he knew that Violet would spot
the language as not his usual style. The message would likely
have the opposite effect of the one his captors intended. His
clever sister would be thoroughly alarmed. She would consult
Preston, and they would look at his trunk, but Frank had not
seen his trunk for days. Anything could have happened to it
to disarrange his message. *Don't let Moldova leave England.*

Since the moment of that dismal realization, Sackett or
Glover, one or the other, had always been in the room or
directly outside the door. Glover liked to have a smoke on
the stairs before he entered, and Sackett had a weak bladder
and a fondness for ale that made him step outside to relieve
himself with some frequency.

It had been a full day before Frank's head had cleared
enough to catch the footsteps of his captors. As soon as he
had figured out from listening to their comings and goings
that he was on the third floor of a derelict warehouse, he
started to look for a way out.

The room had been an office with a wall of open pigeon-
holes for storing orders or bills. Someone had once worked
at the battered desk, and a narrow sagging bed and two

chairs had been added apparently to accommodate Frank and his guards.

The only access to the outside was a high round window covered with slats that let in air and faint light. It had rained twice, and somewhere the building had a leak. Frank could hear the steady ring of drops hitting standing water somewhere beyond the rough board enclosure, and he could smell the ashes of a dead fire. The sound suggested the cavernous interior of a warehouse. Apparently the building was not in use. There was no daytime activity, and his guards seemed to be the only persons who came to the place. Frank positioned himself to catch glimpses through the open door whenever Sackett and Glover shifted their duties. What he saw was a dark expanse of shadowy piles illuminated in patches where a broken window or an opening in the roof admitted some light. He waited for them to get careless or tired of guarding him.

The second day he'd been there, Glover arrived for the evening shift with a glove of Violet's and a note explaining that Frank had erred in his report of the Prince of Moldova's use of English funds. If he could write a proper report of how the funds had helped to build the prince's own royal guard, he could buy his sister's safety.

His head was somewhat steadier by then, and he faced the desk and the papers on it. The glove bothered him. He told himself that the Prince of Moldova and his party were to stay in Milvert's Hotel. The foreign office knew there was a problem. Two dead agents could not be ignored. So how had his captors come to have Violet's glove? They couldn't simply snatch her from Hammersley House with her father and a score of servants around.

He needed some way to let the outside world know where

he was. The first idea that came to him was selling his buttons. Glover admired them and lamented the injustice of Frank's finery.

"'Ere's you going nowheres, dressed like a royal prince with buttons the size o' coppers, and 'ere's me that once shook the king's own 'and practically in rags."

Frank had offered Glover his buttons for a pint of porter. The fellow had looked distrustful, but Frank had talked him round to cutting the buttons off his coat and concealing them from Sackett. It was a gamble. Maybe no one was looking for him. But the foreign office had expected him on the *Madagascar* and would have had a man on the dock to meet him. They wanted his report, and they would want to know what happened to the funds he was authorized to give directly to the prince.

He had to get some message out into the world. His next ploy had been better. He always kept money hidden on his person. While Sackett nodded, Frank had taken a banknote from a pocket in the lining of his coat and slipped it in among the papers on the table. Later when Sackett left the room for a visit to the piss pot, Frank had written on the note. He'd bargained with Sackett before Glover arrived. Sackett had been puzzled by the Spanish banknote, but Frank had feigned surprise about its location. The conversation had unexpectedly revealed the information that he was in Wapping.

He was in a warehouse in Wapping and his captors—he suspected Dubusari—wanted him to produce a doctored version of his report on the finances of the Moldovan army. He knew why, as he knew why he'd heard Russian in his dazed state on the boat. He had discovered that there were those in Moldova who believed the prince too weak to save them from inevitable submission to the tsar. Those forces would sacrifice the weak prince to the much more powerful tsar without a qualm.

Frank had figured that he could delay giving them what they wanted for a week perhaps. In days his actual report and the money would reach the foreign office by the special courier to whom he had managed to slip them on his last day in Spain. The problem was that he didn't know how near to his family the prince's enemies were. The message of Violet's glove was plain; if Frank made a wrong move, they would hurt Violet. Two men were already dead just for being willing to receive his report. Another would be dead if Frank's information did not reach the right hands, and somehow his sister had ended up in the middle of Moldova's lethal politics.

On the third day he sent a version of the report he hoped his unseen captors would buy. He received back a garnet earring of Violet's and a curt note explaining that time was short. He decided that he had to get out of his prison. He considered what he had learned about his surroundings. The building was three or four stories high with a brick exterior. His room was on the southwest side of the building. No street noise came up from directly below the building, and the pervasive odor of the place was of ash and damp. At night it smelled like a damp cellar. In the heat of the day it had a kitcheny smell of steeping tea. A night escape from Sackett was his best hope. The man always came smelling of ale and often dozed as Frank worked. Frank had gone that far in his thinking without any opportunity to act, but he was ready.

Sackett was moving restlessly about, fidgeting as he waited for Glover, complaining that the man was late. He opened the door once or twice, listening for Glover's tuneless whistle. Frank positioned himself. His only weapon, if he got a chance to use it, would be the chair he sat in.

In the same instant, he and Sackett heard Glover on the stairs, and then a shout and pelting footsteps. Sackett heaved himself up and threw open the door. He thrust his head out and looked down the long stairs. Frank was up in a flash. He barreled straight into Sackett, knocking the bigger man towards the stairs.

Frank charged off into the dark, reasoning that there would be another stair at the other end of the building. Behind him he heard Sackett stumbling and cursing and Glover shouting from below. He kept moving as rapidly as he could, his hands in front of him, his boots hitting the bare floor like fireworks exploding. He collided with a metal post. The blow spun him round, and he stumbled, trying to correct his path and tripped over something knee high and sharp edged. He regained his balance, wincing at the blow to his shin. He corrected once more, feeling the outline of a rough pile of wood, and moved forward. Behind him Sackett shouted down the stairs for Glover to come on up. He could hear Glover shouting as well and some kind of a scuffle.

As his eyes adjusted to the gloom in front of him, he could see the faint outline of an arched opening. He made for it until a board gave under his right foot and, with a sudden unexpected plunge, he sank up to his thigh. He caught himself with his hands and hung there, braced, one leg through the boards, the other folded under him.

Pain shot through the leg that had penetrated the floor. He pushed himself up out of the hole. His heart pounded in his chest, and his breath rasped in his ears. He could feel something broken. Once he regained his feet, he stood on his good leg, leaning against an iron column. The open archway was about twenty feet away, but the injured leg would not bear his weight.

Behind him the door of his little prison stood open, casting a beam of light into the cavernous space. Sackett appeared, framed by the light of the small room, peering into the darkness. Frank had not even hidden himself. Sackett stepped out into the gloom framed by the open door. He shouted down the stairs.

Frank shifted, dragging his useless leg, so that he stood behind one of the iron pillars. The water drip sounded loud as a church bell in his ears. He waited for Sackett to descend the stairs. No luck. Sackett came to the edge of the darkness and peered out into the gloom. His big head tilted to one side, as if he listened intently.

"Glover! Come up 'ere, man. 'Ammersely's flown the coop."

Frank waited for Glover's reply from below, but none came. There was only stillness and the usual drip of water.

After a long pause Sackett disappeared, mumbling, back into the room, and Frank dragged himself through the arch. No light penetrated, only a cold musty draft that wafted up from below. He could hear a skittering noise below him. He slid along the wall, dragging his useless leg. Then Sackett's heavy footfalls began to crunch along the floor, and Sackett's lamp sent a beam of light swinging wildly across the open arch. Each swing of the light gave Frank a glimpse of the narrow space—no stairs, but a crude lift for goods, a flat platform with an iron cage around it. He lurched towards it and looked down the dark well of the shaft. It had to be three floors down. No light penetrated.

Frank heard Sackett mutter to himself. Then he shouted, "You'd best not be where oy kin find ya, Frank 'ammersley." Abruptly, Sackett stopped. Frank heard him muttering again. The light sent a faint steady beam along the floor. Frank listened. Sackett appeared to be relieving himself.

He shrugged out of his coat, waistcoat, and shirt, sweating madly. He put the waistcoat and coat back on and wrapped his once white shirt around a sack lying on the lift. Sackett's light showed him the pulley. He released it, and the rough rope slid hotly through his hand. The platform creaked and rattled and began to descend. He braced himself to slow its momentum.

Sackett hollered, and Frank could hear him start to run, and stop and curse. Frank kept feeding the pulley, letting the lift rattle downward. As Sackett neared, Frank staggered back into the shadows. The lift was free-falling now. Sackett burst through the door as the thing hit bottom. Sackett leaned over the ledge, holding his lamp up.

"The idiot's kilt 'imself, 'e 'as," he muttered.

Behind him, Frank slipped back through the arch, sliding along the wall until he could drop and drag himself behind a pile of twisted metal and charred wood. He rubbed his face with black ash and lay still, his injured leg throbbing. He would not be dancing soon.

Chapter Eighteen

. . . she had been blind, partial, prejudiced, absurd.

—Jane Austen, *Pride and Prejudice*

～⁓⁓

Violet stood with her fellow patronesses in the ball's receiving line, Penelope at the head, Violet at the end of the line, reaping the rewards of their bargain. Much of fashionable London appeared determined to squeeze through a narrow plain wainscoted foyer into the glittering hall.

The prince's party arrived early in splendid military fashion. The prince exclaimed over the excess of beauty and declared himself pledged to dance with all the women present if it was permitted. Papa made a fine figure, and the patroness next to Violet whispered to her how very much the gentleman her father seemed to be, as if the notion were a wonder.

The seamstresses' gowns drew exactly the sort of notice Violet had hoped. Every lady, even the little countess, took note, though for all her professed interest in fashion, she wore one of her fragile gowns with three elaborate rows of heavy gold velvet cord around the hem.

Penelope repeatedly presented Violet as the Hammersley
Heiress, as if she were a curiosity, like a new monument
open to public view. She received the acknowledgements of
several young men whose smiles widened and bows deepened at the word *heiress*.

One of them lingered over her hand beyond politeness.
"I beg your pardon, Miss . . . ?"

"Hammersley," she repeated. He appeared ready to make
a note of it if only he had a notebook in his pocket.

Her helpful neighbor in line whispered, "Younger son,
not a groat to his name."

In spite of the happy crush that proclaimed the ball a
success, Violet was conscious of an unreasonable knot in
her stomach. She told herself that nothing could mar the
evening. The room was well proportioned and fitted up with
pots of daffodils and hyacinths in mossy banks. The musicians were of the first quality and knew the popular qua-
drilles and waltzes. Violet's own cook had pronounced the
lemon cakes edible, and no one could object to ratafia and
champagne. If the food was not of some rare, ambrosial
quality, the number of candles gave the scene the sort of
warmth and glow of any large space adequately illuminated.
The ball might not be out of the common way, but it would
not disgrace them.

As the room filled, it became plain that Penelope waited
for Blackstone as consciously as Violet did. To Penelope he
was a free man, a man of interest. His reputation made him
so; a man who belonged to no woman seemed the property
of all women. Penelope saw him as the man in the portrait.
She would never lose her heart to him. To Violet all that
mattered was the plan they had made to distract Frank's
kidnappers by removing the prince from their midst. She

would have to converse with Blackstone to put that plan in motion, but of course, she did not have to dance with him.

As the ballroom filled, the receiving line dwindled, and Blackstone did not come. Violet understood him. He wished to avoid her as much as she wished to avoid him. In the narrow confines of Hammersley House, where they had met and loved, he might not be able to resist her, but in his world he would have as little to do with her as possible.

Penelope shrugged and signaled Violet to assemble her particular guests. The ball was to begin with a brief ceremony, recognizing the women who had made the silk that each of the patronesses wore. Violet ushered them to the dais in front of the orchestra. It was what she'd wished for, a fortnight earlier, a chance to reach fashionable London and touch the hearts of people whose pocketbooks provided work for thousands. The women looked elegant, and the gowns were splendid. She should be very happy with the success of her first ball.

On his way to Violet's ball, Blackstone stopped by the club's card room where Hazelwood and Clare both appeared to be losing, a growing pile of chips rising on the green baize table between them. He couldn't find Wilde, and he had no time to track the youth down at Miranda Kirby's side.

The plan was clear in Blackstone's head. He had conferred with Captain Rodriguez, and a small encampment for the prince had been added to the captain's bivouac in Regent's Park. The last detail in Blackstone's mind was Wilde. He wanted the youth to spend the night on guard outside the prince's tent as an added precaution.

"Blackstone, don't you have all the luck! I suppose you

are off to grace a ballroom and later a bedroom?" Hazelwood laid down an impressive run of royal faces.

"Have you seen Wilde?" he asked.

Hazelwood and Clare exchanged sober glances. "He
didn't return. Miranda came looking for him."

Blackstone stopped midstride. Wilde was used to oper-
ating in the darkest streets of London. He was canny and
clever and he knew the danger of the work. "No word?"

"None."

"Have a care, Blackstone, Goldsworthy sees all, you
know."

"Do you want us to do something?" Clare asked.

"Pray."

The young man who'd made a note of Violet's name and
fortune claimed her for one of the early country dances. As
they made their way down the set, she caught sight of Blackstone in a knot of persons accepting flutes of champagne
from a passing servant. Her heart briefly changed its beat,
and she lost her connection to the music and had to apologize to her partner for a missed step. She saw that Blackstone
was known, more even than he had been at the theater,
where his friends had come to their box. Here, every glance
seemed to recognize him. Men greeted him easily, and
women took his measure, not as a man of title and fortune,
but as a man. That other assessment of his person, subtle or
open, flickered through glances as he passed. Whispers rustled in his wake.

Penelope came to her then. "He's here." She put a gloved
hand to her mouth to cover a quick giddy laugh. "Causing
talk and speculation, as always." She sobered briefly, tamp-
ing down the excitement in her green eyes. "Violet, I meant

what I said to you that day. I will give him the cut direct if you want him still."

"Dance with him, of course, Penelope. He is not my Blackstone."

Violet knew what he was about. He had made some bargain with the government to find Frank. He had used her to make sense of the clues to her brother's whereabouts, but he had made no pretense of loving her this time. If they had given in to old desires, she would overcome those feelings this time as she had before.

She should forgive him and let him go. After all, forgiveness was a gift one gave oneself in the giving. It was like opening the cage of one's heart and letting the miserable huddled creatures, the hopes inside, fly free.

She found herself with a run of partners and very little ability to attend to them. The room had a great many couples now, but she saw only Blackstone dancing with her fellow patronesses, with the countess, with a shy young woman, whom Violet had not noticed earlier, and twice with Penelope.

Blackstone looked over his partner's topaz headdress at the crowd. He did not intend to dance with Violet Hammersley. Let the gossips make of it what they would. Let the Moldovans suspect whatever they might suspect. The prince was in sight, dancing vigorously and pouring his heavy-handed flattery over anything in skirts. Within hours the empty-headed monarch would be surrounded by Rodriguez's men, and in the morning, they would whisk him away to even greater safety in a country house prepared for him by the government.

Still Wilde's failure to report had Blackstone on edge. He had sent Wilde alone this time to keep Goldsworthy from getting to Frank first. If Frank was the thief and murderer that Goldsworthy and the government suspected him of being and Goldsworthy found him first, Blackstone would lose everything. If Frank was honest, but his keepers recognized Wilde as a government man, both Frank and Wilde were at risk.

Between sets Blackstone's friend Slindon appeared at his side with a glass in hand. "Blackstone, what are you doing here, man?" Slindon knocked back his drink. "Tame stuff, don't you think? Wouldn't have come except that Fothergill has a wager going on some sort of intrigue. I say, if you see him, tell him I'm off to Madame Latova's. You should come. It's just your sort of thing."

Blackstone raised his glass and bid his friend good night. Violet was at the other end of the dance. He could see her out of the corner of his eye, and across the room he could see the countess. More than once she had cast him one of her helpless appeals. She was oddly dressed, even for her usual taste, with bands of gold cord around the hem of her white gown. Plainly her husband did not dance, and Dubusari sat with the chaperones, apparently charming them with his quaint eloquence.

As the dancers moved through the figures, Violet advanced nearer. She had chosen to wear something made of petals, or so it seemed to Blackstone, the fabric soft and of a pale dawn pink that gave her skin a pearl-like luster. The cut of the gown fit around her narrow ribs where his hand would go if he danced with her. He laughed at himself. So much for thinking he could refuse to dance with her. He and Violet might think that they had ended it again with his admission that the government was investigating Frank and her confession of her visit to Royce's studio, but whatever had started between them all those years ago was not so easily overcome.

As she passed him, the dance brought her round so that

they were briefly face-to-face. He let her know that he would be coming for her.

At the end of the set he started in her direction when he felt a hand on his sleeve. He turned and found the countess looking up at him with a trembling lip.

He almost left it too late. Violet had seen the promise in his eyes, and then he had gone aside with the countess. He did not come for Violet until the musicians began the last waltz. She told herself it would be a farewell dance, a fitting parting, light and airy as music. It would look odd for them not to converse. They would exchange banalities suitable for the breathless whirl of the dance. There would be no pain that she had not already endured and overcome. This week of wearing his paste ring had been about Frank.

He held out his gloved hand, and she placed her hand in his, lightly, and still the shock of his touch passed through her to her toes.

"I've danced with every woman, from seventeen to forty-seven, who could possibly have a claim on my courtesy, Violet. Now it's time for us." He pulled her out into a waltz and turned her to face him, their hands extended for the opening moves.

She stared at the very fine onyx stickpin in his cravat. "It's good to know my place in the queue."

He laughed as his arm went round her and his hand took possession of the base of her spine, that place from which he would command her movements. Their hands lifted and pressed against each other, his left to her right.

"You don't understand anything." His brows contracted in a frown, his mouth grim.

She lifted her chin, and held her head high. She thought

it a cruel thing to say, the first cruel thing Blackstone had ever said to her. The first steps were a gliding promenade while Violet held herself proudly aloof, their position open, their arms looped around each other's back, then the music changed. The hand at the small of her back drew her closer, arching her spine, lifting her into his hold. She turned her head to look over his shoulder. But there was no escape. His breath stirred against her ear.

"There's really no place to go, Violet," he said. With a shove of his left hand he pushed her back, snapped her into his embrace, and whirled them into the dance.

Blackstone knew she would deny their connection with her last breath if he let her, but her body would not lie. He linked them with his hold so that they turned and whirled and dipped in the sensuous figures as one, and she must look up into his eyes and cling to his hand.

Her scent, sweet and delicate as a single flower opening, filled his head. He could look down into eyes as dark as night and skin as smooth and soft as sea foam. The heat and the motion freed strands of her midnight hair to curl softly around her face.

Violet tried to concentrate on something, anything, that would take her mind off Blackstone's hold, the way his hand moved her effortlessly across the floor. The crisp scent of him enveloped her. Through their gloves she felt the hard edge of the Blackstone ring. She tried to summon the pain of that moment when her young heart had broken, but the pain didn't come.

It felt right dancing with him. They moved well together, their bodies anticipating each other. He raised their joined arms and sent her spinning so that when she came back to his hold, breathless and giddy with the dance, her eyes met his. There were friendly lines around his smile. There was laughter in those deep blue eyes of his, a laughter she had missed, the way dwellers in polar lands must miss the sun in their long winters, and it made her remember another time.

They had been kissing wildly in the long gallery, and he'd spun her in a circle. "Lord, I love you, Violet," he had said. "When you are old enough, you must marry me."

She had stopped their spin. "I am old enough. I am nineteen, and I know my mind. I will marry you, Lyle." She had called him Lyle then before he became Blackstone. "But I won't marry you without knowing."

He'd cast her a suspicious look. "Knowing what?"

She'd drawn a breath and held herself very still so that he would understand she was quite serious. Once before she had told him her position, and she didn't want him to think she jested. "Without knowing what it will be like between us in the marriage bed."

He'd nearly choked. "Violet, you don't need further proof. It will be passionate . . ."

She pressed her hand to his mouth to still him. "But it will be unequal because you know more than I do."

He, too, had grown serious. "While I'm flattered that you think me a man of wide experience, you keep me too busy for any further instruction. So you'll soon catch up with me, once we begin."

Violet had grinned at him then and asked, "So, when do we begin?"

It had not been that day, but they had begun not long after, and he had insisted that she agree to marry him.

The music changed again, signaling a passage in which the dancers circled the room facing forward. Violet felt the stares, the knowing looks. Everyone thought her a great fool. Now she knew why. She, too, had seen the painting of his beautiful Spanish mistress, arching up under her lover's touch. She held her head erect and gripped his hand for steadiness, feeling the hard band of the infamous Blackstone ring on his left hand.

And the painting came back to her, the woman's amorous stretch, the man's arrogant bearing. The man's right hand wore the ring, claiming his possession of the woman. A dizzying sensation washed over Violet. The faces around them seemed to blur.

"The man in the painting is not you. It's not your hand on that woman's . . ."

She lost her steps, faltered, and Blackstone pulled her closer, lifting her off her stumbling feet. "Not now, Violet. Keep moving."

He turned her in a dizzying series of moves, but the whirling sweetness of the music could not drown out the voice in her head. Her mind raced back to Royce's studio, back to years before. The man in the painting wore the signet on his right hand. And that was not the only difference. She could see it all now. It had been there, right in front of her. The man in the painting did not stand the way Blackstone stood, and Blackstone could not have been standing or sitting for Royce. He had been with Violet, nearly every day, in the weeks leading up to his father's death.

She had only a brief note from him. *My father has summoned me.*

Then he was absent from her, with no word, until they had buried his father and Royce had begun showing the painting. The painting had been an instant sensation in London.

The dance was breaking up. The dancers moving into their final turns and bows. He was going to leave her with everything unsaid, misunderstood.

"You didn't know about the painting, did you? You couldn't have known." Violet's chest ached, the pain concentrated in her heart. She wanted to stop dancing and press her palms against her chest. She had lost him not because he was a scandalous rogue who had loved another but because she had doubted and distrusted a good man and believed ill about him without question. She could see how it was. He had counted on her when his world turned against him, and she had failed him.

"Violet, you can't undo the past."

"If I had not broken the engagement, would you have married me?"

"After Royce made the painting public? Could I have involved you in the scandal as well?"

"You couldn't stop Royce, could you?"

"My mistake. I underestimated his power and his greed."

"He knows the truth, but he lets everyone assume." *As she had assumed.* "But you never denied the rumors. You never told the truth." She did not say, *You never told the truth to me.* Her heart ached with the unspoken words.

"Other people would have suffered."

His mother. His sisters. The man in the picture had been his father. It had only been the accident of Royce's timing, and something in the man's manner that had persuaded everyone to think it a portrait of the living son instead of the dead father. But Blackstone had allowed the mistake to stand. He had chosen disgrace rather than expose his father's infidelity.

The room was a blur of noise and heat and faces. She saw the whole selfless imposture. He had not loved the beautiful woman in the scandalous painting. He had loved his family.

"Violet, look at me. Your face will give us away. Think of Frank. Frank needs you to be my fiancé for one more day."

"Penelope believes I've given you up for good."

"Violet, listen to me. We still have to get the prince away and get Frank."

She nodded.

"Find your papa and make him take you home. And do not go anywhere with the countess, not to the ladies' retiring room."

She looked up at him.

"That cording she wears on every gown—that's her weapon."

"Weapon?"

"I'll explain later. I'm going to get the prince and Cahul to the park. Remember the plan. In the morning go straight to Captain Rodriguez. Take someone stronger than Granthem with you, and a pistol."

Her eyes widened at the pistol.

"I mean it, Violet. You're to go up with the prince in the balloon, not Cahul. The captain will set you down in Hampstead or somewhere nearby as the winds permit. We'll have people on watch. You will explain to the prince. And I will get Frank."

Chapter Nineteen

". . . I have thought only of you."

—Jane Austen, *Pride and Prejudice*

Frank woke to the throbbing of his swollen leg in his boot. The boot would have to be cut off him, if he lived, and Preston, his valet, would be desolate. Still he resolved to brave Preston's displeasure. His mouth tasted foul, and when he rubbed his face, his hand came away covered in black grit. The night waned, and faint light from the ruined roof above him showed him his surroundings. He raised himself on one elbow to look through the tangled wreckage of his hiding place. He could see at once that he had to move.

Above him great charred beams stretched the width of the room against a pale gray sky. Beyond his hiding place other piles of debris littered the space. He could see now why Sackett and Glover had not pursued him in the dark. But even if they began a search for his body on the ground floor, it would not take long for them to uncover his hiding place in the ruined warehouse. He lifted himself onto his elbows and began to wriggle forward. He felt like a worm, and his injured leg protested with a stomach-turning jolt of pain. Plainly, he could not pull himself up to the rafters to escape through the roof.

The darkness through the arch at the end of the long room had its appeal, but he had seen no stairs at that end of the building. His heart pumped painfully at the sense of being trapped. He closed his eyes briefly and waited for inspiration. He listened to the drip that had first alerted him to the decayed state of the building. He opened his eyes again and forced himself to scan the room systematically. Somewhere there would be a bolt hole or an escape hatch.

Violet looked across the park at the greening rounded crown of Primrose Hill that made it seem a place for Jack and Jill to tumble down. It was hard to imagine flying over it, but that was the plan.

Across from her, a small encampment of white tents huddled under a stand of Hawthorn trees. Smoke rose from cooking fires. Violet tried to think only of Frank. She would not think him dead, but alive. Wherever he was this morning, he was a captive because he did not want the prince murdered. What had happened between Violet and Blackstone had been inevitable, the playing out of their story for a second time. She had no reason to feel her grief like a fresh wound. This morning she had her part to play, and if she did it well, the prince would be safe, Frank could come home, and Blackstone would be gone.

The prince came striding towards her from the camp with his usual childlike excitement. She accepted his arm as they walked from the camp towards a small crowd gathering on the green. Just a short flight, just to be borne by the wind like a low-flying cloud over a bit of forest and hill, and set down again. That's all she had to do. Then Blackstone promised they would descend on Wapping and find Frank. Violet carried a small pistol in her bag, but she saw no sign of danger in the gathering spectators. The trees offered little concealment, being in their early budding stage.

Captain Rodriguez was just the man to inspire confidence in a woman facing her first air voyage. Tall and darkly handsome with a droll arch to one brow and a dark shadowed jaw, he assured Violet that she would make an excellent air traveler. He told her that he and his assistants had crossed wide spans of ocean a dozen times between Spain and Africa, and assured her that her brief foray into the atmosphere would be a breeze. Violet smiled at the humor.

A small band gathered, took a position on a wooden stand, and began to tune its instruments. The crowd shifted and chatted.

The captain introduced his assistants, a young African, Mr. Ali, in a fine naval lieutenant's uniform, and a Mr. Danner, who wore a close wool cap and a sleeveless gray sweater. After the introductions, Captain Rodriguez turned with easy competence to the business of the launch. A wicker basket about the size of a small pianoforte stood in the center of the green, attached to what appeared to be a giant fishing net washed ashore full of a shimmering green catch. The captain signaled to Mr. Ali to attach a leather hose to a gas cask. While Mr. Ali turned the valve, Mr. Danner watched the unfurled globe begin to take shape. The prince kept the captain busy answering questions as the procedure unfolded. While the captain explained the clockwise winds and their likely speed and direction, Violet scanned the crowd. Nothing looked amiss. Of the prince's people, only Cahul was with him, and he looked decidedly uneasy about the expanding balloon as if he feared some catastrophe. The rest of the captain's men, looking much like Mr. Danner in wool caps and sleeveless shirts, positioned themselves to keep the crowd at a distance.

The crowd murmured and exclaimed as the pale green silk billowed and filled with lighter than air hydrogen, slowly tilting up from the ground until it bobbed lightly at the end of its tethers. The great globe was gaily decorated with crimson ribbons and cascading ivy vines. Captain Rodriguez moved around the wicker gondola, testing lines connecting the passenger basket to the towering balloon and braided ropes that led to four bags of sand lying in the grass, propped against the gondola. An anchoring rope secured the whole apparatus to a stake in the ground, where Mr. Danner stood on watch. His inspection complete, the captain warned Violet and the prince to stand ready. As the prince came forward, Cahul withdrew to a position next to Mr. Danner.

The band played, and members of the British Society of Aeronauts saluted Captain Rodriguez and his assistants. Mr. Ali placed a box of wooden steps against the basket and gave Violet his arm to help her up the steps. She sat on the lip of the basket and listened as he pointed out the difference between the lines leading down from the balloon to the sand bags and those leading up to secure the basket to the globe.

She swung her feet down into the basket and found herself afloat on the air. The basket tilted and bobbed under her, and she gripped the edge for balance. The prince followed, making a theatrical bow to the crowd before slipping between the guide ropes into the gondola.

Captain Rodriguez turned to the spectators. The band paused in its playing. He glanced at his assistants, who stood ready to release the balloon, and began to address the crowd.

"Ladies and Gentlemen, many a sheep, a fowl, and an aeronaut have risen to great heights, but today we have a rare chance for royalty to do the same. Today we are honored by the presence and the adventurous spirit of Prince Andre Sturdzi of Moldova." Spectators whistled and clapped as the prince himself took another bow. The captain nodded to his assistants. The crowd held its breath. The band struck up again with a blare of horns and clang of symbols.

The captain smiled at Violet as he put his hand to the gondola. Then he jerked abruptly and staggered back, grabbing his left arm and slumping to the ground. His hat tumbled into the gondola as the balloon lurched upward.

"Cahul," the prince shouted, pointing at his bodyguard, who stood over a fallen Mr. Danner.

Violet grabbed the edge of the basket, looking down, trying to understand what had happened. People milled and turned, craning to see what happened. From above, Violet could see Mr. Ali kneeling at the captain's side and Mr. Danner lying on the ground by the stake. Out of the corner of her eye she saw one of the captain's assistants spring forward. He began to run towards them from the far end of the field.

"Cahul shot Rodriguez," the prince said. He turned to Violet, utterly dazed.

"Sit down, prince," Violet ordered.

Free of the stake, the anchor rope slid through the grass, and Violet and the prince rose in the air.

Some bystanders grabbed at the trailing rope, but sand poured from the ballast bags, a choking stream, which scattered the crowd. The rope, their last contact with the ground, slithered after them like a snake as the balloon rose fast. The running man never swerved or hesitated. He plunged through the stream of sand and threw himself after the rope, catching it as it lifted from the ground. He twisted it round his arm and it carried him dangling and twisting, knocking him against shrubs and low walls. He turned his face up to hers, and she laughed at his madness.

At last Mr. Ali caught up to him and grabbed his legs. Violet felt a slight tug on the balloon. Then other men joined hanging on, forming a chain. The balloon stopped its upward drift. It bobbed at rest above the heads of the men below like a boat at anchor.

"Are you mad?" Violet shouted down at him.

Blackstone shook his head. "Violet, there's a line that opens a vent in the crown of the balloon. Can you pull it?"

Violet braced herself in the swaying gondola and looked for a likely line. More than a dozen ropes attached the basket to the globe above. She tried to remember Mr. Ali's words when he helped her into the basket. As they bobbed at the foot of Primrose Hill, she reached over the prince for a line wound around a cleat.

"This one?" she called down.

Mr. Danner came running with a stake and a hammer. He gave her a nod. "Aye, lady, that's the one." Violet unwound the line from the cleat and gave it a pull. The balloon dropped with a stomach-flipping abruptness, and Violet slammed against the basket rim, nearly tumbling out. The prince yelped, and men scattered below them.

Blackstone grinned up at her, and she righted herself and tried again more carefully. The balloon settled to the ground. Blackstone reached her and pulled her from the gondola into his arms. For a moment she was lost there. She heard him swear and rail against her ear while his arms held on as if he would crush her. She reached up to stroke his cheek, to let him know she understood his anger. They had been so careless of each other, wounding without realizing how necessary they were to each other, necessary as air.

She pulled back from his embrace. "You do love me." It

was a wonderful discovery. It made her feel giddier than balloon travel.

He nodded. "No matter how hard I try not to."

They had forgotten the prince. Other spectators helped him to the ground.

"Where are my people?" He was looking about in puzzlement. "Where's Cahul?"

Blackstone could not let go of Violet. Mr. Ali quietly explained that Cahul had fired at Captain Rodriguez and knocked Danner on the head. Cahul was plainly long gone.

When Blackstone turned to lead Violet to her carriage, the prince began to follow. Young Ali and Mr. Danner stopped him.

"Lord Blackstone," he shouted, "what's happening?"

"Stay with the captain, Prince. You'll be safe with him. Violet, you are going home with your groom."

"You're going after Frank?"

"Trust me. I'll bring him back to you."

Blackstone returned to the club to find Clare and Hazelwood waiting for him in the entrance hall.

"So you've slipped Goldsworthy's leash, Blackstone." Hazelwood took in the clothes Blackstone had borrowed from Rodriguez's men.

"No use denying it," Clare added. "We know you sent Wilde off on his own. A dangerous game to play."

"And Wilde's still not returned." Hazelwood shook his head. "What are you up to, lad?"

Blackstone nodded grimly. "I'm to meet a 'fair maiden' this morning." Hazelwood's brows shot up. "Oh? Clare and I were rather looking forward to rescuing Wilde from low ruffians and breaking sundry villains' heads."

Blackstone recognized the alteration in the two men. All signs of indolence gone, they were armed and dressed for action. He realized he had never seen Hazelwood in clothes other than his soiled, rumpled evening attire.

"I would by no means deny you the satisfaction." He grinned as he took the first steps up to his room. "Wait here." He needed to make a swift change to keep his appointment with the countess.

Blackstone returned in minutes to explain the plan that had been taking shape in his head. With Wilde missing, he sent one of the cook's boys to the stables. He tossed Hazelwood the little note he had received from the countess.

"Aren't you a lucky sod, Blackstone. Here you are causing a fluttering in the hearts of ladies and girls who are no better than they should be and now some countess declares that"—he read the note—"'Only you can save me, Blackstone. I put myself in your power. Come alone.'" Hazelwood pressed his hand to his heart and tilted his head to one side in an affected way.

Clare grinned. "This lady is of age, isn't she? She writes like a chit of fifteen with her first Minerva novel in hand."

Blackstone shook his head. He had a brace of pistols on him and was pleased to note that Clare and Hazelwood were similarly armed. "The lady is thirty, if she's a day, and she's as deadly as an adder."

Hazelwood opened the door and they strode out. "Charming, and you're meeting her alone to savor her bite?"

The three men descended the club steps. Blackstone kept an eye out for the vehicle they were to use. For once he was glad of the concealing scaffolding. But the first vehicle to pull up to the curb was not one of Goldsworthy's discreet black chaises built for speed and anonymity. It was a familiar barouche with the top up and a familiar coachman on the box, but no footmen.

The door opened. The steps unfolded, and Violet Hammersley emerged, clad in sensible gray skirts and a plain black bonnet. He could see her boots peeping out from under the hem of those skirts.

She smiled at him, a smile that said she perfectly understood his noble manly intention of leaving her behind and was having none of it.

"Violet," he began. "How did you find me here?"

"Captain Rodriguez was kind enough to direct me."

Blackstone was conscious of the awkwardness of persuading his love to act against her will under the amused gazes of Hazelwood and Clare. "You see that I don't go alone, and that we do go armed to this encounter."

She produced a small but effective-looking popper pistol from her muff. "Yes, I suspected the occasion required arms. It's the countess, isn't it?"

He did love her. "How did your papa let you out of his sight?"

"Papa is taking care of the prince and Cahul."

"Cahul?"

"He came blubbering back not five minutes after you left, begging to be forgiven for his part in the plot against the prince. In perfect English, I might add."

"Did he say anything of value to our search for your brother?" Blackstone put out his hand to assist her back into her carriage.

"I believe he did." She did not take his hand.

He understood her at once. There was just a delay while his brain adjusted to the position she'd put him in.

"I believe she has you in a bind, Blackstone," Hazelwood commented.

Blackstone continued to look at Violet. He recognized the flashing eyes, the dusky hair, and that haughty mouth, but she was not the girl he had seen again for the first time a week earlier. The pistol in her hand did not waver.

"You need me, you see," said Violet. "I believe that we have unfinished business. There is an established mode that governs declarations of love."

"Did I make a declaration of love?"

"You did. You distinctly said that no matter how hard you tried not to that you did love me."

"What did I leave out?"

"Your request for my hand in marriage."

"Violet, you are wearing my ring."

"It's paste, however, and no declaration accompanied the placing of the ring upon my finger."

They faced each other in the shadowy portico under the scaffolding. His companions looked on. Trust Violet to take charge and push him to make his proposal before two of the most dissolute men in England. Above them the usual activity of Goldsworthy's workers continued. The coach horses snuffled and blew and swished their tales. Idle passersby glanced at the fine carriage. Blackstone's feet were planted firmly on stone, and yet he felt as if he'd been jerked aloft in one of Rodriguez's balloons, loosed to ride vagrant currents of the air. For a moment he had no name for the unfamiliar feeling. Then it came back to him. *Happiness*.

"I love you, Violet. Will you marry me?"

"Yes, thank you, Blackstone, I will. Shall we go after Frank? I've brought a vehicle that can accommodate us all if you feel there is strength in numbers."

Blackstone stood rooted to the spot, momentarily unable to answer as he mastered the desire to seize Violet in a crushing embrace.

"Well then." Hazelwood stepped forward. "Clare will drive. I will ride on the box. Coachman, may we borrow your cape?"

A very few minutes were consumed in making changes and taking their places before Clare set the horses in motion.

Violet began to interrogate her love at once. "Why does the countess want to meet you?"

"To tidy up loose ends. They suspect that I know too much. They believe they have already killed you."

"In the balloon. Cahul? We always believed he knew no English."

"A convenient ruse."

"Have they killed Frank?"

He reached over and squeezed her hands. "We don't know. If the countess is waiting for me at the rendezvous, she can't be where Frank is, and likely she's not alone."

"They'll take care of you first, then Frank?"

"That's my hope."

She elbowed him in the side.

"Well, not the hope, but if the plan is to dispose of me first, and they don't, we have a chance to save Frank."

"Cahul says they have kept Frank in a derelict tea warehouse belonging to someone named Waring."

"Wilde was right."

The countess had named a churchyard near the docks for their meeting place. When they could see the church's white tower from the highway, Clare pulled up, and Hazelwood leapt down to help Violet from the carriage. She turned to Blackstone and pulled him to her by the lapels of his coat and kissed him with all the fierceness of her passionate nature. It took a moment to recover his senses.

"I cannot lose you again."

Chapter Twenty

"But disguise of every sort is my abhorrence."

—Jane Austen, *Pride and Prejudice*

Blackstone drew the carriage up where his arrival might be seen from the open churchyard with its crisscrossing paths and bare chestnut trees, in bloom with spikes of pale creamy blossoms. He could see the countess in one of her distinctive gowns huddled on a granite slab where a few tall headstones clustered on the south side of the church.

Lichen-covered monuments, crumbling low walls, and gnarled tree trunks suggested places where her companions might find concealment. Blackstone kept himself in the open and took his time crossing the lawn. Hazelwood, Clare, and Violet would follow and find their own hidden vantage to watch his meeting with the lady.

The countess saw him, and, as if on cue, started up from her dejected pose, a picture of a woman welcoming her rescuer. "Thank goodness you've come," she told him, extending her hands to him, and clutching his as if she depended on him to pull her from the Thames.

Mud and grass stained her cloak and her hem, and bits of thread hung where one of her usual velvet cord bands had come off. Two of the heavy bands remained.

Blackstone made a concerned face and held her at a distance. "Dear countess, what's happened?"

She turned tear-washed eyes up to him. "I have done a very brave thing, which I will tell you soon, but you must help me."

"Of course, how?"

"You see I don't wish to return to Moldova. I should never have let them marry me off to Alexi, and now that I am here and I see how English women live, I want to stay in England. You will arrange it, yes? You will be my protector, is that what they say?"

"You wish to leave your friends and separate yourself from your countrymen?"

"Yes." She gave an emphatic nod. "They leave soon, but if I had a position here, I could stay. I am a wretched countess. I could be a happy waiting woman." She leaned towards him so that her bosom pressed against their clasped hands.

"Not many women would give up marriage and a title for so modest a circumstance."

"Oh, how can I convince you? I was so sure you would understand. You are a sympathetic man, no?" She pulled free of his hold and reached in the silk bag dangling from her arm.

It was too small and light for a pistol, but Blackstone nerved himself nonetheless. She pulled out no weapon, but a scrap of a lace handkerchief. She pressed the lace just below her eyes, so that he could see the silver tears shining against the blue. It was cleverly done. He suspected that two men had seen that bit of treacherous feminine helplessness just before they died.

Her lip trembled. She hiccupped, and with a smile she straightened her spine. "You will see, Lord Blackstone. I have done this brave thing to prove myself to you."

"Dear lady, you have nothing to prove. I am only concerned for your honor."

A quizzical look passed in her eyes. He had not offered the anticipated line, and it had thrown her off. She glanced over her shoulder briefly, just enough to give Blackstone a hint of where her hidden partner might be. He tilted his head to the left to indicate to Hazelwood and Clare where to look.

The next instant she recovered. Her hand came out to touch his sleeve. "You must let me tell you the brave thing I have done."

He nodded.

"I have found Miss Hammersley's missing brother."

Blackstone did not have to feign surprise. "Missing? I thought Frank was merely delayed."

"I overheard my countrymen plot against him. I listen well until I learn where it is they keep him. Here near the river. Today when they are sleeping from the ball, I go. I free him and hide him."

It was a preposterous tale, impossible to credit. There was not an honest breath in the woman's body. As she looked up at him, he noted again the missing cord from her hem.

"You need the foreign secretary's help then, not mine."

Her lids came down briefly over the startlingly blue eyes. "But you are with the government, are you not? That is why you can help me."

"I have some connections with the government." He wondered how much she knew. It did not bode well for Frank if the Moldovans had seen through their ruse.

"You frighten me, Lord Blackstone. I told him I would bring you here, only you, so he would be safe."

"I would like to see Frank."

"You must agree to help me, to keep me with you, so that Alexi cannot hurt me ever again."

That he could agree to. He imagined separate prison cells for each of them. He nodded.

The countess climbed a sunken granite slab and waved her lace handkerchief towards the trees at the far end of the churchyard. A man emerged from the dappled shade and strolled towards them.

One minute he thought Frank Hammersley was walking towards him through the green churchyard, and the next moment he knew it was not Frank. The clothes were Frank's, but it was the count who wore them. In the same instant the countess was on him from behind. A velvet cord passed over his head and dug into his throat, and he felt the countess twist at his back, so that her shoulders pressed against him.

Instead of pulling against the cord, he shoved back hard with long strides, using his legs and his weight to unbalance her and force her into a stumbling run. She did not let go of the choking cord, but she could not keep it taut without his resistance.

The count shouted and began to run towards him, and from behind him two pistols fired, almost simultaneously.

The countess stumbled and went down. Blackstone let himself fall with her. He heard the harsh exhalation as the wind was knocked out of her. The cord went slack round his neck. He pulled free of it and rolled off of her. She writhed on the grass, her face livid, trying to recover breath.

The count turned and began to hobble away. Clare sprinted after and brought the man down. Blackstone looked for Violet. She was coming across the grass toward him with swift, eager steps, her little pistol in her hand.

He opened his arms and folded her in them. "I knew it was not Frank, but I wasn't quick enough to fire before she sprang."

Blackstone sent Hazelwood a look of gratitude.

"Nothing to it. I shot all my father's birds as a boy."

While Blackstone directed two pistols at the count and countess and Clare and Hazelwood secured the prisoners in the carriage, Violet reloaded her gun.

Hazelwood chuckled as he used the countess's cords to bind their feet. Her face was a cold porcelain mask, a purple bruise forming along her jaw. "You will not defeat us," she warned. "It is you who will suffer." The count silenced her with a harsh sentence in that other tongue. Clare mounted the carriage box, and drove off.

Lord Chartwell read with growing irritation the report from Samuel Goldsworthy. The man was cursed, cheeky, and damned secretive. The worst thing about Goldsworthy was that he got results without ever letting his superiors know the state of his investigations. One was supposed to wait and trust in Goldsworthy's mysterious methods no matter how one's own superiors frowned.

Chartwell found his patience particularly thin in the matter of dead agents and missing sums of money to the tune of a hundred thousand pounds. Nothing in Goldsworthy's report of visits to hat shops, theaters, beekeepers, and balls seemed likely to produce the essential result.

Lord Chartwell's secretary interrupted as Chartwell stood at the window considering whether he could prod more definite information out of the laughing green man.

"Sir, there's a woman to see you. She refuses to leave."

Chartwell frowned at his secretary. The man was paid to deal with anything that might disturb Chartwell's day.

"She says to tell you that Frank Hammersley sent her."

Chartwell spun from the window. "Frank Hammersley?"

His secretary nodded.

"Send her in. Find some tea or coffee."

Chartwell glanced at the state of his office. It would do. He removed a red dispatch box from his desk and put it out of sight on the floor.

The woman his secretary ushered in was perhaps forty and extraordinarily handsome, a great beauty. Even Lord Chartwell, who ordinarily dismissed such qualities in his fellow human beings, felt the effect of the woman's striking looks. There was something familiar in her smile, and he thought he might have seen her somewhere before, but dismissed the notion. She stood with quiet dignity, her hands gripping a rust and gold tapestry carpetbag, the unfashionable but practical device of ordinary travelers.

"I have something I believe you are looking for, Lord Chartwell."

Her English was impeccable, but still there was an accent. Again a sense that he should recognize her struck him.

Chartwell did not at first realize she meant the bag, but when she lifted it, he gestured to his secretary to help her.

"You'll want to open it at once and count the money," she said.

Chartwell signaled his secretary to place the bag on his desk. He opened it and found himself looking at neat bundles of Spanish banknotes. Lord Chartwell felt that perhaps the lower part of his jaw was no longer attached to the upper.

"How? Frank Hammersley, you say?"

She smiled. "Your countryman did me a great service." She shrugged.

"My countryman?" Chartwell was certainly puzzled.

"Lord Blackstone. He ransomed my son from the bandit, Vasiladi."

Blackstone. The name brought it all back. That painting. Chartwell had not seen the actual thing, but he'd never forgotten the parodies that had appeared in the print shops for months, the lovely woman wearing nothing but her smile. No wonder she had been familiar and unfamiliar at once.

He felt himself reddening at the thought of the painting and tried to recover a professional air. He cleared his throat. "Madame *you* have done a very great service to his majesty's government, is there any way we may do you a service in return?"

She smiled. *That smile.* Almost Chartwell thought that he had blundered in his offer.

"*Sí.* There is something you can do. It would be a great kindness."

Chapter Twenty-one

Do not give way to useless alarm . . . though it is right to be prepared for the worst, there is no occasion to look on it as certain.

—Jane Austen, *Pride and Prejudice*

Waring & Sons Bonded Tea warehouse was out of the way at the end of a huddled row of derelict buildings with rubbish piled against fire-blackened brick walls. The bustle of the docks ended abruptly where the sloping rutted road turned to the river. Trade had moved elsewhere.

It was midday, but the window openings of the burned-out brick building gaped like sightless eyes, except where they glowed a lurid red like the grate of an iron stove. Violet felt her heartbeat falter and start again. The building was on fire, and she had every reason to believe that Frank was inside in some form of captivity. In the general reek of the neighborhood, where furnaces burned condemned cargoes, no alarm had been raised. No fire bells clanged.

Blackstone's grip on her wrist held her in place in the shadows opposite the structure. His gaze scanned the building and the deserted street that led to the river.

"We don't know Frank is in there," he told her.

"But if he is?"

"We get him out, but we've still the rest of the prince's party unaccounted for."

"How many?" Hazelwood asked.

"Maybe three or more. Dubusari and any bully boys he's hired. If the valet and chef are in on it, they're likely managing some conveyance to make their escape." Blackstone glanced at the river. Violet could see the top of a flight of stone steps at the edge of the vast muddy roll of waters gleaming dully in the spring light. "Easy enough to head down the Thames to catch a ship putting out to sea."

Blackstone's gaze narrowed, and Violet followed his lead. Towards the river at the bottom of the building's southwest corner, a dark green door stood open, a heavy chain hanging from its iron door pull.

She heard Hazelwood chuckle. "Does your villain think we're idiots, Blackstone? He leaves the door open and might as well put up a sign—'Come on in, dearies, I've set a sweet trap for you.'"

"It looks that way, but Dubusari's not expecting us. He's expecting the count and countess with a report of my demise. But his fire is burning too slowly. The open roof has let in the heavy rains and dampened the timbers. Opening the door is like opening a flue in a chimney."

"Where's Frank then?" Violet felt the hard restraint of Blackstone's hand. She knew he was right that they needed to be patient and cautious, but her heart was beating madly at the thought of Frank trapped in a fire.

"I've an idea, Blackstone. Let me go up the stairs to spring the trap, if it is a trap, while you two go around along the river's edge."

While Blackstone and Hazelwood debated the plan, Violet studied the building. It was four stories tall and shaped like an L with the long wing extending to a rounded end like the stern of a ship above the river embankment. The glow of the flames seemed strongest on the topmost floor right in the center of the long wing. At either end of the building, the windows had their lifeless gray aspect. She tugged Blackstone's sleeve and reported what she saw, asking him what it meant.

He squeezed her hand in his. "It means they don't know where Frank is. They are trying to smoke him out. That's why the door is open. They're waiting for him to bolt."

"Why hasn't he?" She didn't want to think why Frank couldn't escape.

"He can't or he knows they're waiting." Trust Blackstone to be direct with her. She could appreciate that honesty of his now.

Hazelwood shook his head. "If someone is watching that door, he's likely seen us, friends. I say we go boldly forward."

Blackstone looked at Violet. She saw that fear for her was holding him back. She smiled and pulled her pistol from beneath her cape. He smiled back, a gleam of admiration in his eyes.

They entered the building and found wooden stairs that turned around a dark narrow well. A layer of smoke hung in the air.

"I'll take a quick look, shall I?" Hazelwood bounded up the stairs without waiting for an answer.

Blackstone had Violet's hand in his, keeping her close. Stinging smoke curled down the stairs and out into the main section of the building. The fire was taking hold. They could hear wood popping and beams collapsing.

Hazelwood called down from above. "There's some kind of office here. Look's like a makeshift jail, but Hammersley's not here, Blackstone." They heard him stomping about, dragging something heavy. Then he appeared again at the top of the stairs. "It seems our countess has been here. Two dead fellows inside. Local citizens by the look of them, one strangled with a velvet cord, still around the fellow's neck."

He tossed a bit of cloth down the stairs, and Blackstone caught it. A wool tweed cap. He kept his expression blank and stuffed the thing in his pocket.

"No sign of Wilde," Hazelwood shouted. "What do you want to do next?" He didn't wait for an answer, but disappeared again.

What Blackstone didn't want to do was to take his love up the wooden stairs of a burning building. Nor did he want to leave her alone where Dubusari or his hirelings might find her. Violet had edged as far as his hold would allow to peer into the murk of the first floor.

Blackstone leaned forward and shouted up the narrow stairwell. "Hazelwood, let's regroup." As he pulled back, he was aware of a warning squeeze of his hand from Violet.

He turned and found himself facing a very different man than he expected. Dubusari blocked the way, but he was not the quaint elderly gentleman of the powdered wig and steepled fingers, but a powerful man of little more than twoscore with short-cropped black hair. He pointed a pair of lethal dueling pistols their way.

Blackstone kept his gaze on Dubusari. The man never blinked. The frame was just as lean, but without the effeminate loose clothes, the sinewy strength of the man was evident.

He could hear Hazelwood moving about above.

"Where are my companions?"

"In custody. Why are your hirelings dead, Dubusari?"

"Because they failed."

"They let Hammersley get away." Blackstone hazarded a guess.

"It doesn't matter. You've made a mistake, Lord Blackstone. England has made a mistake, and history is unkind to those who back the wrong player, as you have done."

"You mean Prince Andre?" Blackstone could hear Hazelwood moving somewhere up the smoke-filled staircase. It sounded as if he were dragging something down the stairs. Blackstone needed to keep Dubusari talking and keep Violet from moving. He had her left wrist in his left hand, but he could feel the tension in her, the desire to bolt up those stairs to look for Frank.

Dubusari sneered. "Moldova deserves better. We will see that she has a prince who can truly defend her, not an English puppet."

"By selling out to the tsar? That's your plan, isn't it?"

"England is weak. Nicolai will be a strong ally to Moldova."

"Nicolai?" Blackstone could not help his surprise. "You mean Alexander, don't you?" At the moment Alexander was the Russian tsar as far as Blackstone knew.

"Nicolai." Dubusari's certainty was chilling.

Blackstone had a fleeting thought that if they lived, the foreign secretary would find that piece of conversation most interesting.

Dubusari turned his gaze to Violet. "How convenient that you have come, Miss Hammersley. Your brother has eluded us until now, but now I think he will come out of his own accord when he hears your voice. Will you be so good as to ascend the stairs and call his name?"

"No need for Miss Hammersley to come up, Dubusari, I'll call." Hazelwood's cheerful voice came down the stairwell. He bellowed into the burning building. "Frank

Hammersley. Your sister's come to find you. Now would be a good time to turn up."

Hazelwood came back to stand above them, choking and gasping in the smoke, a red glow outlining his dark figure. "Nothing. I suspect he's got away."

Blackstone could see they were at an impasse. The heat was growing. The stairs could go up any minute. Hazelwood might be plunged to his doom, and they had no idea where Hammersley had got to. Plainly he'd escaped the room at the top of the narrow stairs and eluded the now dead guards. He'd had nowhere to go but down the stairs or out into the shell of the building. They had no way of knowing whether he had heard them, though Hazelwood was making enough noise to wake the proverbial dead.

Dubusari broke the impasse. "Call your friend, Lord Blackstone," he said quietly. "Tell him to come down the stairs at once or I shoot Miss Hammersley."

"I'm unmoved, Dubusari. You intend to kill her anyway."

"Blackstone," Hazelwood called. "Tell the bastard not to shoot. I'm coming."

Dubusari allowed himself a thin smile of satisfaction. The smile, more than anything, threatened to crack Blackstone's patience.

Hazelwood's heavy-footed steps came thumping down the stairs as if he weighed eighteen stone or more. At his back, Blackstone felt Violet shift and position her pistol so that she could slide it around his ribs and fire. For the moment he was all that stood between her and a bullet from Dubusari.

"Blackstone?" Hazelwood's voice rasped now with the smoke. He spoke in an exaggerated stage whisper. "I think I've found Hammersley. Can you come up?"

The words broke Dubusari's concentration. His gaze flew up. Violet shifted her gun and fired. The bullet caught Dubusari in the left shoulder and threw him off balance. He staggered back, and the gun in his left hand discharged into the floor.

Blackstone had time to draw his own pistol as Dubusari righted himself. Violet was exposed now, and Dubusari turned his pistol on her when Hazelwood shouted again. "I'm sending Hammersley down. Give him room."

Again Dubusari glanced up. Blackstone shifted to stand in front of Violet at the side of the stairs. There was a pause, a loud thump, and a body plummeted feet first between Blackstone and Violet, and Dubusari. As Dubusari sprang back, Blackstone fired. Dubusari crumpled, his pistol clattering to the floor.

Blackstone sent Violet outside. He sat her in the grass, and went back in. Hazelwood had heard a faint cry. The smoke was the worst of it. Though it was still day, the inside of the building was like the worst of a London fog, and hot besides. They soaked their coats in a pool of rainwater and laid a beam from the stair landing across the uncertain floor to the exposed top of a brick column. Blackstone scrambled across. The cry came again, and when, gasping for air, he leaned his head out of a gaping window frame, he found Frank Hammersley lying below him on a hollow ledge.

They broke in to the opposite end of the building where Hammersley said he had found a lift, and found ropes with which to lower him to the ground. During the painstaking process, Violet paced the weedy grounds.

A groan from behind a pile of rubbish caught her ear, and when she investigated, she found a young man lying in the weeds with a bloody gash across the back of his head.

She knelt and touched his shoulder.

He groaned and rolled over onto his back. His eyes opened and blinked against the light. She shifted to put his face in shadow. "Who are you?"

"Nate Wilde, Miss Hammersley." His voice rasped dryly.

She rocked back on her heels. "You know me?"

"I've been looking for your brother. He's here, isn't he?"

"We found him. Alive," she said.

The youth's eyes closed. "Good."

She touched him gently. "What happened to you?"

"I fell, must've broke something. I was running from . . ." He drifted off.

"Don't worry. We'll get you help now."

Chapter Twenty-two

"We will not quarrel for the greater share of
blame annexed to that evening . . ."

—Jane Austen, *Pride and Prejudice*

Blackstone returned Violet and Frank to Hammersley House
and watched as servants spilled from the entrance, colliding
with one another in their eagerness to do something for Master Frank. When Frank had been carried off with painstaking
care on a bench that arrived from below stairs, Violet came
to stand at Blackstone's side and reached up a hand to his face.

"I must go and be with him now, but I must see you soon."

"Meet me tonight, Violet."

She leaned into his chest, and he let himself hold her
close. Then she pulled back. "Oh dear, we can't meet in
Frank's room. He'll be in it."

"The long gallery then. Where we began."

"Yes, where we'll begin again."

He nodded. "Right. Now I've got a patient to tend to as
well."

He gave her a brief kiss and turned to care for Wilde. He
still had to look as she ran lightly up the steps to her door.

* * *

Violet met Blackstone in the long gallery sometime after midnight. The house had settled into quiet rest. Everyone performed amazing exertions from the moment she and Frank had arrived. The physician found himself with a half dozen helpers more than he needed at any given moment, but he'd seen at once that all needed to be employed, and had suggested ways that Frank's comfort could be assured. There was now a quantity of ice on hand and towels and shallow basins, enough to ice a dozen injured limbs.

The doctor had done all he could for the present and would return when they had the swelling down sufficiently to set the bone.

Blackstone rose from a couch, which Violet instantly recalled had been a favorite of theirs before they had progressed to more earnest lovemaking. He offered his arms, and she stepped into them, laying her head against his chest.

"Papa is with Frank. He'll be there all night. It feels miraculous to have him back. We owe it all to you."

"Don't thank me, Violet."

"Oh, but I must, and I must beg your forgiveness, too. I think you will tire of the regularity with which I do both."

His arms tightened around her. "Violet, you are wearing a wrapper, and . . ." He shifted and slid a hand inside her wrapper to cup one breast. "And a nightgown."

"Yes." She spoke to his chest, right above his heart. "I thought perhaps it was best, after all, if you simply came to my bedroom."

She felt his heartbeat change at the words.

"Ah, so that the thanking and the pleas for forgiveness can begin."

"Exactly." She laughed softly against his chest, and lifted

her head and took his hand, leading him on through the dark house he knew as well as he knew any place on earth.

In her room they lit a brace of candles and faced each other and took time undressing and studying one another.

Blackstone had returned to London over a month earlier, but now he knew that he was home. When he pulled the tie on the rose silk wrapper and pushed it from her shoulders, and reached to cup both of her breasts in his hands and lift them for his kiss, and when her hands in turn clung to his waistcoat so that she might steady herself and catch her breath, it was home he breathed.

And when she tugged at his neckcloth and unwound the white linen from his throat and found all the buttons that needed releasing so that she might free him from waistcoat and shirt, it was home that touched him.

For a time they were content to stand in the flickering light and press against one another and savor the meeting of all the points—soft and smooth and round, rough and hard and flat—that could express their longing. Hands stroked, lips met and clung.

When, belatedly, he freed her hair from its braid so that it fell around them, a more urgent tempo drove them to a final hasty shedding of garments and a laughing retreat to fall upon the bed.

When they were well and truly naked, warm skin pressed to warm skin, he said, "I've missed this."

"You said you never thought of me."

"I lied." He rolled them so that his body covered hers.

Violet welcomed the long, lean strength of him, the smooth symmetry and the rough places, the soft texture of hair on his arms and chest and on his legs where they twined with hers. She took hold of his hips to feel the flex of muscles as he came into her.

Then they met in the movements they knew so well, that made them gasp and strain upward towards a distant sun of pleasure, until it burst in a bright shaft of joy that left them heated and shuddering in each other's arms.

Violet closed her eyes and let tears come, not tears of hollow ache but of fullness, of joy brimming over. Blackstone caught them with his thumbs and tasted them. "I love you, Violet."

"I love you, Blackstone." She pushed herself up on her knees, and kneeling over him, she began to explore. She found and kissed all the purpling bruises the day had raised and saw the way his time in Greece had worn his belly thin. She traced lines and angles and claimed for herself with her touch all the parts of him that seemed the most wonderful because they were him and not her.

He moved to pin her under him again, and when they had had a second fill of one another, she let him take her back against the pillows in the circle of his arms, their hands twined together. "I changed my room, you know, because of you."

"I guessed that when I saw it. It shocked me, shocked me out of my side of our quarrel. I felt my responsibility for the change in you, my fearless friend."

"I thought changing the paper would help me to banish thoughts of you. I could not look at those walls without thinking that you had been here with me."

"It was pretty paper, Violet."

"But those vines and flowers had seen you love me and leave me. They missed you, too, and I couldn't bear their reproaches." She turned his hand to see the bold Blackstone signet on it.

He withdrew his hand from hers and pulled off the ring. "Maybe I should not have felt so bound by that promise."

"No." She took his hand again and restored the ring to its proper place, turning to face him then, easy in her nakedness with him. "The ring is you," she said solemnly. "It is your loyalty and your honor. *You* wear it now, and it means you, not him, nor any other man."

"Is this where you ask for my forgiveness again?" he asked hopefully.

"Will you forgive me again?" She settled back against his chest with his arms wrapped around her, under her breasts.

"I denied myself the pleasure of thinking of you, which makes me all the hungrier now. I told Rushbrooke—"

"You told Rushbrooke about this?" She twisted up to look at him. He kissed her, and kissing her was like drinking from a cold rushing stream, so that for a time he was lost in it. Then he moved so that they lay side by side.

"I told Rushbrooke that when you were my bride, I would keep you in bed no more than eight hours of the day, so that you could continue your charitable works."

"You didn't!"

"I did."

"He must have choked." Her eyes flashed with amusement, and he remembered the moment on the *Redemption* when he wanted to see that flash again.

"Nearly. But I don't think I can honor that promise. I may need you to be naked for a longer period of each day."

Naked was how he liked her best, lying soft as snow beside him. He let his hand drift over the smooth, rounded hills of her, over the deep dip of her waist, and down the long slope from her hip to her knee. She shivered under his touch and a laugh shook her. Her laughter, like a bracing draft of winter air he drew into his lungs, made him laugh in answer and know he was alive.

"We could talk all night, but I need to kiss you again, Violet."

"Do you? Then I propose a bargain, because I need to touch you, all the parts I like."

Chapter Twenty-three

"I declare after all there is no enjoyment like reading! How much sooner one tires of anything than of a book! When I have a house of my own, I shall be miserable if I have not an excellent library."

—Jane Austen, *Pride and Prejudice*

"Congratulations, lad. You got the lot of them and Frank Hammersley. I don't think a professional could have done a neater job."

Blackstone set the paste ring Violet had returned to him on Goldsworthy's vast paper-strewn desk. He was conscious of what Goldsworthy was not saying, and he was not sure how much Goldsworthy knew of Blackstone's plan to free Frank whether it served the government or not.

Goldsworthy picked up the velvet box. "That's a good thought. You'll want to buy Miss Hammersley the real thing now."

"When I finish my year and a day, you mean."

"No need to wait on us." Goldsworthy waved a dismissive hand. "You want to marry the girl now, marry the girl. No reason you can't be married and working for us."

"I can't see myself living apart from my bride or betraying her."

Goldsworthy rose to his towering height. A laugh shook him, like a tree in a sudden breeze. "Not necessary."

Blackstone was missing something, some piece of the puzzle still eluded him. He let his gaze take in Goldsworthy's office, the grand scale of the furnishings and their martial simplicity and the concealing canvas curtain. "I thought you chose me for my scandalous name. Blackstone, the charming rakeshame."

Goldsworthy looked grave for once, the knowing gleam in his eye quiet. "I can't change your reputation, lad. London has a long memory for scandal, but I didn't choose you because you made fodder for the print shops in your salad days."

Blackstone was once again glad to be sitting. An encounter with Goldsworthy had a way of unsettling a man, like a ship dropping in a trough of the sea, or a minor earthquake rattling the china in the cupboards. "Why did you choose me then?"

"Why? Because you went to Greece to save your brother. You managed Vasiladi for near a year and kept your head and the heads of those captives of his, too. Now that was a piece of work. Had to have you, don't you see?"

"How do you know I have a brother? I've never told anyone."

"Now that is a club secret, lad. I can't be telling you how I know things. You may be bound to secrecy, but other people aren't. Now, you go, marry the girl, move into Hammersley House, if you like. Somewhere here, I've a draft for you, a first installment on our bargain. It should help you take care of your mother and sisters until you finish your time with us."

Once again Blackstone watched Goldsworthy disturb the piles of paper on his desk. It took a great deal of rustling before the right document emerged from the disorder, time in which Blackstone could rearrange his thinking about the big green man and his role in their lives.

"Aha!" Goldsworthy lifted the draft for which he'd been searching, like a magician producing a hare from a hat. He stuck out his hand, and Blackstone rose to take it.

He didn't fully understand the club and its workings, but he knew one thing. "Hazelwood's got it all wrong."

Goldsworthy gave a slow shake of his great head. "The lad's a hard case, but we'll get to him. We'll set 'im straight in time."

Miranda had never ventured into the living quarters of the club. It was unthinkable that such a male place would admit a female visitor, but now Lord Hazelwood was breaking the rules. He was leading her up the servants' stair to see Nate Wilde. "The cub needs cheering, Miranda, and you're the one to do it. He's lower than a coal cellar. Thinks he failed some grand test."

Privately, Miranda could not imagine Nate Wilde low. He was impudence itself, sure of himself when he had no right, born in the Seven Dials, better at lifting the coins out of person's pocket than earning a penny to put in his own. But Lord Hazelwood had taken her hand and told her how pretty she was and promised that Nate Wilde would heal in a flash if he could just see her face looking at him instead of seeing the sawbones.

When Lord Hazelwood asked her to go as a favor to him, Miranda could not say no. Still she held back a little at the door, so that Lord Hazelwood turned to look at her with a knowing look. "You're not shy, now, are you, Miranda?"

She shook her head.

Lord Hazelwood knocked.

A muffled voice, groggy and low-spirited, answered.

"Wilde, are you decent?" Lord Hazelwood called, pushing the door open a crack. "There's someone who wants to see you."

Miranda glared at Hazelwood. She wasn't the one who

wanted to see Nate Wilde. But Lord Hazelwood only grinned at her with that lazy smile of his. He pushed the door fully open and bowed her into the room.

Nate Wilde wore no shirt.

Miranda had assisted her father countless times as he measured the young lords of Mr. Goldsworthy's club, but they had not been shirtless. She dropped her gaze at once from that smooth white breadth of shoulder. But the impression had been made. A wide linen bandage crossed his chest and held his right arm in a sling. There were contours and muscles and an interesting valley down the middle of his chest. She had seen, too, in the glazed eyes, that he was in pain. She didn't move.

"Now then, Wilde, say hello to your visitor." Lord Hazelwood found a chair and pushed it up near the bed. "Come, Miranda, have a seat so you can visit." He took her arm and propelled her into the seat. She cast him a look of appeal.

"I'll come back for you in half an hour. Don't tire him out. The gudgeon won't take the drug."

Miranda couldn't look at him. She let her gaze wander the room. She had not imagined that he kept his room as neat and ordered as the shop itself. The narrow bed had a hessian coverlet in dark blue and green. Beside the bed was a small chest of drawers with a lamp, a book, and a glass of some liquid. To the left of the door stood a tall walnut wardrobe and next to it a brown wicker standing screen. To her right was a dormer window and a writing table under a pair of shelves neatly filled with books. Miranda could not read the tiny gold titles, but the books had plain, dull colors—rust and dark green and blue. It was all plain and manly.

She could feel him looking at her. "You've seen it all," he said.

"Why won't you take the medicine?"

"It makes me sleepy. If I take it, I can't read." He pushed himself more upright, exposing more of his chest and ribs. His face tightened with some twinge of pain.

"How long will you have to stay in bed?"

"The sawbones says another week. I'm not to move till then."

"You have a great many books."

"I like to read. Are you surprised?"

"No."

"You are. You think I'm going to say *cawfy* and *tyke* and drop every *h* and *g*. I might have been born in the Seven Dials, but now I can be who I want to be."

"Then why do you tell me I can't be who I want to be."

"It's just teasing. I like your airs, Miranda." He leaned his head back against the pillows, and his eyes fell closed, and he drifted off, just like that.

Miranda bent over her sewing. A few minutes ticked by, and she glanced at him again, and an odd thought struck her that she did not know the color of his eyes. How could she not know the color of his eyes when they had met and talked nearly every day for a year?

She did not care what color Nate Wilde's eyes were.

The door opened and Miranda looked up to see three fine, handsome gentlemen, two with dark curls, and one with an angel's golden hair. They were as fine as Mr. Goldsworthy's gentlemen. One of the dark-haired gentlemen stepped forward.

"Whelp, what have you done to yourself?" The gentleman asked.

Nate Wilde came back from wherever he'd drifted off to with a smile. "Devil, what are you doing here? Sir Xander, sir. Daventry!"

"We've come for two reasons, but it looks as if you're in good hands. Are you going to introduce us?"

"Miss Kirby, Sir William Jones, Sir Alexander Jones, and Lord Daventry."

Miranda stood on shaking legs and dropped a deep curtsy. The gentlemen smiled. She hoped her knees would not crumble and embarrass her. The laughing gentleman winked at her and went to the head of Nate Wilde's bed. "Don't let us interrupt, but we've come to take you away, Wilde. Our wives insist. The fair Helen won't take no for an answer. She's going to be the first to nurse you back to health."

The second gentlemen spoke next. "But, I assure you, Wilde, that Lady Jones, and Daventry's lady are equally determined to have a share in healing your wounds."

"We'll be back, Wilde," said the third gentleman, the serious golden-haired one. "I'll see that no one jostles you on the trip."

Miranda watched Nate Wilde grin. "Who am I to argue with the Jones women?"

The first gentlemen looked at Nate. "At the quarter hour then?"

Nate nodded. "Thank you, Devil."

The three magnificences took themselves out of the room. Miranda took her seat again and began to fold up her sewing. "I guess you're leaving the club."

"For now. I'm not much use here at the moment. My friends will take care of me."

"Your friends, are they?"

"They are."

He said it with no pride. Miranda felt small. She knew she would boast of knowing such gentlemen, but she would cut her tongue out and feed it to a jackdaw before she would ask Nate Wilde how he came to know so many sirs and lords.

"Then I will wish you well and see you when you return." She gathered up her sewing. It made no sense to her that he had such friends and yet he worked for Mr. Goldsworthy and served the gentlemen of the club. She didn't understand him. If he could disappear into the care of the great and the rich, why would he return to her?

She looked at him. The white shoulders were just as broad and beautiful as she had noticed at the first, and the eyes were glazed with pain.

"Are you going to kiss me good-bye?" he asked.

"Kiss you? Oh the fall has knocked your brains loose, Nate Wilde."

"I think not. I think it makes me see things clearly. You want to kiss me, Miranda."

"*I?* Want to kiss *you*?" The idea of it. But a voice whispered that no one would know. He would be gone.

"You do. So come here."

She did. His eyes were blue, blue like birds' eggs and summer skies. She did not know why she had not noticed them before.

Violet now spent most of her time at her brother's side, but it was nearly a week before he could sustain any conversation. "You wanted to talk to me? How are you getting on?"

"I've been better, but the doctor doesn't think I'll lose the leg."

Violet pulled her chair closer and sat where he could see her. He was able to stay awake for longer periods now than when they'd first brought him home. For days the regimen had been sleep and laudanum with Violet or Papa sitting at Frank's side. Yesterday he had begun to wean himself of the drug. "I'm sorry we did not get to you sooner."

"Not your fault, V. I thought I'd outfoxed them putting a false report in my valise and taking the real one off to . . ." Frank's gaze shifted away with some thought.

"When did you realize what Dubusari was about?"

"Almost at once, but I couldn't tell how far it went, or who else was involved at first. I didn't know whether the prince was playing dumb . . ."

"Or if he just didn't see what was right in front of him?"

"The money, of course, revealed the truth. I realized I had to show them a false report just to get out of the country alive. In Greece, I thought I could pass the real one along to our agent, but the fellow was dead when I got there."

"Our friend, the countess. Did you realize she was involved?"

Frank shook his head.

"You tried again in Naples?"

"By then I was pretty desperate. I knew they must not ever see the real report, and I had to give it to someone they'd never suspect of British sympathies."

"The person you went to see in Spain?"

"Yes." Frank plucked at his coverlet.

Violet jumped up. "Is it too heavy for you? Is it bothering the leg?"

"No." He held up a hand to stop her. "There's something I ought to tell you."

"Oh dear, a confession?"

"I'm afraid so." His gaze met hers and slid away again. "Blast it, V, I don't know how to tell you this."

Violet smiled at him and sank back into her chair. "Directly and honestly will do."

He laughed. "For you, yes." He shifted once more, pushing himself to a more upright position. "I took the report to Blackstone's former mistress. Only she never was his mistress."

"I know. That is, I know now. I should have figured it out five years ago, but I wasn't thinking then."

"How could you have figured it out then? Everyone thought he was a rakeshame of the worst sort. That painting was in all the print shops. His ring was unmistakable."

"On the wrong hand. But how did you figure it out?"

Frank studied the coverlet. "Did he tell you why he went to Greece?"

"No."

"Well, he's a stubborn, honorable fool. Anyway I learned his reason for going to Greece, and that got me to thinking about the past and what I'd been willing to believe of him. He was my friend. I never should have believed he would engage himself to you while he had a mistress."

Violet stood and crossed to the window. She pressed her hands to her chest. She didn't deserve to be so happy, but she was. The least she could do was tell her brother the truth. She turned back to Frank. "My turn to confess. I should have known that Blackstone was not the man in the picture because he had been with me so often and so . . . intimately that he could not have been in Royce's studio."

Frank was staring. "You mean I should have called him out."

Violet shook her head. "I'm going to marry Blackstone next Sunday. It's five years late, but it is what we intended."

"Next Sunday?"

"We have such a dismal record of believing in each other and such a hopeless attraction, you see. There's no other way."

"Did he tell you why he went to Greece, V.?"

"No. I don't need to know. You don't have to tell me. I know I can trust him. Whatever the world thinks he is, I know he's honorable."

"A stubborn, honorable fool," Frank repeated. "Do you think he'll want me at your wedding?"

"He will. Can you manage a bath chair?"

"I'll be there."

Chapter Twenty-four

"You are then resolved to have him?"

"I am only resolved to act in that manner, which will, in my own opinion, constitute my happiness, without reference to you, or to any person so wholly unconnected with me."

—Jane Austen, *Pride and Prejudice*

"Violet, I came as soon as I heard. You don't mean to do this thing. You can't seriously contemplate becoming Blackstone's bride." Penelope looked round Violet's straw-colored drawing room with surprised approval.

"I do."

"I beg your pardon, but are you mad?" Penelope sank on the Aubusson-covered sofa, and paused to stroke its elegant pattern.

"Tea?"

Penelope nodded.

Violet smiled. She couldn't help it after all. Her happiness had a way of bubbling up to the surface like a spring. "I think I am mad, but it's a lovely form of madness."

Penelope accepted a cup from Violet. "People will call him a fortune hunter."

"I don't think he will mind."

"How do you mean to handle his family? They will not rejoice at his connection with you."

"I acknowledge that it may take time for his mother and sisters to accept me. They have had trials enough in these past years, but it is for Blackstone first to make his peace with them. He's gone to Bath to speak with them, and we will see what reconciliation is possible."

Penelope set down her tea untouched. "No one will support your charities any longer. No one will seek your acquaintance. People will cut you direct."

"I will have to rely on Blackstone for company, won't I?" Violet brightened at the thought. She supposed that they would often be naked, at least in the early days of their marriage, and that definitely meant that other company would be unwanted. What an empty blank place London had been without Blackstone. Though she had tried to fill every page of her calendar with appointments and meetings, in his absence, the million-peopled city of London had been a hermitage.

"That's the maddest notion of them all. Rely on Blackstone?! The whispers about his intrigues will begin before the ink has dried on your marriage lines."

"Yes, I suppose his name will always be synonymous with scandal. People will imagine that he has a harem or a Spanish lover or an actress or a lady love."

"The vain imaginings of bored ladies of fashion will be nothing to endure, but the knowledge of his infidelities will pain you." Penelope was quite serious.

"You are right, Penelope. If I had to endure knowledge of any infidelity on Blackstone's part, it would be impossible to be his bride."

"Violet, you may not think me the most sincere of your friends, but I do know my world, the world from which Blackstone comes. I have been trained from childhood to exist in it. You have not."

"You think I would do better as Mr. Rushbrooke's bride."

"I do not. But there are hundreds of sensible, worthy men between Rushbrooke and Blackstone. I only ask you not to connect yourself with Blackstone."

"I think I have been connected with Blackstone for years now."

"You are resolved then to have him? You'll let yourself be known as Blackstone's bride?"

"I like the sound of that, Blackstone's bride. It suits me, I think."

"Hazelwood, I have a job for you."

Hazelwood dropped into one of Goldsworthy's large leather chairs. The scale of the man required grandeur even in the club's furnishings. The man's office reminded him of visits to his father's study, except for the canvas backdrop and the noise of workmen, and except that Goldsworthy was an amiable fellow, and *amiable* was a word one would never apply to the Earl of Vange.

"I thought you'd never ask, Goldsworthy. You want me to ride a white horse to the rescue of a fair damsel. Do I get to keep her if I save her?"

"You've got the right of it, lad, but sadly you can't keep this one."

"Goldsworthy, old man, I don't think you realize quite how wearing this celibacy regimen is. I suspect you've been sneaking off to tup Mrs. Goldsworthy on the sly while Clare and I sleep chaste as nuns in our beds."

Goldsworthy's russet brows contracted. He looked quite serious for a moment. "You and Clare would do well to become acquainted with chastity, I think. Quite a new experience for the pair of you."

"But you're willing to let us run free for a bit to rescue this maiden?"

"To restore a lady's honor."

"Ah, then Clare's your man. He's stuffed with honor that one. You know what he did at Waterloo, don't you?"

Goldsworthy nodded and began absently pushing the papers around on his desk, like a man with a broom trying to push a load of snow off the pavement.

"Of course, likely you saw him do it. You know everything about the unfortunates who have fallen into your trap."

"Hazelwood, do you want the job, or don't you?"

"I do."

Goldsworthy leaned down, opening and closing the drawers in his desk, obviously looking for something.

"Well, what is it?"

Goldsworthy stretched a hand across the desk and offered him a wad of banknotes.

Hazelwood took the notes. A man could have a long run at the faro tables with the wad in his hand.

"The job is to buy a painting from the artist Reynolds Royce and ship it to Spain. I'll write out the directions for you." Goldsworthy started writing.

"You mean Blackstone's painting? The painting of his Spanish dancer?"

"Don't take *no* for an answer." Goldsworthy held out a slip of paper. "Your first assignment, lad. Report back when you've got the fair lady shipped off to Spain."

Hazelwood looked back at Goldsworthy from the door. "You do realize that you're seriously thinning the ranks of our little club. Blackstone's going to be married, solvent, and sober. He can hardly claim membership any longer."

Goldsworthy looked up at last with a grin. "Don't worry, lad. I won't let you down."

Epilogue

"My affections and wishes are unchanged."

—Jane Austen, *Pride and Prejudice*

A great deal was said and written about Blackstone's bride. Though the wedding party was exceptionally small and varied for persons of such consequence as Lord Blackstone and his banking heiress, Miss Violet Hammersley, there are those persons in London, alert to the doings of the fashionable who will note the day and time of a wedding and contrive to witness the event.

So it was that as soon as the parties involved had secured a special license and a parson, speculation arose in many quarters as to the fabric and design of the bride's dress. Such a quantity of blond lace and silk tulle had been ordered by a particular Spitalfields dressmaker that some persons declared Violet Hammersley was getting above herself, a rich cit marrying a lord, even such a rakeshame as Blackstone. Other persons simply made note of the dressmaker's name and resolved to make use of her services.

Those who did manage to insert themselves into the modest crowd in the church or to obtain a spot upon the pavement outside were not disappointed. The ladies of Spitalfields had outdone themselves. The simple gathers of the bodice, the rich floral appliqué of the overdress, the delicate figured lace of the veil gave the gown an ethereal beauty, fitting both the dignity of the bride and the church, with its soaring arches and ancient windows.

A particularly bold young painter who had managed to attend the affair through the good graces of the Duchess of Huntingdon offered to paint the new baroness and was told that Lord Blackstone had tossed his card upon the fire.

As for the new bride herself, once the solemnities had been observed, and a tearful parting from her father and brother had passed, she discovered that her new husband meant to make good on his threat to keep her naked as much of the time as he could. In a country inn, within walking distance of a pretty bay, they had a large sunlit suite with a substantial bed, famous for the royal persons who had once laid their heads there.

Violet sat cross-legged in the middle of the bed on the third afternoon of her married life gazing at her sleeping husband. A faint sea breeze cooled the warm afternoon. She stroked the dark waves back from her husband's brow and sighed. "How soon do you think you will stop wanting me?" She kissed his forehead.

He opened one eye and stretched with lazy masculine pride. He was as naked as she, after all.

Violet unfolded her legs and reached for her wrapper. She would never stop wanting him, and maybe that was all that mattered.

Blackstone's right hand shot out and snagged her wrapper, whisking it out of her hands. "Violet, why do you think I'll stop wanting you? I wasn't able to stop for five years when you broke our first engagement."

"You must, mustn't you?" She watched him closely. The blue of his eyes seemed to have deepened with their marriage, but that must be a trick of her own besotted senses. He looked perfectly at his ease, lying in naked splendor. She knew him, knew that at any moment, he could spring and pin her under him, but he might not, given the way they had spent much of the afternoon.

"Did your friend the duchess suggest that husbands must inevitably tire of their brides, or only that Blackstone's bride must not expect constancy from her scandalous husband?"

Violet swallowed and nodded.

His eyes drifted closed again. She waited.

"I think that if I stop wanting you in English, I will start wanting you in other languages. How do you feel about Spanish?"

"Try me."

"*Yo te quiero.* I want you."

"I like the sound of it."

The words barely left her lips when Blackstone sprang. He snagged her waist with a warm strong hand and flipped her onto her back, and surged over her. He held himself above her, his eyes full of love and laughter.

"*Yo te quiero*, Violet." He made her laugh, too, even as his knee made a place for him between her legs. "And if we grow weary of wanting each other in Spanish, we will move on to other tongues."

"Greek and Latin?"

"Sanskrit, I think. I know a Sanskrit word that will always make me think of wanting you." He dipped his head to kiss her breasts.

"What?" she whispered.

"*Yoni.*" The word came out rough and low as she felt the light graze of his jaw waken the ache of desire in her core.

"*Yoni.* What does it mean?" She framed his face in her hands and lifted his head from her breasts. His laughing blue gaze met hers.

"*Divine passage,* my love."

Turn the page for a preview of Kate Moore's

To Seduce an Angel

Now available from Berkley Sensation

Chapter One

England. 1824

Emma faced the two gentlemen in front of the massive stone fireplace. A painting on the wall above the gray stones depicted a hunting dog pinning a spotted fawn in agony between his forepaws. Emma's sympathies were with the fawn.

They had her pinned, the duke and his nephew. The Duke of Wenlocke, tall, gaunt, and imperious, his face as unyielding as granite, leaned heavily on a black cane. His gnarled hand curved over its golden head like an eagle's talon. His other hand clutched a document.

"This is the girl?" His haughty gaze sent an icy wave of alarm over her. "She doesn't look like a murderess to me."

Emma willed her knees to remain steady. It took steady knees to run.

"Oh, she's the one, Uncle. Emma Portland." The other man, the duke's nephew, the Earl of Aubrey, turned from prodding a great log with an iron poker. A shower of sparks vanished up the flue. *If only escape were that easy.*

"What's your age, girl?" the duke demanded.

"Twenty, Your Grace." Her voice came out thin and reedy, unrecognizable to her own ears over the pounding of her heart.

The duke's gaze fixed her to the spot. "Stuck a knife in some fellow's ribs, did you?"

Don't deny it, Emma. She clenched her fists in the folds of her shawl. Let them think her a murderess. Let them stare as if she were a beast in a menagerie to be baited.

"She's accused of the deed, Uncle, not convicted. I'm sure she'd rather do a favor for a pair of gentlemen than face the law." Aubrey had a smooth voice and a powerful body, his muscled thighs bulging in skintight riding breeches, his calves sheathed in gleaming black leather. Emma had seen him return his pretty mare to the stables with bloodied sides. She had not imagined that he noticed her.

The duke's stare pierced her. "She'd better. I'm done with the law and courts. Hang all lawyers. I want that *whore's get* out of Daventry Hall and back in the gutter where he belongs."

He shook the paper in his fist at Emma. "You know what this is, girl? A request for the king's pardon. The duchess wants me to sign it. If I don't, you'll be had up before the justices at the next assizes in Horsham."

Emma drew a sharp breath and blinked hard against a sudden sting in her eyes. Somehow in spite of all their care, the law had connected her with the spy's death. She knew what that meant. Once more she and Tatty had been betrayed. Her thoughts raced back through the long chain of coins and jewels pressed into willing palms and hasty bargains made with low characters. Their enemies might have bought off anyone on sea or land in the thousand miles between home and England.

"You'll hang, you know." The duke handed the paper to Aubrey. "Read it to her."

Aubrey circled her, making a slow deliberate perusal of her person, the privilege of a man with power. A mad desire to pick up her skirts and run passed in an instant. She would not make half the distance to the library door. She would never make the first set of stairs or the grand entrance or the drive, let alone the unfriendly woods below Wenlocke Castle. Escape took care and planning and, above all, luck. No one knew that better than Emma. How many times had she and Tatty and Leo tried and failed in seven years, until their jailers had hanged Leo?

Aubrey stopped so close to her she breathed his scent, a heavy male mix of musk and leather with a tang of sweat.

"Not pleasant to contemplate, is it? Much better to hide here at Wenlocke, teaching servants' brats. That's what you do, isn't it, Miss Portland?"

Her downward gaze caught at the flimsy paper in Aubrey's hand. A pardon meant that the duchess, her grandmother's friend, still believed in her. When she and Tatty had reached her grace, all their difficulties had melted away. Until now. Now the duchess had gone to London to visit her daughter. Tatty was on her way to a ship at Bristol. There was no one at Wenlocke to help Emma. Still the duchess's wishes must count for something. "The duchess kindly gave me a position."

"Don't think to hide behind her grace, girl," the duke snapped.

"But she's done it for weeks, Uncle. Look at her. With her pink cheeks, golden curls, and round blue eyes, a man thinks butter won't melt in that sweet mouth, but that's a lie, isn't it?" Aubrey lifted her chin, the cutting edge of his nail against her throat. Her stomach roiled at the touch. "You're a lie, Emma Portland. There's a dead man in Reading whose reeking corpse says you're someone else."

His broad back was to his uncle. He let go of her chin and reached down and dealt her breast a swift, stinging blow with a flick of his middle finger.

Fear cramped her insides, but Emma knew better than to show it. She had wanted to be a girl again, but she'd made a mistake to brush the walnut dye out of her hair and scrub her skin and accept an old-figured gown from the duchess, sweet and clean and scented with lavender and verbena from the clothes press.

"Listen to Aubrey, girl." The duke's voice brought her gaze back to him. "If you don't want them to break your pretty neck and feed you to the crows, you'll do as he says."

Crows. She steadied her treacherous knees. *Don't think about crows, Emma.* Tatty and the babe must reach the coast and the waiting messenger.

The fire crackled. Outside, a March gale howled against the windows. The Englishness of the place, which had seemed so warm and comforting when she first arrived at Wenlocke, now seemed chillingly cold. The baroque grandeur of the room dwarfed her. Its dark oak cases held thousands of morocco-bound tomes with gold-tooled spines, crushing slabs of history and law. The English liked their law to do the killing. They did not send assassins to kill babes in their cradles as her countrymen did, but they would hang the merest child for stealing.

Aubrey called it a favor, but Emma knew better. The prickle of the small hairs of her neck warned her. He and the duke wanted her for some ruthless business because they believed her to be a murderess. She could tell them what a joke that was. Tatty, older than Emma by three years, was the fearless one. Leo had always admired her for it, married her for it. Her brother and her cousin had been well matched in courage.

It had been Emma's duty to kill the flies and spiders in the cell she'd shared with Tatty. Once Emma had even been so bold as to kill a rat. But if these gentlemen knew the truth about her, if they saw that she would be of no use to them, they would simply give her over to the law. And the crows would get her.

Aubrey handed the paper to the duke. His voice turned coaxing. "We want you to teach a different group of brats. That's all. Here, read this notice." Emma swung her gaze back to him. This time he offered her a newspaper, and she was pleased with the steadiness of her hand as she took it. Inside her everything quaked as if she would shake apart in spite of the name she had taken for herself. *Portland* for the stone and *Emma* for the lover of the great English hero Nelson. She had vowed to be as unshakeable as her new name.

The paper was folded open to a small notice inquiring after a schoolmaster. *Private instruction wanted in letters, mathematics, and geography. References required. Inquire at Daventry Hall for interview.*

Emma handed the notice back. Asking a suspected murderess to tutor children in a private gentleman's house was not the favor Aubrey meant. "What makes you think this person will hire me?"

She did not know where her boldness came from. Tatty would say a cat pent up becomes a lion.

Aubrey watched her with a twisted smile. A ridge of vein marred his smooth broad forehead. "We will send impeccable credentials with you."

Aubrey's smile was the slow, complacent smile of power. Emma waited for the trap to close.

"In return, you must do something for us. It's simple

really. I'll keep a man in the village. He'll tell you what to
do, and you'll report to him everything you discover about
your new employer's habits and plans."

"I must spy?" She tried not to betray any relief. They had
not asked her to kill anyone. *Still she would have to report to
a man, Aubrey's man. Aubrey would know where she was.
Escape would be very, very hard.*

"Or hang if that's your preference."

"On whom must I spy?" Her mind raced. Let them think
her agreeable. Let them think she could be bought with a
piece of paper. There would be time while she spied for them
for Tatty to reach the coast and Emma to plan another
escape. She was the planner, not Tatty.

"On the Marquess of Daventry."

"A lord?"

"Whore's get." The duke's cold voice insisted.

She turned to him. The lines cut deep in his harsh face.
The hooded eyes were unreadable. "May I know why I am
to spy on this lord?"

"He's an enemy of this house, Miss Portland."

"Is he dangerous, then?"

"He's damned hard to kill."

She stared at the duke, but his closed expression revealed
nothing. Emma's brain could make no sense of it—to send
a schoolmistress to spy on a dangerous lord. "For how long
must I spy?"

"As long as it takes. And we may ask you to obtain certain items for us, certain papers and objects."

They wanted her to spy and steal. "You will sign the
pardon request if I spy?"

In answer the duke tossed the paper aside. The weary
gesture told Emma all she needed to know about her pre-
dicament. The duke's unsteady leg buckled, and Aubrey

took his arm to help him to a leather chair. Emma understood the gesture. The duke relied on Aubrey now, and Aubrey only waited to take power as it slipped from the duke's grip.

"When do I leave?"

"Today."

Chapter Two

Daventry Hall stood on a low rise with a wide view of surrounding woods and fields, still bleak and bare in March. An arched bridge over a smooth-flowing blue river led to a curving drive. Four stories of warm golden stone rose with the stern and stately symmetry of an earlier century to a series of flat roofs with nearly a dozen small towers domed with copper cupolas blue-tinted with age. Hundreds of windows caught the afternoon light.

Emma saw at once that the house had no defenses to keep out an army. Apparently the English believed themselves protected from attack by their little ribbon of choppy sea over which a man could easily row. The house's only defense was its unobstructed view. A spy could not escape undetected in such an open setting.

The gig from the inn rocked to stop under a two-story porch that projected from the main house. Its weathered stones, carved and ornamented with columns and tracery, gave the impression of a hundred staring eyes. Emma was glad to step inside.

When she explained that she was expected for an interview, a cheerful manservant in a plain brown suit led her up a stairway dark with heavy old timbers to an ancient stone chapel. Entering its shadowy vaulted nave, she experienced a moment of confusion.

On Sundays when their jailers took them to chapel, she and Tatty had counted the painted cherubs on the ceiling with their tiny fluttering wings, peeping around clouds or dangling their bare feet over the architecture. Here the ceiling had apparently crumbled with age, dumping frescoed cherubs onto the floor. She looked down to see sturdy fallen angels lying tangled on one another, round limbs protruding from snowy linen, rosy cheeks and tumbled curls in a jumble.

At her footfall on the stone, the heap of angels stirred.

A midsized angel opened one blue eye and peered up at her. "'Oo the devil are you?" he asked with a surprisingly earthly accent.

His words prompted other angels to stir and scramble to their feet in a row. Emma counted seven earthbound angels, staring openly at her. They came thin and round, dark and light, rough-hewn like carved figures, or rounded with curls about their rosy cheeks, not angels after all, but barefoot boys in white shirts and gray wool breeches. One last angel lay on the stone floor. He was no cherub.

A thin lawn shirt, open at the throat, clung to a powerful chest and shoulders. One sleeve was sheered off completely, exposing a gleaming muscled arm like living marble, and a lean hand gripping a great sword. The words of a childhood prayer—*archangel defend us*—rose to her lips.

The warrior angel rolled to his bare feet in a fluid move, tall and lithe and fierce. His shirt billowed about him. Char-

coal wool trousers hugged his lean hips and legs. He took
Emma's breath. Angels such as he had fought each other for
the heavens with fiery swords when Lucifer revolted.

His bold gaze met Emma's and held.

"I came about the position," she told the angel. She had
no idea what his place on the household staff was, but the
boys around him must be her intended pupils.

He leaned his folded arms on the hilt of his great sword
and regarded her with frank interest, a sardonic lift to one
brow. "I don't remember advertising for anyone with your
qualifications."

"I beg your pardon. *You* placed the notice in the paper?"

"*You* are hardly the expected result."

Emma blinked. "*You* are Daventry?"

"None other." He bowed slightly. "You are E. Portland?"

Emma tried to pull her wits together. She was talking to
a man, not an angel, a dangerous man who was hard to kill.
She found herself babbling her qualifications, real and false.
"Emma Portland. I speak French, German, and Italian. I
know Latin, maths, and geography. Do you wish to see my
credentials?"

"Can you teach?"

"Of course."

"Let's find out." With an effortless sweep of his bare arm,
he brandished the sword in the air. Emma retreated a step
before she realized the sword was made of wood. "To the
schoolroom, lads."

The ragged cherubs erupted into motion and noise, surg-
ing around her. In a blink they had snatched her reticule and
letters of reference and whisked them away. She could see
her bag bobbing from hand to hand above their heads as they
disappeared up the dark, narrow stair.

"After you, Miss Portland." The warlike angel lord, whatever he was, grinned at her discomposure. It was not a good start. Her escape plan was not in place. She could not go back to Aubrey's man at the inn. She needed this man to hire her, not to mock her.

The girl turned an assessing gaze on the schoolroom. Dav had held no proper lessons there since his old tutor Hodge had left. The books he'd purchased for the boys lay in a heap in one corner. Their slates were scattered about the floor. He had continued to read to them a tale of exploring the great pharaohs' tombs. The result of that tale dominated the room—a dark pyramid built of desks and chairs that nearly reached the ceiling. A tunnel led to the interior of the structure, where the boys had disappeared.

Dav doubted she would last the afternoon, and a stab of disappointment accompanied the thought. He needed someone to take charge of the boys. They could not play games forever as if time would stand still for perpetual youth. But his idea of a tutor was nothing like this girl. From the letter he'd received, he had expected E. Portland to be a shabby scholar with his mind on the ancients. He should have told her at once that she wouldn't do for the job and arranged her escort back to wherever she came from. Even now he should stop her before his band ate her for luncheon, but it would only be polite to offer tea before he sent her away.

He righted a chair in the back of the room, straddled it, and waited to see what she would do. The sword had startled her, but now she ignored him, her brow puckered in a little frown of concentration, as she removed her plain black bonnet and gloves. She was thinking, stalling for time, he suspected.

Her hair, gold as sunbeams and springy as waves, was pulled back from her face with only a few curls escaping. A part of him just wanted to look at her. She undid the strings of her cloak. He hadn't seen the style, but he recognized an old, secondhand garment when he saw it, like the velvet coat he had in his wardrobe, a garment with a past. The cloth was faded rose wool, and the collar had a fringe like the petals of a wilted rose. Her gesture in removing it spoke of pride even when necessity made one bow.

He imagined helping her undo it, a missed opportunity. Gentlemen did such things, didn't they? And he was a gentleman now. The courts had made him one in spite of his grandfather's opposition. Daventry. He'd actually said the name rather easily.

Under her cloak she wore a dove gray muslin gown, too loose for her light figure. An overdress of pale sky blue closed under her bosom and gave some shape to the gown. Her eyes were vivid against that blue. Something about the dignity of her bearing had made him expect elegance, and not a woman in a secondhand gown applying for a humble household post. The upward tilt of her chin with its slight dent seemed regal, a dent made for a man's thumb.

Inside the pyramid, the boys squirmed and positioned themselves to spy on her. At any moment he expected them to erupt from their hiding place with wild whoops. He prepared himself to step in and put a comforting arm around her shoulder. If she sensed the boys meant mischief, she didn't show it. She circled the pyramid, collecting slates and pencils and stacking them on a chair facing the dark entrance.

When the room grew quiet, she stopped and touched the pocket of her gown, as if she had something tucked there. He smiled to himself. If she had something there, a good luck talisman perhaps, and still possessed it, the lads had lost their touch. Lark and Rook could lift the feathers from a strutting cock, and he'd not miss them.

Her gown fell back in its near-shapeless line, and she folded one hand over the other, a gesture of perfect self-containment. It irked him. He felt his fists tighten on the sword and his jaw clench that she should be an expert at retreating into herself. It spoke of a past about which he wanted to know nothing.

Her voice, low and sweet and surprising in its authority, interrupted the thought. "Once upon a time," she began.

He did not know the story. It was like the old stories he had heard as a child, but unfamiliar, too. He doubted it was English at all. A part of him believed she was making it up on the spot, or at least altering it to suit her audience, for there were seven sons of a poor woodcutter and his wife who had no more money. The wife took a threadbare cloth and wrapped it around the last of the bread, and they sent their two oldest sons out into the world.

Dav thought he could listen to her voice if she talked about laundry, and he certainly did not mind looking at her. The story continued with the journey of the woodcutter's sons.

"Off they went down the road, and passed men working in the fields, and building a great church, and selling goods, but no one offered them work. As they sat at noon to eat their bread, a flock of little brown birds landed in the branches above and hopped about their feet. The birds chirped and chirped."

Here the storyteller paused and wrote upon a slate, her pencil making a birdlike cheep. She put the slate aside and resumed the tale of the hungry boys, who ate and went their way, leaving the empty cloth but not a crumb for the birds.

As the sun was setting, they met an ogre, and the storyteller lowered her voice to a gruff growl. " 'What do you have to say for yourselves?'

"When the woodcutter's sons replied, 'Nothing,' the ogre said, 'Then you'd best come work for me.' He led them to his house at the edge of a wood and opened an oaken door crossed with iron bars. 'In here,' he invited. The boys stepped forward, and he shoved them down stone steps and locked them in darkness black as pitch."

In the way of such stories the second pair of sons met the same fate as the first. They, too, waved away the birds and left behind their mother's scrap of cloth but shared no crumbs. Again the girl wrote on the slates. Again the woodcutter's sons had nothing to say for themselves when questioned by the ogre, and down into the cellar they went.

She paused, and the room held its breath. Her gaze didn't waver, but Dav felt her awareness of him. He had tightened his grip on his sword. She told the story as if she knew just what it was to be locked in that fairy-tale cellar, and she made him feel it, too, his heart beating in his chest. When she began again, his hands relaxed.

"At last the woodcutter and his wife were so hungry they sent their youngest sons out into the world with bread tied in neat bundles. These three passed the men in the fields, the church builders, and the busy market, but no one offered them a job. Hungry and weary they sat on a log to eat their bread. When a flock of birds flew near, the youngest said to his brothers, 'Listen, the birds want to speak.' He held out his hand with crumbs upon it. A bird hopped down at once and pecked them up. And when the three brothers rose to go on their way, they brushed the remaining crumbs onto the ground for the flock."

This time when she paused, Dav knew that she had

reached the turning point. Now the brothers would get it right. Kindness, that was the point of the story, he felt sure, an easy moral lesson and there an end. He felt disappointed.

Her concentration was perfect. She seemed so caught up in the world of the story that she did not notice rustlings and whispers from inside the pyramid.

Consciousness of her femaleness thrummed in him like the low vibration of some powerful machine. Her gown seemed insubstantial, like cloud or water, loosely clinging to her form. He liked the look of her springy golden hair that might escape its bonds and her wide blue eyes and the way she wavered between trembling courage and contained purpose. He put her age at twenty or so. It occurred to him that she would have to be a prodigy to have the scholar's knowledge of languages and maps and math she claimed to have.

"The last three of the woodcutter's sons soon met the ogre, who asked them, 'What do you have to say for yourselves?'

"The youngest opened his mouth to answer when the flock of birds flew round and set up such a din of beating wings and chirping that a person could not hear himself think. The ogre shouted and waved and drove the flock to the rooftop except one bird who settled on the shoulder of the youngest son and chirped in his ear."

The girl stopped speaking and put down the slate in her hands. Her voice dropped as if she had come to the last words of the tale. Dav could sense the edge of anticipation in the boys. She stood contained and cool, unmoved by the tension of the unfinished story.

"Well, wot 'appens?" came a voice from within the pyramid. Slaps, grunts, and rustling hushed the speaker. Someone whispered, "Let 'er finish it."

Dav did not know whether to be amused or annoyed that

she had engaged him in this test of patience. She had violated the fundamental rule of storytelling by leaving the woodcutter's sons trapped in the ogre's cellar and her audience unsatisfied.

He could call a halt to the lesson and thank her, but if he did so, he, too, would not know the story's end.

He was sure the boys could see her, but she gave no sign of impatience. Again there was movement in the pyramid, and Robin, at eight, the baby of the band, poked his blond head out of the tunnel. "Please, miss, are you going to say wot 'appens?"

In a flash Dav realized the unfinished story had been her strategy all along. But she showed no sign of triumph at this first victory. She was patient, Dav would give her that.

"Only you can finish the story."

Robin crawled out and sat at her feet. Savage whispers hissed at him from the tunnel. "'Ow can we finish yer story?"

She looked as solemn as the little boy. "Each must answer the ogre's question."

"'Ow do we know wot to answer?"

Swallow's head emerged. "Robin, ye nodcock, it's wot the birds say, isn't it?"

The girl handed Robin a slate. "I've written their words for you on these slates. There's a word for each to tell the ogre."

Jay and Raven crawled out next, a matched pair of ruffians at ten. She handed out more slates.

Finch came out, bringing her bag. He gave it to her and accepted a slate in exchange. The boys sat, looking at each other's slates without speaking until a voice from within the pyramid muttered, "Idiots." Dav knew their dilemma and wondered if they would admit it to a stranger.

At last Swallow admitted, "We can't read."

Lark and Rook slid out of the tunnel and stood, arms crossed over thin chests. "And wot do we care? Words don't slay ogres."

"Besides Daventry can read. As long as we've got 'im, we don't need 'er." Rook looked to Dav for support.

Instant debate started.

"She could stay until she teaches us to read."

"But only seven words."

"A week, then."

"'Oo wants a blinkin' girl around for a week? Girls, useless as warts."

Dav held up his sword, and they fell silent. "We vote then. Who wants to keep her for a week?"

"A fortnight." The girl's voice shocked him. There was an unmistakable hint of desperation in it that woke all the instincts that had kept him alive for three years in the streets of London. She was not the ancient scholar he'd expected, nor was she what she appeared to be.

"I will stay a fortnight. No less, or not at all," she declared firmly. She had control of herself again, except for her eyes.

He felt the boys' gazes on him. He knew the smart thing to do, the thing his brothers would advise. But his street self was awake in him now, alert to snatch any good thing that came his way. She was a prize, a windfall from a passing wagon, a treasure washed in on the tide. The desperate flash of need in those blue eyes told him so, told him that whoever had once possessed her had let her go. She was his for the taking. He would have the end of her story.

"Miss Portland, you may have your fortnight. Prove yourself a worthy tutor to my boys, and you may have the position." He made it sound like a gentlemanly request, reasonable and aloof.

She did not thank him, but he did not miss the relief in her eyes.

"Tea, lads. Take the sword," he ordered. Lark took the hilt, and Jay and the others lined up to carry the long blade. Where he could lift it with ease, the weight of it made them stumble awkwardly, like pallbearers shuffling solemnly under their burden.

Dav was left with the beautiful stranger he'd hired without a glance at her credentials, wondering irrelevantly, where she would sleep.